D0887883

Far Out Man

By Chuck Snearly

Cover Design By Jessie Gontko

Far Out Man

©2022, Chuck Snearly

ISBN: 978-1-66783-090-2
ISBN eBook: 978-1-66783-091-9

For Denny

English 343

Course Title:	*"What's So Funny 'Bout Peace, Love and Understanding?"* *A Review of 1960s Counterculture Literature.*
Course Description:	*An examination of works in the American literary tradition exploring the themes of a turbulent and transformative time.*
Course Material:	*A wide variety of books from before, during and after this decade will be read in part or whole and discussed:*

- *The Catcher in the Rye (J. D. Salinger)*
- *On the Road (Jack Kerouac)*
- *The Feminine Mystique (Betty Friedan)*
- *One Flew Over the Cuckoo's Nest (Ken Kesey)*
- *Catch-22 (Joseph Heller)*
- *The Autobiography of Malcolm X (Malcolm X)*
- *Trout Fishing in America (Richard Brautigan)*
- *A Confederacy of Dunces (John Kennedy Toole)*
- *Slaughterhouse Five (Kurt Vonnegut)*
- *The Teachings of Don Juan (Carlos Castaneda)*
- *Steal This Book (Abbie Hoffman)*
- *Rules for Radicals (Saul Alinsky)*
- *The Electric Kool Aid Acid Test (Tom Wolfe)*
- *Fear and Loathing in Las Vegas (Hunter S. Thompson)*

Course Guidelines:	*If you are not fully committed to understanding this material please DO NOT take this course as an elective or to fulfill a non-major Humanities Requirement. (Per Prof. Crost.)*

Part One

When A True Genius Appears

"When a true genius appears, you can know him by this sign: that all the dunces are in a confederacy against him."

—Jonathan Swift

ONE

Ghosts And Dreams

If this was a premonition, it was bullshit.

The ghost who haunted his dreams had told him he was going to meet a woman who would change his life. It was all downhill from there; the promise of great revelations implied, but only vague generalities delivered.

"She's pretty, smart," she said again.

She's pretty smart?

Or pretty and smart?

For Christ's sake, what's her name?

If she was trying to tell him something why be so cryptic?

She was beautiful, as always, breathtaking and heartbreaking in ways she would never understand. Her words were meant to console him, absolve him of his sin. But her presence, even in a dream, brought him more pain than any words could erase.

"You did nothing wrong," she said. "I was where I wanted to be."

"I should have been here in our home with you," he replied.

"It wasn't your time. You still had work to do."

"The work I'm doing is crap. Most of the kids don't get me. The book is stalled."

"There's other work. Important work."

"What kind of work?"

"Mysteries to be solved."

"Mysteries to be solved? What does that even mean?"

"Mysteries to be solved."

"I gotta believe you know that repeating something doesn't make it any easier to understand. You mean like Sherlock Holmes and Dr. Watson? That kind of mystery? Are you saying that because you know they're two of my favorite characters in literature?"

"More like Shaggy and Velma in Scooby Doo."

He started to say she could always make him laugh but the scene shifted and turned grim. They were somewhere dark and damp, a closed-in space with a single light far in the distance. It was not a place he recognized from any of his haunted dreams.

"This is different," he said. "We haven't been here before."

"Lots of things are going to change. You need to be ready for it."

"What's going to change?" he asked.

"Watch out for those meddling kids," she replied.

"What do you mean? What's going to happen?"

"You'll be joining me soon."

He woke up with a huge smile on his face.

Terrified.

TWO

Flying Over Rooftops

It was the greatest feeling in the world.

Where others saw obstacles, they saw opportunities.

A wall was an invitation to rise. A bench could be transcended. A car parked on the street was a launch pad.

Except when it wasn't.

"Hey you assholes, what the fuck do you think you're doing?"

The angry voice called out after them, so they stopped.

Starting at Old Main, the three men had been freestyling a perfect parkour down Cass Avenue toward their favorite bar. Running at full speed, they had climbed on rooftops, run parallel along walls, jumped over orange and white construction barrels. It was only a half-mile, but they made it as difficult as possible.

They were young, strong and free, surfing a wave of adrenaline down a gentrified street that was the most dangerous in Detroit in the not-too-distant past. Now they were the princes of the city, racing toward a king's ransom in craft beer. Going up and over a parked Mercury Grand Marquis was their right as royalty: jumping onto the trunk, running across the roof and launching off the hood down the road.

Until somebody yelled at them.

The three young guys slowed the forward momentum from their jump, stopped, and turned around. One of them replied with the universal question of those seeking conflict: "What'd you say?"

"I said, what do you assholes think you're doing?"

The man who posed the question was standing outside of a party store holding a six-pack of Stroh's beer. A woman stood beside him, looking less than happy about the situation.

"We're running down the street, minding our own business. What are you doing?"

"That's my car you just ran over; you dented the hood."

"I don't think so. Let's take a look."

The three young men, breathing deeply, walked slowly back to the car they had just launched from. The car's owner met them in front of his Grand Marquis.

"Where's the dent?" one of three asked.

"It's right here, look," the man replied as he bent over the hood.

That was a mistake.

One of the three came up from behind him and slammed his head onto the hood of the Grand Marquis. The man threw his head back, blood streaming down his face. The young man behind him slammed it down again.

This time it stayed down.

The woman screamed. The young men picked up the six-pack, twisted the tops off of three bottles, and drank them down on the spot. Two of them looked on with great anticipation until the head slammer unleashed a pitch perfect belch. Then each of them grabbed one of the remaining three bottles and tossed them into the air randomly.

They ran down Cass Avenue laughing as the bottles exploded around them.

THREE

All You Need Is Love

Jack Crost desperately wanted to make a difference in the lives of his students.

That was his first mistake.

His second mistake was asking his class what he thought was a simple question: "In his novel *A Confederacy of Dunces* what message was John Kennedy Toole sending us?"

That started and ended it all.

On a good day his students would blow his mind with fascinating insights into the books he loved. Those were the days he lived for.

Judging from the averted eyes and flop-sweat silence in the amphitheater classroom this would not be one of those days. A fluttering hand in the back row raised his hopes, but the answer that followed made him question his career choice once again.

"We should land a man on the moon?"

It took Jack a moment to process the depths of oblivious ignorance this answer came from and another to temper his response. He reminded himself not to use any profanities, especially those with multiple syllables. Then he took a final moment to silently repeat his classroom mantra:

Be cool.

Be cool.

Be cool.

"I appreciate the effort, man," he said finally, "But this is American literature, not American history – you might want to check your class schedule, make sure you are in the right place."

"Ask what you can not do for your country?"

"Please stop, you're not even close and you're embarrassing both of us. Your answers are the worst thing to happened to John Kennedy since Dealey Plaza."

Really-bad-answer guy smiled blankly and the rest of the class appeared to be frozen in time. Jack considered the source of his failure out loud.

"Too soon? Too late? Too obscure?"

He began to pace back and forth in front of the rising semi-circle of seats, a formal hipster in sport coat and blue jeans with a short crop of what he called "hit record" hair – going from gold to platinum. As he paced he searched his brain desperately for a way to engage the class. There were two things in life he cared about passionately: writing and teaching. So far teaching was the only one he'd had any success with, but today he was off to a slow start.

It was what they used to call a bummer.

Another fluttering hand offered a glimmer of redemption. But when he recognized the student waving it the glimmer faded and he braced himself for the familiar answer.

"Man's inhumanity to man."

Once again Jack paused to consider his response and repeat his mantra. It wasn't that the answer was wrong.

It just wasn't right.

"It's Dave, right? Dave, that's actually a quote from Robert Burns. He's an 18th century Scottish poet, and this is a class about 20th century American literature."

"But I'm right, aren't I? One of the messages in *A Confederacy of Dunces* is man's inhumanity to man, isn't it?"

"When it comes to interpreting literature, there aren't a lot of wrong answers. The problem I have is that you keep giving that same answer to every question."

"But aren't people mean to other people in the book? So my answer is right, right?"

"There is kindness also, and love. The two main characters are in love, or at least their version of love. They try to save each other."

"So my answer is wrong?"

"We're not trying to solve a puzzle or check off a 'Right or Wrong' box. Great literature is meant to engage you, intellectually and emotionally, broaden your perspective and make you think. The Sixties were about opening your mind and your heart. They were about love, something highly underrated and badly needed these days."

Love meant a lot to Jack.

He was certain love was all that had kept him alive and functioning all these years on his own. He wanted to tell his class it really was all you need, but he was too embarrassed, what they used to call uptight, so he said something else.

"You're missing the point if you interpret everything you read the same way."

"But I would at least get partial credit if it was on the test, wouldn't I?"

At this point several more hands flew like birds into the air, but Jack shot them all down with a simple statement.

"Yes, this will be on the test. So it would be groovy if someone had an answer."

It was at this exact moment that his lecture went from bad to worse to last.

The moment the Wise Guys answered his question.

FOUR

A Confederacy Of Dunces

Jack spotted the three Wise Guys huddling in the far corner of the room in a conspiracy of whispers and braced himself for another helping of sugar-coated smart-ass.

The hand of the one in the middle went up and he acknowledged it.

"Thank you, Professor Crost. Toole's main character, Ignatius T. Reilly, believes in a set of outdated values from an earlier time. He talks a lot about fate. His message is that people are powerless to control the circumstances of their lives, but instead are guided by something outside themselves."

"Thank you, that's actually a very good answer. Well done."

Jack waited for a moment while all the other students in the class began writing frantically in their notebooks. It was a thoughtful answer, unfortunately one taken straight out of an Internet study guide. His problem with the three pre-law students he called the Wise Guys, besides their barely concealed disdain for liberal arts, was that they didn't want to actually engage with these great works and grow as human beings, they just wanted to game the system for an easy A.

He had warned them it wouldn't be easy, but they didn't listen.

At the beginning of the first class he explained, very slowly and carefully, that in the spirit of the Sixties his grading methodology put more emphasis on engagement, insight and personal growth than it did on the ability to memorize a checklist of answers.

For the past twenty years he had fervently believed, or needed to believe, that people were basically good. His life's passion was to bring out the best in them, especially young people. It had started as a tribute, turned gradually into a mission, then grew into an obsession. He wanted his students to open their minds and hearts, challenge convention and live passionately in the moment.

As the saying went, those who can't do, teach.

In recent years, as the world grew more narrow-minded and hateful, he had become increasingly fixated on fulfilling his mission and more dogmatic in his approach.

"This is not an easy class," he said that first day. "You have to do more than regurgitate facts to get an A. Please leave now if that concerns you."

He was well aware that his grading methodology often did not please the pre-med and pre-law students who took his class as an elective or to fulfill a humanities requirement because of its catchy name and his reputation as a weirdo who told bad jokes. It especially displeased them when, true to his word, he began handing out B's, C's and even D's to students who desperately wanted to maintain an A average.

The three Wise Guys were the most desperate of all.

All three had nicknames they used with each other, based on bodily functions or something else, he couldn't remember what. After his first few encounters with their special brand of bullshit – interruptions, digressions and thinly veiled derision – he had labeled them the Wise Guys and left it at that.

With a crushing sense of hubris and entitlement, they had stayed enrolled in his course past the date when they could have dropped out without receiving a grade. Now it was well past the halfway point, and all three were carrying a C in a class for the first time in their lives. After weeks of being contemptuous class clowns, they were trying to catch up by memorizing study guide boilerplate off the Internet and repeating it with a cloying Eddie Haskell charm.

Jack was onto their game and didn't want them to get away with it. He wanted the material to change their lives, or at least have some kind of impact on them, so he challenged himself to reach and teach them.

"I like your answer, but I think there are more layers to what Toole was doing. Even though Ignatius doesn't see himself as being in control of his own destiny, he acts as an instrument of fate to many of the other characters in the book. He causes the more deserving characters to have good things happen to them, and the less deserving characters to have bad things happen to them. So maybe we *can* move beyond what the fates deliver to us and help ourselves and others get what they deserve."

The Wise Guys stared and said nothing and the rest of the class continued scribbling notes.

"I'm not trying to make you look bad here: I just want to have an honest discussion. I want you to get real with me, as they used to say."

More stares, more scribbling.

This time Jack did not be cool.

"Why do we study literature?" he asked.

A number of hands shot into the air.

"It's not just so you can pass this class, graduate and get job."

The hands shot back down.

"The purpose of this class isn't just to punch your time card in the education factory," he continued, his voice rising. "Stories can change our lives and make us better people. They can change our world and make it a better place."

The vacant stares surrounding him made Jack even angrier.

"The people we are reading about lived in the moment. They shared their love freely, opened their minds to new ideas and experiences, fought injustices and pursued great causes with tremendous passion. These stories could save your life."

It was obvious from the awkward silence that greeted his emotional outburst that his earlier instinct was right; today was not going to include one of those rare moments when he connected with his students and the discussion carried them off to a magical realm of mutual discovery and moving epiphanies.

Today was going to be more of the same old shit.

He was failing them, failing himself, failing her.

From then on Jack did all the talking and the students took notes. He walked them through the main characters and major themes and messages of the book. They seemed relieved not to be challenged to do any thinking of their own and rewarded him by laughing when he quoted a series of passages in character as Ignatius T. Reilly.

"Apparently I lack some particular perversion which today's employer is seeking."

Mild laughter.

"I am at the moment writing a lengthy indictment against our century. When my brain begins to reel from my literary labors, I make an occasional cheese dip."

Louder laughter.

"Is my paranoia getting completely out of hand, or are you mongoloids really talking about me?"

That one killed.

At one point he noticed the Wise Guys huddling again, but he ignored it and continued on with his lecture. He was on a roll doing his Ignatius impersonation and thought nothing of it when one of the Wise Guys got up and moved down to a seat on the end of the front row. Later, as he basked in the glow of his student's laughter, he saw that one of the Wise Guys still sitting in the corner had raised his hand.

Thinking that perhaps he had finally gotten through to them with the material, Jack gave a self-satisfied nod to his would-be questioner.

"Professor Crost, there was a line you quoted a few minutes ago that I really liked and I want to write down. Something about paranoia. Can you say it again?"

Score one for the hip, relatable professor who could connect with his students. Jack gathered himself and channeled his most pompous, angry and self-absorbed Ignatius T. Reilly – the trick was to think of Comic Book Guy from The Simpsons.

"Is my paranoia getting completely out of hand, or are you mongoloids really talking about me?"

As the class burst into laughter he noticed one of the Wise Guys in the corner kept a straight face and shook his head. It seemed strange, but he was too busy wrapping up the class to think any further about it. He would have forgotten it completely if it wasn't for the equally strange encounter he had with the Wise Guys when the class ended.

As they shuffled past him on their way out the door, the one who had moved to the front row near the end of class said goodbye in a classic Wise Guy way, combining a surface innocence with an ominous undertone.

"We learned a lot in your class today, Professor Crost. It's too bad everybody can't see the kind of teacher you really are."

FIVE

Physics Lecture

"I'm not judging you, Ajeet, or trying to interfere with your personal life. But when your partying disrupts my experiment I have to register my objection."

She was a middle-aged woman who looked younger, due in part to the way she dressed: blue jeans, cardigan sweater, sneakers. He was a young man who looked older, due in part to the way he had spent the previous evening.

"I'm sorry, Dr. Stollard. I drove down from the Upper Peninsula a day early so I would be here in plenty of time for our meeting this morning."

"So what happened?"

"I hooked up with some of my homies from the hood last night. They were having sort of a going away party and I got caught up in the fun. It won't happen again."

"Can I ask you a question Ajeet? How long have you lived in this country?"

"Three years."

"That's what I thought. You might want to check on that phrase, 'homies from the hood.' I'm not overly familiar with street slang, but I'm fairly certain nobody says that anymore. I assume you meant your friends from Grosse Pointe. Who's going away?"

"Some professor I never heard of, I forget his name. He wasn't there, they were celebrating that he's going to be leaving soon. We had a few and drinks and went to the Joe Louis Arena. They were having a concert there and we hacked the roof."

"You mean you raised the roof."

The young man thought about it for a moment, then reluctantly agreed with her.

"Okay, we *raised* the roof. The important thing is the equipment is in the mine and ready to go. I'm leaving for Hancock after lunch. You'll get your results, I promise."

Maggie Stollard pushed away from her desk, leaned back in her chair and sighed.

Her office was dominated by the large dry-erase whiteboard behind her, which was filled with mathematical equations that only a handful of people in the world could understand. She was using these equations and the experiment that was about to get underway to try to unlock the mysteries of the universe. Right now that seemed a lot easier than trying to unlock the mysteries of human behavior.

She leaned forward again and looked him in his bloodshot eyes.

"You are a gifted young man with a bright future ahead of you. If these experiments succeed you'll be able to do important research at any university in the world."

"I know. I am very grateful for this opportunity."

"Unlike the material we are experimenting with, I can't be in two places at once. You earned the privilege of conducting the experiment at the Hancock site because you are one of the most brilliant students I've ever had. You have the potential to be one of my best research assistants, as well."

"Thank you, Dr. Stollard. I appreciate the confidence you have in me."

"You're doing your thing, I get it. But you show up two hours late for our final debriefing looking like you slept in your clothes and smelling like a frat house basement. And it's not the first time you've missed a meeting."

"I promise you this was the last time I'll ever be late for a meeting."

"I really hope so, Ajeet. It's taken me years to pull all of this together, to get the grant funding, the permissions, the right equipment and the right locations. I don't have a lot of time to waste. What we're doing could change the world. But if we screw it up, I won't get another chance."

"I understand what's at stake. That's why I'm willing to risk my life."

"We've been over this many times, Ajeet. The chance of a disruptive event is smaller than the particles we are observing. It is virtually non-existent. I wouldn't be doing it myself on this end if it wasn't safe."

"I'm sorry I'm brought it up. I trust you, and I trust the science."

After a few more last-minute instructions, several more apologies, and a handshake that turned into an awkward but heartfelt hug, the young graduate student left. Looking more her age after their discussion, Maggie put her elbows on her desk and her face in her hands, and had the last word.

"Shit."

SIX

The M-1 Avenue Crosswalk Song (Feeling Groovy)

Jack Crost was trying hard to be spontaneous and live in the moment.

He began the morning feeling groovy, as the old song went. Not groovy enough to talk to a lamppost – he assumed that would require taking drugs, which he didn't do – but enough to whistle the tune and hatch a far out plan.

He would walk to work.

It was a sunny spring day in Detroit, a season of renewal in a city being reborn. His beloved hometown was on the rebound; and now maybe he was as well. If fate really was smiling at him at last, a whimsical walk would return the favor.

The shabby old Victorian mansion in the dangerous neighborhood he had purchased for next to nothing twenty years ago was now a beautifully restored historic home in a thriving community of artists, intellectuals and cash-infused hipsters. He had finished his Thursday class on a high note with his crowd-pleasing Ignatius T. Reilly imitation and followed it up with an incredibly productive weekend of writing.

He was especially happy because he had managed to get the Great American Novel monkey off his back, at least for a short time. By holing up in his home for three days, skipping meals and not answering the phone he was able to write two double-spaced pages of promising prose.

Not wanting to spoil his good mood, he decided to read them over later and use the time saved for a free spirited ramble.

His office on campus was only a mile away.

For most of the way his triumphant walk to work was even better than he had imagined it. Brilliant sunshine and a cool but comfortable temperature made it one of those rare moments in life when everything seems promising and new.

"Slow down, you move too fast," he sang to himself. "You've got to make the morning last."

Jack thought "groovy" was the dumbest expression to come of the Sixties, a decade he otherwise revered for its brilliant slang. But he liked saying it, and he especially liked feeling it. He rambled on feeling groovy until he reached the Woodward Avenue crosswalk and spotted an Action News van parked by the opposite curb. As walked toward it he amused himself by imagining they were here to ask him about the wonderful day he was having.

They didn't ask him that.

Instead a young woman holding a microphone, followed closely by a cameraman, jumped out of the van and started shouting at him.

"How does it feel to be the most hated man in Detroit?"

It was a tough question, especially for a Monday morning.

Jack wasn't sure how to respond, so he kept walking.

"Do you think you're the monster they say you are?"

Once again, he had no idea what to say, or even what she was talking about.

He kept walking.

He thought it might be a case of mistaken identity, then supposed it was a joke one of his friends was playing on him. Confused and embarrassed, he tried and failed to think of something to say.

So he just kept walking.

"What do you think about the student protests here on campus?"

Wait. This was something he could respond to. He loved the spirit of the Sixties, when students stood up for what they believed in, and fought back against hatred and injustice by taking to the streets. There must be some of kind of protest on campus.

He kept walking but started talking.

"I've always felt that today's students are a bit too comfortable with the world they live in. The college years should be a time for pushing limits and questioning social mores. I'm glad to hear students are getting engaged and involved."

It was the young woman's turn to look confused.

"You do realize they're protesting you? They want you fired from the university and banned from campus."

Jack kept walking as he tried to process her statement. He decided this was a very bad joke and walked on in silence, rounding the corner to the wide, grassy pedestrian walkway that led to the refurbished house where his office was located. It was here that his groovy walk became a bad trip, and his daydreaming morphed into a full-blown nightmare.

A large group of young people stood in front of the house waving signs and shouting. It was the student protest he had secretly hoped for his entire career, but there was something wrong. It took a moment for him to realize they were chanting his name.

"Crost must go! Crost must go! Crost must go!"

As he got closer recognized his name and likeness on several signs:

"No Hate at Wayne State"

"We Can't Bear This Crost"

"Don't Teach Hate Speech"

He was 30 feet away when someone recognized him and shouted, "There he is!" The crowd started booing, and two more news crews ran up to him shouting questions. His mind raced to make sense of what was going on, but shock and confusion made it hard to think.

"I don't know what going on. I thought this young lady was playing a joke on me."

"You think this is funny?" someone shouted from the crowd.

"I don't know what's going on. I haven't done anything wrong."

"Do you deny it's you in the video? That's not you saying those horrible things?"

It was the young lady who had followed him onto the campus. He looked at her and kept walking toward the house.

"I really don't know what's going on here, but I'm sure it's some kind of mistake. If you'll excuse me, I have work to do."

At first the crowd parted to let him through, but as he got closer to the front porch they began to stand their ground.

"Please let me through. I'm sure we can straighten this out, whatever it is."

A chorus of boos and obscenities erupted from the crowd, and he felt himself being pushed and jostled back and forth. The obscenities got louder, more ugly and more personal. Someone tugged on his coat, and his foot was stepped on. From somewhere in front of him he heard a command shouted so loud it cut through all the boos and curses.

"Don't let him get through! Stop him!"

Jack looked up and saw it was Professor Tanner, the head of the English Department, who had an office down the hall from his. He tried to think of what he could have done to deserve the look of pure hatred this person – his boss – was giving him.

Then his thoughts stopped.

SEVEN

The Troll Under The Bridge

The call from dispatch came just as they were pulling out of Java Joe's with two large coffees to go.

"Tourist family said they seen a dead body in the water at Bridge View Park. Go check it out, eh?"

"Tourist family?"

"Mom and dad and a couple of kiddies, boy and girl. They'll be waiting for you in a blue and silver Ford Flex in the parking lot. Dad will show you where the body is."

For a moment the two police officers debated whether or not to put on the siren and race to the scene. The younger one wanted to, but was overruled by his older partner.

"Probably just a log or a bag of trash someone threw off the bridge. We're three miles away, no need to going flying through town and scare the tourists."

Spring was not the prime tourist season in St. Ignace, but early visitors were already starting to fill up the town, hopping on the ferries to Mackinac Island or stopping in the park to gawk at the Mackinac Bridge, the five-mile span that connected Michigan's lower and upper peninsulas. They walked in clusters past the shops along State Street, dressed in winter coats and knit caps that seemed to contradict the bright sunny morning.

"It's going to be colder than hell down by the lake," the young cop said.

When his partner didn't respond he made a few more attempts at conversation.

"I never seen a dead body before. I mean, outside of a funeral home. I'm guessing it's pretty cool, eh? It's what we're here for, right? If it is a dead body, there'll probably be a lot of paperwork. I wouldn't mind doing it. Hope it's not a log."

Having failed to get a response from his partner he finally lapsed into silence.

When they got to the park the father took them to the end of the path where he had posed his family for a photo with the Mackinaw Bridge in the background.

"The zoom lens on this thing goes from 28 to 200 millimeters," he explained. "When I finished taking pictures of my family I zoomed in on the bridge, and that's when I saw the body. It's by the rocks where the bridge reaches the shore."

"Do you mind if I take a look?"

The older cop looked through the camera lens, then sent his partner back to the Flex with the father to get a statement and contact information. When the young cop finished this task he walked back to where the path ended, then kept going until he reached his partner on the rocks below the bridge. The older man's blue uniform pants were stained darker by water up to the knees, and he was blowing into his cupped hands to warm them up.

The body of a young man was sprawled across the rocks at his feet.

"Did you pull him out of the water?"

"He wasn't going to come out by himself."

"This is a crime scene. I thought we're supposed to secure the area and not touch anything."

"It's not a crime scene, it's a big, cold lake. From the looks of him, he jumped off the bridge and drifted over here. I pulled him out so he wouldn't float away before the medical examiner got here."

"You can tell he jumped off the bridge just by looking at him?"

"I seen a few jumpers in my time. Doesn't happen too often, but when it does it isn't pretty. From that height when you hit the water it's like hitting concrete."

"His face is kind of messed up, but I'd know him if he was from around here. Where do you think he's from?"

"He's a graduate student from Detroit."

"Really? That's awesome police work. How did you figure that out?"

"The license in his wallet was my first clue. After that, his student ID. Our friend here is a Warrior from Wayne State University."

"Oh. Yeah. I get it. Is it okay that you touched him?"

"If you're so worried about the crime scene, why don't you go back to the car and call this in. Tell them to send the medical examiner and I'll try not to mess things up any worse, eh? And have them check and see if anybody reported any abandoned vehicles on the bridge last night. Better call the State Police, too. If I'm right and this guy is a bridge jumper they're going to want to be involved, especially since he's a troll."

"What's a troll?"

"You never heard that expression? Anyone who lives in the Lower Peninsula – under the bridge – is a troll."

The young cop laughed and started back toward the parking lot.

EIGHT

The Trolls On The Net

"When I woke up I thought I had slept funny the night before, because the side of my face hurt and my shoulder was killing me," Jack explained. "Then I realized I was lying on my back on the sidewalk surrounded by an angry mob."

"So campus security took you to Henry Ford Hospital?"

"Yeah, and by the time I got out the university had already begun the proceedings against me. I went straight from the hospital and got there just in time to hear their decision. This whole thing really sucks, Baxter."

"I agree that it sucks. And it's the first time in the history of academia that a faculty advisory committee made a quick decision. But it's the best deal you're going to get."

This was not the advice Jack wanted to hear. He had come to Baxter Fineman's office to develop a battle plan that would let him keep teaching, but his old friend and colleague was advising him to give up the ghost.

"I can't just walk away from this fight. If I give up it will make it easier for students to do this other professors."

"You need to do what's best for you, Jack. Your fellow professors aren't exactly going out of their way to help you. Even the union is backing away from this one."

Baxter was right about that.

He was right about a lot of things, that's why Jack had come to talk to him. Baxter was a law professor at the university and a long-time friend. Over the years his proud Afro had gradually yielded to total baldness, and his piercing gaze was now assisted by thick glasses, but he remained a fierce warrior fighting to bend the arc of the moral universe toward justice.

Baxter's office was in Old Main, an iconic campus building that looked like a low-budget version of Hogwarts Castle, complete with turrets and a big clock. Jack had come there hoping to find a magic spell that would make the nightmare of the last week vanish. Instead he got advice that was as easy to understand as it was difficult to accept.

Shut up, take the deal, and go.

Jack found it hard to do any of those things.

"You're right about our colleagues," he said. "A few of them said nice things about me, but no one protested too loudly. Nobody threatened to quit if they forced me out."

"They all support you. But we have to pick our fights, Jack. Nobody knows that lesson better than me. I learned it the hard way, I don't want you to do the same thing."

"Tanner doesn't support me. He picked his fight and won by a knockout."

"That's the professor who told the students not to let you through?"

"Yeah. My boss, the head of the English Department, can you believe it? The university isn't disciplining *him*."

"He didn't actually punch you, someone else did."

"And I ended up in the emergency room with a concussion. Campus security says they don't know who punched me. No witnesses have come forward, and for some reason the security cameras on the mall weren't working that morning."

"So that's it. Justice won't be served, but you can make the best of a bad situation. It's not just the video, you have a history of students filing grievances against you."

"I push my students because I want them to understand the material on an emotional level as well as an academic level. I want it to change their lives, and it has. For every grievance against me there are ten lives I have changed forever for the better."

"The university doesn't keep track of lives changed for the better, Jack – but it does keep track of student grievances. Sometimes you push too hard. Yourself included."

"What do you mean?"

"You understand the material on an academic level better than anyone in the world, you've been published in all of the prestigious journals and your work is highly acclaimed. But on an emotional level, the capability you demand of your students?"

"Yes?"

"Well, no one would describe you as laid back. You're not exactly a hippie, Jack."

"I'm not asking them to be hippies. I have standards I ask them to meet, a certain level of commitment. You can't just bullshit your way through my class. The university doesn't understand that. They don't want me to enforce the same rigorous standards of excellence they would apply to math or science."

"The university is actually on your side, more than you know, but the public pressure is enormous. They're not forcing you out, they're asking you to go on a sabbatical."

"They've frozen my tenure until I return. I'll lose a year."

"It's a year off with pay to do whatever you want. By then this whole thing will have blown over and you can go back to teaching. It should be easy for you, you've got that thing that Finnish thing you're always bragging about – scissors?"

"Sisu."

"You've got sisu. Grit, guts, perseverance, whatever it is. You can take it."

"I have to take sensitivity training, too."

"Isn't that what you English professors call irony? That's what you're trying to teach in your class every day."

They looked at each other across Baxter's massive old desk and shared a laugh, which felt good. Jack hadn't enjoyed many laughs in the past few days. Someone in his last class had used a smart phone to shoot video of him quoting lines from *A Confederacy of Dunces*. They edited it to make him look like a maniac who was yelling at his students, and ended it with him shouting the line about paranoia and mongoloids.

It was put it online with the title "Crazy College Professor Goes on Hate Rant."

The impact was immediate and devastating.

Over the course of a weekend, while he was holed up in his house ignoring his cell phone, laptop and TV to write the Great American Novel, he was branded an insensitive monster by an online jury that seemed to grow larger and angrier by the hour. Past transgressions, real and imagined, were posted and shared. The iconic issues of the Sixties he had discussed in class – dropping out, drugs, civil disobedience, casual sex – were portrayed as values he demanded his students embrace.

The hastily convened academic review panel assured Jack that all of its members believed his version of events – he was set up, the words he was quoting were taken out of context, he was a good person and a great teacher. They also assured him that it would be in the best interests of the university to relieve him of his teaching duties immediately. His replacement would grade the class on a Pass/Fail basis that wouldn't affect grade point averages, and he would be allowed to leave on a sabbatical until things died down.

"So you don't think I can take the university to court?"

"You can take them to court if you like, you might even win. Freezing your tenure was especially egregious, a bridge too far in my opinion – we could take them on there. But if you go to court they will no longer be on your side. The gloves will come off, and it will cost you a small fortune to have every dumb thing you ever did or said in your entire life made public."

"What if I can find the students who did it? I have a pretty good idea who it was."

"Whoever posted the video hasn't broken any laws."

"The way they edited and posted the video makes it look like I'm some kind of lunatic spewing hateful insults at my students."

"The trolls who attacked you…"

"Trolls?"

"You've never heard the term 'trolls'? A troll is someone who goes online and attacks other people."

"I don't do a lot of that Internet stuff."

"You might want to learn a little bit more about it, if for nothing else than self-defense. The trolls who attacked you actually got a two-fer, in terms of hate speech. Some people consider the word 'mongoloid' to be an insult to Asians, others consider it an offensive way of referring to mentally challenged people."

"I told you, they took what I said out of context and edited it to make me look bad. Isn't that against the law?"

"What they did with the video was unethical and immoral, but not illegal. You've already lost in the court of public opinion, going after them would only make things worse."

"You know I'm not hateful or prejudiced."

"You are the most loving and unprejudiced person I have ever met. Almost to a fault, I might add. You believe people are basically good, but that's not always the case."

Jack looked down for a moment, then spoke in a soft, sad voice.

"She believed it, so I believe it," he said. "I have to or else nothing makes sense."

He raised his eyes and his voice and spoke again.

"I might make an exception for the little shits who did this to me. If they had put half as much thought and energy into the class I would have given them A's."

"You know their names?"

"Yeah. There's three of them. I call them the Wise Guys."

"You have proof that they did it?"

"No, but I'd bet my pension it was them. They were worried that I was going to bring their grade point average down."

"Like I told you, Jack, whoever did this didn't break any laws. It's not going to help if you confront them, it might even make things worse."

"Things can't get any worse. Teaching is what keeps me going, it's the only thing I'm good at. But if you help me prove they did it, I promise I won't do anything stupid."

"I'm a lawyer, Jack, not a detective."

"But you know people. You have connections."

Baxter said nothing at first. The traffic sounds outside the room died down, and they could hear the clock on the wall ticking. He stared out the window for a moment, then sighed, shook his head, and spoke.

"For what it's worth, I know a guy who can help you prove who did it. He's a little different, he rubs some people the wrong way. But I think you'd like him."

"Is he good?"

"He's the best. If I ask him to look into this, will you promise me that you will give the university's proposal serious consideration?"

It was clear to Jack that his plan to wage a legal battle against the university would not work. He had other plans, but this was not the time to share them.

"I promise," he said.

NINE

OM

"Yeah?"

"Murphy, it's Baxter. Do you have a minute?"

"Always have a minute for you, counselor. Just doing my meditation."

From the sounds he could hear in the background, Baxter was fairly certain Murphy was not sitting in a quiet mediation retreat, but he let it pass. There were certain things about Murphy you had to accept if you wanted to take advantage of his remarkable skills.

"A friend of mine at the university is in trouble. I'm certain he was set up. I need your helping us prove who did it."

"What's your friend's name?"

"Jack Crost."

"The nutty professor who was all over the TV news?"

"That's him. But he's not crazy, he's a good man."

"Of course he is. He looked good on TV before he got his lights punched out in the middle of that riot they were having in his honor."

"Murphy, you know me. If I tell you this guy is okay, he's okay."

"You've always been straight with me, counselor. I believe you. What do you need me to do?"

"Have you got a pen? I'm going to give you some names, I want you to check them out. Your standard daily fee and expenses all right?"

"Forget about it. There are two people in this world I owe my life to, and you're one of them. No charge for you, counselor."

"Thanks, Murphy. You're doing a solid for a good man."

Baxter spent the next few minutes giving Murphy details about the case that weren't covered in the media, and the names and small amount of background he knew about the people he wanted checked out. When he finished he asked Murphy if he thought he could find anything with so little to go on.

"The Buddha said three things cannot be hidden for long: the sun, the moon, and the truth. You just gotta know where to look."

"I don't believe Buddha ever said 'you just gotta know where to look.'"

"You're right, I added that part. It makes more sense when you say it my way."

"Thanks again, Murphy. I really appreciate your help. The university is under a lot of pressure to resolve this issue as soon as possible, and my friend needs to make a decision. I'm going to need whatever you can get right away."

"No problem. Just one more thing, if you got it. Is there any place around here where these kids like to hang out?"

"The Old Miami Lounge on Cass Avenue."

Murphy started laughing.

"What's so funny about the Old Miami Lounge?"

"I'm sitting there right now, counselor."

"I thought you said you were meditating."

"Old Miami – OM. This is where I come to meditate. I'm doing it right now with my old friend Jack Daniels. Namaste. And cheers."

Baxter's phone beeped off before he could say another word, but he was smiling.

Murphy was on the case.

TEN

Heaven and Hell

"Here's to Pass/Fail, the grade that doesn't count!"

The three students Jack Crost called the Wise Guys – known to each other as Casper, Melch and Baltimore – clinked their mugs together and gulped down a large amount of Amber Alert, their favorite craft beer. They were sitting on a well-worn couch in the Old Miami Lounge, celebrating their recent triumph and planning the next one.

The one in the middle, Melch, issued his trademark melodious belch, then spoke:

"I heard they're not going to fire him. They told him he could just go away on a sabbatical if he wants."

"A what?"

The question came from Casper, who earned his nicknamed because of his ability to materialize out of nowhere in places he shouldn't be.

"A sabbatical. It's like a paid vacation."

"They're giving him a paid vacation? That sucks. They should have fired his ass," said Baltimore.

He was from Baltimore.

"We got him good, he looked like an idiot, and our grades are safe," said Melch. "The Crazy Professor Hack worked."

"Sending a guy on a paid vacation isn't my idea of payback, not for all the shit he gave us," said Baltimore. "I think we should figure out a way to send him off with a bang."

"We don't have time for that, and we don't need to draw attention to ourselves," said Melch. "It was an awesome hack. He got punched out and kicked out – that's enough. Let's focus on the tunnel and roof hack. It's going to be even more legendary."

"To Heaven and Hell," said Casper.

They clinked their mugs and finished their beers, then finalized the details of their new plan over several more.

Almost all the details.

"Dammit, I forgot. I have to work at the Jam on Thursday."

"It's too bad you have to keep that shitty job, Baltimore," said Melcher. "Why did you ever want to work there in the first place?"

"My dad thinks I have too many things handed to me, so he says I have to have a job in college like he did."

"Sounds like an ABC After School Special – 'The Boy Who Had To Work.' I might start crying."

"Fuck you. My shitty job is what got our business started, and it's what keeps it going, or have you forgotten?"

"I guess that makes you a regular Donald Trump. What time do you get off work?"

"I'm working the afternoon shift. I get off at eight."

"Then we'll start at nine. We want a nighttime shot anyway."

Heads nodded and Melcher continued.

"If this thing works like I know it will, our next party is going to be sold out. We're going to need a lot of party supplies this time, twice our normal order. That's a lot of product – are we still cool, Baltimore?"

"Yeah. I had a law clerk at my dad's firm check it out. Whatever this shit is, there's no laws against it. We can sell as much as we want and not get in trouble."

"This guy had it analyzed?"

"Yeah. He's not sure exactly what it is, but it's definitely not illegal – yet."

"And he's cool? He's not going to rat us out?"

"He's cool. He's a young guy, he's been to our parties. He's a paying customer."

Melcher nodded and turned to his other partner.

"How about you, Casper, is your man in the U.P. going to be able to handle that much business?"

"I'm sure he will. He said something about the people he deals with up there wanting to raise their prices, but that shouldn't be a problem – we'll just raise ours. I need to get ahold of him again to find out what the deal is, that's all. I haven't talked to him since the party we had to celebrate Crost going away."

"You haven't told him how much we're going to need yet?" asked Melch.

"He hasn't been answering his phone or text the last few days. The coverage up there isn't that good to begin with, and he spends a lot of time in the mine. I'm not worried about it – he'll turn up."

"If you say so," said Melch. "Anything else before we go?"

"Yeah, I just thought of something," said Casper. "We need to change the name around. We should call it the Hell and Heaven Hack."

"Why's that?"

"Because it starts in Hell."

ELEVEN

The Last Supper

No one at Jack's going away party could have known how far away he was going or how fast it would happen.

Not even Jack.

The stated purpose of the party was to celebrate the upcoming sabbatical he had agreed to take. In reality it was a last-minute tonic his friends had concocted to make that bitter pill a little easier to swallow. What his friends didn't know was that Jack had ideas of his own about what was going to go down.

He hadn't lied when he told everyone he would use the time to hunker down in his family's old house in the Upper Peninsula and finish writing his book. But he had other plans as well, and tonight he would share them with his friends and colleagues.

Fifty people were gathered in a private room in the Traffic Jam, a restaurant that had been a Wayne State University mainstay since before the area had gentrified. In the twenty years Jack had been teaching there he remained a loyal Traffic Jam customer, even more recently when trendy new bistros had begun sprouting up like free range mushrooms.

It was the perfect place to say "goodbye for now" and reveal his going-away surprise.

Nearly all of Jack's friends and colleagues were there, with the exception of Professor Tanner, who had sent his regrets along with a long, rambling note of apology via e-mail. Professor Chandler kicked off the speeches and established the central theme for the evening by making fun of Jack's fascination with the counter culture of the Sixties. The speakers that followed fell in line, and Jack became increasingly uncomfortable as what began as a fond farewell turned into a roast:

"We all know Jack is a hippie wanna be. So why did he come to Detroit? He heard there weren't any jobs here."

"Jack got high and told his dog to play dead, and his dog said 'Nah, man, play Floyd.'"

"Why didn't the lifeguard try to save Jack? He was too far out man!"

His friends were comfortable making fun of him because Jack was known for his sense of humor and easy-going nature, at least when he wasn't fixated on getting through to his students. But as he listened to them he felt his mind being clouded by anger as his stomach churned and his body oozed cold sweat.

The grand finale came when poetry professor Jeffers Stillwater unveiled the cake he had commissioned from the nearby Buns 'N Roses bakery and flower shop. The big square sheet cake sat on a small table at the front of the room, covered with white parchment paper. Two waitresses stood beside it, waiting for a sign.

Professor Stillwater paused for dramatic effect, cleared his throat, and began speaking in a loud, theatrical voice.

"When I think of Jack Crost, I am reminded of a quote from Wayne State graduate and legendary Detroit poet Dudley Randall: 'It's the people in this town that make it such a poetic place, more than New York, London, even Paris.' Jack, you are one of those people. To celebrate the poetry you bring into our lives, I have written a poem on this cake that expresses what I think you are feeling right now. A dieu vous comant et bon voyage!"

He nodded and the waitresses pulled off the paper and tilted the cake up so everyone could see it. Against a white background there was a blue outline of Michigan with a red star in the Upper Peninsula that marked the spot where Jack would stay in the Keweenaw Peninsula at the top of the state. Inside the familiar mitten-shaped contours of the Lower Peninsula Professor Stillwater's poem was written in frosting:

Kept In Short Supply

My Years

Are Somehow Sweeter

JC

To make sure nobody missed the point, the first letter of each word was red and the rest were pink.

Nobody missed the point.

When the laughter died down and Stillwater took a seat, it was Jack's turn to speak. By this point in the proceedings he definitely wasn't feeling well, having become increasingly cold, clammy and angry as his friends poked gentle fun at him. He'd only had three drinks; Moscow Mules served in a copper mug in honor of the Copper Country where he would be staying. Not enough alcohol or sugar to cause his cold sweat or racing heart.

Whatever it was, he didn't have time for it – he had something important to say. He moved to the front of the room where everyone had stood to talk. Tradition called for him to offer humorous rebuttals, warm reminisces and tearful goodbyes.

He did not honor tradition.

"There really isn't anything funny about peace, love and understanding."

Laughter.

"Look around at the world we live in. Fear and hate are winning the day. Where did we go wrong?"

The laughter trailed off into silence.

"I'm being railroaded out of town by a few over-privileged students who took my class for all the wrong reasons and publicly humiliated me to avoid a bad grade. I don't have proof of who did it yet, but I'm going to get it – and then I'm going to get them."

There was a gasp followed by a buzz of conversation and few nervous chuckles.

"What did we do when these spoiled, spiteful students attacked one of us? You all kept your mouths shut because they weren't going after you, at least not yet. And I folded and ran scared. I'm headed into exile while you all go back to work and pretend that nothing happened. We confirmed their twisted view of the world. We let ignorance and hate triumph over knowledge and compassion."

The room had grown completely silent, so much so that Jack felt like he could actually hear his heart racing even faster. A wave of nausea came and went, followed by a sharp pain in his chest. He ignored them and pressed on to finish what he had to say.

"Nobody is going to fight an obvious injustice unless we do it ourselves. They organized a protest, why can't we? Not just for me, but for all of us. Why can't hold a rally against lies, ignorance, and hate? You joined me this evening, and I thank you for that, but tonight I want to ask you to join me one more time."

Another wave of nausea.

"If you would please…"

More pain.

Change of plan.

"Take me to a hospital. I think I'm having a heart attack."

Everyone laughed, and then they stopped laughing.

TWELVE

Panic In Detroit

The question the two graduate assistants faced was far from academic: would the equipment they were testing for an experiment in an isolated underground chamber blow up in less than an hour?

After they raised the alarm and double-checked their instruments, another question was more relevant: if the experiment wasn't going to blow up, would their professor?

The equipment in question sat in the center of an immense room carved out of what looked like white sand. A grey metal tube, three feet wide and fifty feet long, rested on a framework of steel bars, illuminated by a half dozen spotlights on tripod stands. The tube had large metal boxes attached to each end from which a tangled web of cables ran to a table crowded with computers and a variety of sinister looking electronic devices.

Another bundle of cables ran along the ground into the semi-darkness at the far end of the room and disappeared into a tunnel. It was from this tunnel that the two graduate assistants who sat monitoring the computers heard their leader approaching, her loud footsteps and muffled curses giving them ample warning.

Maggie Stollard burst out of the tunnel and came running toward them, sprinting the final 100 feet to where they sat opposite the computers.

"Your text said it was an emergency. What's going on?"

The young woman looked at the young man sitting next to her for a moment before she responded.

"Dr. Stollard, I'm afraid we – that is, some of us – may have overreacted."

"Donna, there are only two of you here. From the way you are looking at him I assume you are talking about Robert."

The young man spoke up.

"We were running the test protocol and there were fluctuations in the vacuum chamber. I thought we might lose containment."

"You thought it was going to explode," Donna said.

"It turns out I was reading the instruments wrong," Robert continued. "I sent another text message to update you, didn't you get it?"

"I only check my messages if I'm stopped at a red light. I didn't stop at any lights after I got the first message – in fact, I might have run a few. I'm just happy we are all still alive, especially me. Show me the data you were looking at."

She peered over his shoulder while he clicked through a number of different databases and real-time monitor readings on a computer screen. They walked through what he thought he had seen and she explained what was actually happening. When they finished he apologized, then tried to explain what caused his irrational fear.

"I'm sorry I overreacted," he said.

"Why do think you overreacted?" Maggie asked.

"Because he's a chemical physicist," Donna said. "They're all about explosions."

"That's not it," Robert said. "I kept thinking of the Large Hadron Collider."

"The LHC? What about it?" Maggie asked.

"When they fired it up for the first time a bad solder connection caused an explosion that put it out of commission for a year. I didn't want that to happen here."

Maggie looked away and with great effort managed to keep from laughing. The LHC was the largest and most complex scientific research facility in the world, a 17-mile long underground circle in Switzerland that took decades to build and cost billions of dollars. Compared to the LHC, her little setup was two tin cans and a piece of string.

"First of all, Robert, I'm flattered that our operation made you think of the LHC. But what I really want you to remember is this: you didn't overreact. Don't ever hesitate to contact me if you think there is a problem. Safety comes first, last and always. You thought there was a problem – you did the right thing."

The young man searched the young woman's face for signs of approval, or perhaps something even stronger, as Maggie continued.

"The other thing to remember is that this experiment is perfectly safe. Even if the power failed completely the liquid nitrogen would have remained in containment. We've had this discussion before, but it's worth having again."

She pulled a chair out from under the table, sat down next to them, and began reciting the facts she had been repeating for the last year. The experiment was intended to induce and measure quantum effects in tiny particles as they affected each other's behavior instantaneously at a great distance.

There was nothing dangerous about it.

Dr. Stoddard had explained this over and over again, to university officials, city bureaucrats, peer review panels and others. The hard part was getting them to believe that an experiment that had to be carried out in an isolated underground chamber was safe. As she had repeated ad nauseum, they had to isolate the equipment to protect it from the environment – not the other way around.

She had given this pitch so many times that she had almost forgotten about the one minor detail she always left out, a caveat that was as unlikely to occur as it was hard to explain. It was an extremely remote possibility even her peers had failed to recognize.

She felt bad about the omission but she was running out of time.

After months of pleading the last organization that stood in her way – the Detroit Salt Company – gave her the final approval she needed. After receiving ample assurance and substantial remuneration, they had been kind enough to provide her with a large empty chamber at the far end of a salt mine 1,200 feet below the city.

Shortly after that she was painfully reminded of the adage, "Be careful what you wish for."

The experiment was about to get underway, but the conditions were terrible. Detroit's salt mines were like an underground city of their own, covering more than 1,500 acres connected by 100 miles of roads. They'd had to dissemble a lot of their equipment to get it to fit in even the larger cargo elevator, then reassemble it in a room made of salt that threatened to jam or rust everything it touched. The only communication with the outside world was by text or e-mail from a hard-wired computer – phones didn't work down here.

Not to mention her claustrophobia.

It wasn't so bad riding in the golf cart down wide, well-lit roads, or in the chamber where the experiments took place. But the elevator that brought you down was a nightmare, as was the smaller tunnel you walked through to get to the chamber. Because the text she received said it was an emergency, she didn't have time to take her medicine before she plunged below the surface.

At least the fact that it was an emergency gave her an excuse to run through the tunnel swearing the whole way.

"So, once again, please do not hesitate to contact me if you have any concerns," she concluded. "But, be assured, this experiment is perfectly safe. Is there anything else before I head back?"

Robert thought about asking her why they had to sign a lengthy waiver to participate in this perfectly safe experiment. Instead, he asked what he thought was a routine question.

"Have you heard from Ajeet lately?"

"No, I haven't. Have you?"

"Not for a few days. He's supposed to be in the copper mine getting ready to start the experiment by now. We ran tests last week and the hard wire connection worked fine, so he should be able to read our texts. But he hasn't responded to any of our messages since he went back on Friday."

Maggie's response was simple and succinct.

"Shit."

THIRTEEN

Up On The Roof

At first Jack only heard voices.

"It's over. He had a heart attack and died. Time of death 9:39."

"I told you we shouldn't have given him metoprolol. The blood tests showed he had a substance similar to an amphetamine in his system. Amphetamines can cause beta blockers to trigger unopposed alpha vasoconstriction. That would have increased his tachycardia and caused a cardiac arrest."

Jack could see them now, two men in hospital scrubs standing in an operating room. There were other masked people in the room looking on as they argued.

"Are you giving me a lecture, doctor?"

"I'm not giving you a lecture, I'm stating a fact. We should have used a different drug to slow down his heart."

"We could have given him labetalol instead of metoprolol but it wouldn't have made any difference. Nothing we could have done would have saved him. He had a cardiac arrest. He's dead. We're done here."

"We're not done."

Jack's perspective shifted, he was looking down on the two doctors and the people around them. There was someone lying on a table between them.

It was Jack.

"I'm going to give him another shot of adrenaline."

"You've already given him five shots, that's enough."

As their argument continued Jack felt himself rising.

He rose up out of the room and found himself looking down on the hospital grounds. Across the way was a taller building, what he saw when he reached its roof level convinced him that of all his crazy dreams this one was the strangest.

Seated by a wall on the roof of the taller building was a TV star from the 1950s.

As Jack tried to wrap his mind around that everything began turning brighter.

Then he saw her.

It was the woman of his dreams.

FOURTEEN

Puppet Masters

Luc and Jasper went over what they had done on the ride back from St. Ignace.

"The smallest details are important, because the tiniest mistake can fuck you up," said Luc. "I learned that lesson the hard way, eh?"

They didn't stop for a drink when they got back to Houghton like they normally would do. Instead they crossed over the bridge into Hancock and headed north on Highway 41. Luc wanted to have a beer and go over everything one last time without interruptions.

They knew the House would be empty this time of day.

They climbed the steep hill to the other side of town, passing by Quincy Mine and the No. 2 Shaft Hoist House, where the world's largest hoisting engine had given up the ghost and stopped hauling copper up from 7,000 feet below the surface nearly a century ago. Shortly after that they pulled into the parking lot of the Hoist House Inn, where the signs out front proclaimed "We're No. 1!" and "Come on in and Hoist a few!"

Inside was a large open room with a plank floor, roughhewn wood furniture and walls decorated with mining helmets, shovels and chunks of unrefined copper ore. In the middle of the room was an island bar surrounded by tall stools. They sat in the back and split a pitcher, talking quietly despite the fact that there was no one else in the place.

"You wiped down everything you touched in the car?" asked Luc.

"Like I told you before, I wiped down everything. Even the things I didn't touch."

"You checked his phone to make sure we weren't in any e-mails or pictures?"

"Yeah. There wasn't anything like that. He had my cell phone number in his phone directory under "Puppet Masters" but I deleted it."

"Puppet Masters? What a smart ass. Not so smart about negotiating prices, eh?"

Luc laughed long and hard, Jasper didn't join him. Then they sat in silence until the waitress finished delivering another pitcher of beer.

"He *really* didn't want to go back to Detroit," Jasper said. "He bitched about it the whole trip. I almost told him, 'shut the hell up, you're not going to Detroit asshole.'"

"If he knew where he really was going he would have begged to go to Detroit."

More laughter from Luc, then he became serious again.

"You sure he didn't try to tip off his friends, tell them we were coming?"

"You saw me, I took his phone when we told him we were going to Detroit. I deleted my cell phone number, added his Facebook post, and checked his messages. He had texted a friend in Detroit that morning, asked him to pick up a package for him."

"What kind of package?"

"I don't know, a package. He said pick up the package we talked about. The guy texted back he couldn't pick it up until Wednesday."

"This guy have a name?"

"He called him Chemic in the text he sent. I'm guessing it's a nickname, all these assholes Ajeet was dealing with have nicknames."

"Anything else?"

"Nothing."

"And you left the phone in his car like I told you?"

Jasper hesitated.

"You put the phone back didn't you?"

"You think I'm stupid?"

"I do think you're stupid, eh? That's why I'm asking all these questions."

They kept going over the last 24 hours until Jasper pleaded with Luc to stop.

"It won't just be the local yokels from St. Ignace checking things out," Luc reminded him. "The State Police investigate every time someone jumps off the bridge."

"We're good, Luc. We didn't miss anything. They can't connect us."

"I hope so. I gotta get this shit straight before I talk to my uncle. He's going to wanna go over every detail, and I guarantee he's going to give me a lot of shit."

"I though you already told him what we did."

"I called him to give him a heads up when you were buying those pasties in Mackinac City. I didn't go into a lot of details over the phone, but I did tell him our former partner had been staying at the Copper Crown. I knew it wouldn't take them long to connect the abandoned car to the motel. I want my uncle there when they check it out."

"So what do we do now?"

"I'm going to meet with my uncle after he makes sure the motel room is clean. After that we'll take a trip to Detroit – this time for real. We'll introduce ourselves to his partners, offer our condolences for his loss, and tell them we can still do business."

"On new terms – *our* new terms, not theirs."

"That's right. What's the name of the guy we want to meet?"

"I told you, he never said what his friends' real names were, but we can find them easy enough. I heard him talking on the phone a couple times, and he said the guy's nickname and where he hangs out – some bar called the Old Miami Lounge."

"So what do they call this guy?"

"Casper."

FIFTEEN

The Third Day

"Say kids, what time is it?"

As soon as it came out of his mouth Jack regretted saying it.

It was weird and condescending, not like him at all. And the fact that he had no idea why he said it scared him.

He had opened his eyes to discover he was lying in a hospital bed. Two young nurses were standing next to the bed checking the blinking machinery that surrounded him. They looked startled when he started talking, but one quickly composed herself and answered his question.

"It's eleven o'clock."

"I remember being taken to a hospital, but it gets a little fuzzy after that. Are you telling me I slept all morning?"

"Mr. Crost, it's Sunday. You've been unconscious for three days."

"Sunday? Are you sure"?

"I'm sure. You're in Henry Ford Hospital, I'm Sue and this is Janet. We just started our shift and we came in to check your vitals. You must have woken up when you heard us talking. I'm going to have Janet stay with you while I get the doctor. How do you feel?"

"Never been better."

He wasn't sure if that was a true statement, but it seemed like the right thing to say.

The nurse who spoke to him bolted out the door and left Jack smiling sheepishly at Janet. He felt as if he'd done something else wrong, far worse than calling them kids, but had no idea what it was. She turned back to the blinking machinery and said nothing.

After several minutes of writing down notes on a clipboard, she turned back to him.

"You were dead."

"Beg your pardon?"

"You died. You were dead, and then they brought you back. After that you were in a coma the whole weekend. You're a very lucky man."

Before Jack could ask her any one of a dozen questions that immediately crowded into his mind a middle-aged man in a white coat rushed into the room, followed closely by a younger man in a suit.

They did not look happy to see him alive.

The man in the white coat went right to the machinery, checking it closely before turning to Jack. Without saying a word he proceeded to hold his wrist, shine a small flashlight in his eyes and poke and prod him for what seemed like a very long time. When he finished with the last prod he introduced himself.

"I'm Dr. Foster. How are you feeling?"

"Never been better."

When he said it this time it definitely felt like the truth.

Dr. Foster asked a series of simple questions – his name and address, the city they were in, what month it was – that Jack answered easily. They had asked him the same questions in the emergency room earlier in the week. He started to make a joke about cheating on the test, but stopped himself.

From the looks of this doctor laughter would not be the best medicine right now.

"You've had quite an ordeal, but it looks like you're doing fine now," Dr. Foster said finally. "We'll keep you overnight for observation and if everything checks out you can go home tomorrow."

"Did I have a heart attack?"

"No. You had the symptoms of a heart attack when you arrived, and that's what we treated you for initially. But it turns out you were just having a bad reaction to a drug."

"What drug?"

"It appears to be some form of methamphetamine. A street drug with an unusual chemical composition and, apparently, extreme side-effects."

"I took meth? That's crazy. I've never taken a hard drug in my life."

"You most certainly took one Thursday evening, that's what brought you here. Now if you will excuse me, I have to continue my rounds. I'll be back to check on you again this afternoon, in the meantime we have some forms for you to fill out."

When the doctor left the young man stepped up with a clipboard full of forms for Jack to read, fill out, initial and sign. Most of them asked for the usual medical background information: name and address, insurance company, medical history. But the ones at the back were more about the hospital and its practices. In convoluted legalese they made it known that shit happens, then went on to excuse the hospital from any wrongdoing in the past, present or future.

"I seem to be signing a lot of waivers," Jack said finally.

"Standard hospital procedure," the young man replied.

"I didn't have to sign all these waivers when I came here a few weeks ago."

"What was the reason for that visit?"

"I got punched in the face."

The young man looked at him but said nothing.

"Are you like a resident or an intern or something? Do you work for Dr. Foster?"

"I'm a hospital administrator. I work in the legal department."

When Jack handed back the clipboard and pen the young man looked over the forms for a moment, then turned and walked to the door. He turned in the doorway and paused for a moment before giving Jack a final surprise.

"Thank you for your cooperation. We're done examining and processing you. Now the police would like to speak to you."

SIXTEEN

Hidden Connections

"Professor Stollard, do you have a minute?"

"Sure, Donna. What's up?"

"I'm calling to give you background on why Robert panicked yesterday."

"Okay. Can I ask why?"

"I don't want you to get the wrong impression about Robert. He's very smart and very competent, it's not like him to make a mistake like that."

"First of all, I know he's smart and competent, that's why I asked him to assist me with the experiment. And it's never a mistake to point out a potential safety hazard."

"You're being very kind and understanding professor. We both know there was never any safety hazard, it was a mistake a freshman might make, but not a doctoral candidate. Robert knows better, it's just…"

There was a long pause.

Maggie assumed Donna was considering her next words carefully, perhaps about to cross a line that couldn't be uncrossed.

"Just what?" Maggie asked finally.

"He hasn't been himself lately. He's worried about Ajeet."

"I've been worried about Ajeet myself. I'm afraid he's been enjoying himself too much since he went up north. I don't think I'm betraying any confidences by telling you what I told him a few days ago: his partying has put the experiment and himself at risk."

There was another pause before Donna spoke again.

"It's not just partying. Robert says Ajeet is hanging out with some rough characters up there. He may be doing drugs."

"You mean like marijuana?"

"I mean like amphetamines. Robert's really worried about him, he's nervous and preoccupied, that's why he made such a dumb mistake."

It was Maggie's turn to consider her next words carefully before speaking again.

"You really care about Robert, don't you?" she asked.

"I care about Ajeet, and I care about the experiment."

"And you care about Robert."

This pause was shorter.

"Yes."

"So why don't you two get together?"

"He's not interested in me."

"I wouldn't be so sure. I've seen the way he looks at you. I think he's in love."

"Then why hasn't he asked me out after all the time we've worked together?"

"You said it yourself, he's preoccupied. Or maybe he just doesn't know how to ask a girl out. Sometimes the most brilliant scientists are lacking in social intelligence. It happens so often it's become an old cliché."

"I'm as much as fault as Robert – I haven't asked him out, either."

"Well then, I'll leave it to you two to figure it out. I just hope Robert has been able to talk some sense into Ajeet."

"That's part of the problem, professor."

"What is?"

"Robert wasn't able to reach Ajeet all weekend."

SEVENTEEN

A Few Questions

While he waited for the police to arrive Jack frantically searched his brain for memories of his going away party. He was even more eager to remember what happened during the three-day after-party.

He vaguely remembered being loaded into an ambulance at the Traffic Jam and racing through the streets of Detroit with the siren screaming and lights flashing. There wasn't much after that, except for a vivid recollection of two doctors arguing about how to treat him.

As he recalled the sights and sounds of their argument another memory began tumbling into place after it, one so bizarre that at first he dismissed it as a dream. But the more he thought about it, the more convinced he became that he was fully conscious when it happened, and that it actually happened.

Which was impossible.

He was still trying to separate the improbable from the impossible when the police arrived. The two officers walked in and stood next to his bed, one started writing in a notebook when the other started talking.

"I'm Lieutenant Preck, this is Officer Markowitz, we're from the Central Precinct. We have a few questions for you if you don't mind."

"I don't mind, but if I can ask you first, why am I being questioned by the police?"

"You're a college professor at Wayne State who overdosed on a dangerous street drug that we've been tracking for several months. A number of young people, mostly students from your university, have ended up in the hospital after they took it. Then there's the video."

"The video? You mean thing on the internet?"

"Clearly you have some anger issues in regard to your students."

"You think I gave my students drugs to hurt them? They edited that video to make me look bad. I'm the victim here."

"We just want to know how all these facts fit together, and how you are involved in all this. So tell me, who did you get the drug from?"

"No one."

"Did you make it yourself?"

"No, I didn't make it myself, and I didn't take it."

"You didn't take some pills? White pills with red spots?"

"I didn't take any pills of any color."

"How do you explain the overdose?"

"I don't know. I was at a going away party with fifty people for two hours. I never left the room, not even to go to the bathroom. Ask my friends who were at the party, they'll tell you I didn't take any drugs."

"What about before the party? What were you doing then?"

"I was at home getting ready for the party."

"Any witnesses?"

"No, I was by myself."

As the questioning continued Jack began to feel as though he had landed in the middle of one of nightmarish stories written by one of his favorite authors, Franz Kafka. Making things even more surreal were the newly recovered memories of what had happened when he first got to the hospital.

He couldn't deny them and he couldn't explain them.

"Mr. Crost, we may want to check out your house at some point. Would you be okay with that or will we need to get a search warrant?"

"Check out my house? Do you think I make drugs in my basement?"

"We're not accusing you of anything, but we might want to look around to try to find a possible explanation for what happened."

"I'd like to find an explanation, too. But you're not going to find one in my home."

After a few more questions Lieutenant Preck declared they had enough and Officer Markowitz closed his notebook. As they turned to go Jack felt compelled to give them one more fact about the case.

"I died, you know. Did they tell you that?"

They turned to face him again and Lieutenant Preck spoke.

"They did tell us that. If you don't mind, I'm just curious – what was that like?"

"Surprisingly pleasant."

"Really? What happened? Did you see God?"

Jack hesitated. They already suspected he might be a criminal, he didn't want them to think he was crazy, too.

"You wouldn't believe me if I told you," he said.

EIGHTEEN

The Circumstances Of My Death

"I know it's hard for you to believe, Jack, but I'm telling you the truth. It may be painful to acknowledge, but I owe you that as a client, and especially as a friend."

For the second time in less than a week, Jack had returned to Baxter Fineman's office for legal advice and moral support. Once again, he didn't like what he was hearing.

"You know me, Baxter – I'm not someone who sues people just to make a buck. I'm not trying to win a big settlement. I just want to know what happened that night."

"What happened that night was that you were rushed to the hospital exhibiting the symptoms of a heart attack. You died and they brought you back to life. I think you owe Henry Ford Hospital a great deal of thanks, not a lawsuit."

"But they're the ones that killed me. They gave me a drug that reacted badly with the street drug that someone else had given me. That's when I had a real heart attack."

"You said the hospital refuses to share the details of what happened to you. So tell me how you know all this."

Jack sighed and looked around the office. Wooden desk and chairs, brown metal filing cabinets, map of the world on the wall. It was definitely old school and no-nonsense, like Baxter himself. That made what Jack was going to say next all the more embarrassing. But it was the truth, which was what Baxter needed to hear.

"I told you, I heard the doctors talking. They were arguing. I heard what they said about what was happening."

"What did they say?"

"They talked about giving me a drug to slow my heart and lower my blood pressure. One of them wanted to do it and the other didn't.

"What happened then?"

"They gave me the drug, but instead of slowing my heart and lowering my blood pressure, it did the opposite. I had a heart attack and died."

"We keep going over the facts, and they haven't changed. You were brought into the hospital exhibiting the symptoms of a heart attack. At some point you actually had a heart attack and died and they brought you back to life."

"But they are the ones who caused the heart attack."

"They were following medical protocol. You, on the other hand, had taken an illegal street drug."

"I was *given* an illegal street drug – I didn't take it."

"Either way, there are no grounds for a lawsuit. They won't even try to settle out of court."

"I don't want money. I just want them to tell me what they did after I died."

"Why is that so important to you?"

"Because I already know. I need them to confirm what I remember."

"What you remember? When you were dead?"

Jack looked across the desk at his friend, who was staring back at him through thick glasses that made his eyes look even more wide open than they already were. He had reached the point in his story where things stopped making sense, but he was determined to keep pushing on.

"When I died, something happened. I felt like I left my body and floated up over the room. I could see the doctors and nurses standing around my body, and I could hear what they were saying."

"You had a near-death experience?"

"I know they call it that, but it's not really accurate. I wasn't near death – I was dead. I had a death experience."

"So what happened then? What is it that you think you saw and heard?"

"I don't think it, I know it. One doctor said it was all over, I'd had a heart attack and died. He said they could have given me a different beta blocker to slow down my heart – labetalol instead of metoprolol – but it wouldn't have made any difference."

"You remember the names of the drugs?"

"I remember everything. The other doctor – the one who didn't want to give me the metoprolol –said my blood tests showed a substance similar to amphetamine in my system. Amphetamines can cause beta blockers to trigger 'unopposed alpha vasoconstriction,' which would have increased my tachycardia and *caused* my heart attack."

"How do you know all those medical terms?"

"That's the point – I don't. I heard them being said and I saw the people saying them. I felt like all my senses were heightened. I could see and hear better, I could even think better, and I remember every detail of what I saw and heard."

"So what happened next?"

"The two doctors argued for a while, the first one wanted to call it…'"

"Pronounce you dead?"

"Yeah. The other one – the one who thought I might be on some kind of amphetamine – wanted to give me an adrenaline shot. He finally just did it."

"And that brought you back to life."

"No. It took six shots before I came back to life. While all that was going on I kind of wandered around a bit."

"Wandered around?"

Jack hesitated, knowing that from this point on his story went from strange to bizarre and beyond. It would test Baxter's credulity and his friendship, but he couldn't *not* tell him. If it really happened, it was life altering.

If it *didn't* happen, he was going crazy.

"I rose up out of the room. I was looking down on the hospital grounds, on the roofs of the buildings."

"You went through the ceiling?"

"I guess so. It just felt like I was floating up. I was higher than the tallest building, and I was looking down on its roof, and I saw something really strange."

"I would think flying around like an angel would be strange enough. A lot of people who have a near death experience claim they see God. Is that what happened?"

"No. I didn't see God, but I did see somebody strange and wonderful."

"Who?"

"Howdy Doody."

NINETEEN

Bad Call

"Robert, this is Maggie Stollard calling. Have you got a minute?"

Maggie took the long silence that followed as a yes.

"I spoke with Donna. She said you still hadn't heard from Ajeet."

"Professor…"

"Donna said you're worried about Ajeet. I'm worried, too. This experiment means everything to me. Ajeet's partying is putting it at risk, and putting him at risk."

"Professor…"

"You've made excuses for him in the past; covered up his mistakes and failures, or at least trying to. That's not helping him."

"Professor Stoddard, please listen to me."

"I'm not blaming you, I've ignored many of the signs myself, making excuses, rationalizing things away. We've got to stop doing that. We need to confront him with his problem and hold him accountable. I assume he's been out on some kind of wild weekend binge. When you get ahold of him, tell him to call me immediately. We're going to get some help for Ajeet."

There was another long silence before Robert spoke again.

"I've been trying to get it together to call you for the last hour," he said finally.

"What do you mean?"

"Ajeet doesn't need our help."

"Of course he does. We can't just keep looking away when…"

"Ajeet is dead."

TWENTY

Uncle Vladimir

"So you hung him over the side of the bridge?"

"Yeah."

"And you thought that was the smartest thing to do?"

"Yeah."

The slap came so fast that it didn't seem real until Luc felt the stinging pain.

"What did you hit me for?" he asked.

Luc was sitting on his Uncle Vladdie's back porch, watching the occasional boat go by on Portage Canal and trying to explain his actions of the last two days. Uncle Vladdie was not following his logic.

"I hit you for being stupid. Tell me again what you did and why."

"We been selling our stuff to this kid for six months. His buddies in Detroit sell them at raves."

"What the hell is a rave?"

"It's like a party, only you charge people money to come."

"Where'd you meet this kid?"

"At a bar in Houghton. He had been drinking all night and was looking for something to keep the party going. We gave him a Howdy Doody and he loved it. He told us he had friends in Detroit who would love it. He said they threw big parties, so we figured we could move a lot of product. Once they tried it we went into business with him."

"How did you know he wasn't a cop?"

"He said he was a graduate student from India, so we checked him out online. He was all over the place – Facebook, Snapchat, Instagram, Tinder."

"Cops set up fake accounts online."

"He wasn't a cop. No offense or nothing, but you can tell when a cop sets up a fake identity online."

Luc flinched slightly in anticipation of a slap that didn't come. Instead Uncle Vladdie had another question.

"He's from Wayne State, not Michigan Tech. What was he doing up here?"

"He was helping one of his professors set up some kind of science experiment in Quincy Mine."

"Quincy Mine? Where they take the tourists?"

"It's set up at the back of the mine, past where they take the tourists. Looks like a big sewer pipe with computers hooked up to it."

"You seen it?"

"He took us there one morning after we partied all night with Howdy Doody."

Another slap stung the other side of Luc's face.

"What the hell, man? What was that for?"

"I've told you time and time again – you make the shit, you don't take the shit. Plus, you were partying with this kid, people saw you with him."

"Okay, before I say anything more you got to promise you will quit hitting me. That shit hurts."

"Not as much as getting sent away to Marquette and becoming someone's bitch. Or getting killed, like your dad."

Luc and his uncle locked eyes for a moment, then looked away. They watched a sailboat with its sail furled powering down the canal towards Lake Superior. When it disappeared around a bend his uncle spoke.

"I ain't gonna hit you no more. Keep talking."

"We took Howdy Doodys with him the first couple times to prove it was safe. After that he gobbled them down on his own. I told you before, the only time I take it is to make a sale."

"But you partied with him, right? If there's any reason to be suspicious about his death, the Sheriff's Office is going to be looking for people who knew him. I won't be the one that questions you, you'll be lucky if they even let me in the room to watch."

"He partied with a lot of people, not just us. And there won't be any reason to be suspicious, we took care of that."

"How'd you do that?"

"After he fell we used his phone to post something on his Facebook page."

"You posted something?"

"Yeah, it said, 'I can't take it anymore. I'm going to kill myself.'"

"This was just you and Jasper, right?"

"Yeah."

"And why were you dangling him off the side of the bridge?"

"He told us he had been paying too much for the Howdy Doodys. He wanted us to cut the price in half or he would start making his own."

"How was he going to do that? We invented that formula ourselves. Nobody knows how to make it but us."

"He said he'd done a chemical analysis of the pills could make them himself."

"So you killed him?"

"I didn't mean to kill him, I was just trying to scare him. I wanted to show him he couldn't mess with us."

Uncle Vladdie gripped the arms of his deck chair tightly, but did not move.

"Tell me exactly what happened again," he said finally.

"We told him we needed to go to Detroit and meet with his buddies to renegotiate our deal. We took his cell phone and said he had to wait until we got there to call them so they wouldn't have time to plan any funny business in advance. Jasper drove in his car with him and they followed me in my car."

"And what happened on the bridge?"

"There's a section of the bridge where they've been doing repairs for months, I pulled over there like I was having car trouble. When they got out to help I pulled a piece and told him we were going to throw him off the bridge for fucking around with us."

"So you were planning to do it all along."

"No, I swear, it was just a bluff to scare him. We wanted to make him beg for his life and swear he would never make his own stuff. After he did that we were going to drive him back to Hancock and charge him double."

"Did he beg for his life?"

"Hell no, the dumb shit. He started laughing, which pissed me off. I dragged him over to the railing and sat him on top of it. I told him I wasn't shitting around. He quit laughing then."

"Then what happened?"

"I told you, he slipped out of my hands and fell. It was an accident."

"And I told you nobody is going to believe you. What'd you do then?"

"We left his car on the bridge and drove into Mackinac City. We got some gas and pasties, that's when I called you. Then we turned around and came back home. You said yourself that everyone in the Sheriff's Office thinks it's a suicide."

"You been lucky so far, but this ain't over. I'd hit you again if I thought I could smack any sense into you. You fucked up and we have to deal with it. There's a million ways something like this can go sideways. He could have left notes in his motel room, something that would tie you to him and drugs. He could have left the formula there."

"That's why I called you."

"Like I said, you're lucky. I was on patrol and I circled the Copper Crown until the dispatcher called for someone to check out his room."

"And you didn't find anything that tied him to me. So why are you so pissed off?"

"I didn't find anything that tied him to you. But I found something – a receipt for a Fed Ex package. It was on the table."

"So?"

"So it's dated and time-stamped for Saturday morning. He sent this package out right before he met with you."

"So?"

"So maybe he put the formula in it, just in case, sent it to his friend. The formula wasn't in the room, that's for sure – I tore it apart looking for anything suspicious."

Luc almost said out loud what he was thinking – that must be the package in the text message Jasper talked about. He stopped himself just in time to avoid getting slapped again. There was no sense upsetting his uncle: Jasper also said the friend who was supposed to pick up the package wouldn't be able to pick it up until Wednesday.

"Jasper and I can check it out. Who'd he send it to?"

Jasper pulled a rumpled pink slip of paper from his pocket and read from it.

"Somebody named Chemic, at a Wayne State address in care of someone else."

"Who?"

"Dr. Magdalene Stoddard."

TWENTY-ONE

When I Saw
Her Standing There

Jack had never seen Baxter laugh so long and hard. When he finally stopped laughing he took a moment to catch his breath before he spoke again.

"So you saw the puppet from a 1950s children's TV show on the roof of the Henry Ford Hospital Clinic Building?"

"I don't know what building it was, all I know is that it was the tallest one."

"That's the Clinic Building. And you recognized Howdy Doody? I didn't think you were that old."

"I'm not. They have him on display at the Detroit Institute of Arts. I saw him there a few months ago, he's the star of their puppet collection."

"I'm very familiar with the collection, and with Howdy Doody," Baxter said. "It pains me to admit it, but I'm old enough to remember watching the show."

"He's behind glass on display at the DIA, which I assume has a very good security system, considering the priceless collection of art they have there. How did he end up on the hospital roof?"

"Jack, it's obvious that you were having some kind of hallucination, either from the street drug or the drugs the doctors gave you. You remembered what you saw at the museum, and that became part of what you imagined you saw."

"It wasn't a hallucination, Baxter, I promise you that."

"Okay. Let's put a pin in that for a minute. What happened next?"

"This really bright light appeared, like at the end of a tunnel…"

"And you saw people from your past who had died."

"Actually, yeah. How did you know that?"

"It's in all the reports of near-death experiences. People who are dead show up and tell you it's not your time, and you go back into your body."

"That's what happened. I went back down into the hospital room and I heard someone say 'That's six shots of adrenaline and no results, give it up already.' The next thing I knew I was waking up three days later."

Baxter stood up and began pacing back and forth behind his desk.

"Have you told anyone else this story?" he asked.

"I almost told the cops who questioned me at the hospital. But it was obvious they would think what you think, that I was tripping on drugs, so I shut up. Can you believe they still consider me to be some kind of suspect – either a drug user or a drug dealer."

"Have you spoken to anyone else besides the police about any of this?"

"There was someone from the legal department at the hospital who made me fill out a bunch of forms to cover their ass. I started to tell him, but he was aggressively uninterested – he *really* didn't want to hear it. They wouldn't let me talk to the doctors who worked on me. If nothing else, I wanted to thank the guy who saved my life."

Baxter walked over to his window and stood staring out for a long time. When he finally turned around, he was ready to give his advice.

"I don't know what to tell you about death and the afterlife, you're going to have to figure that out on your own. But there are two earthly mysteries that need to be solved here, and I can help you with them."

"Two mysteries?"

"The first is what happened in that hospital room. Even if it corroborates your story, I'm not sure proves anything– maybe you heard them talking while you were under anesthesia and dreamed the rest. But knowing what really happened would be a good start."

"It would."

"To me, the other mystery is the more important of the two: who drugged you? You have a lot of haters on the Internet who saw your video and said terrible things about you. If one of them did it, they could be planning to do something else nasty to you."

"So what should I do?"

"As I've been telling you, a lawsuit against the hospital would be costly and time-consuming. There's no guarantee you would get the information you want, and it would do nothing to help you find the person who gave you the drug."

"What's the alternative?"

"I got a guy."

"A guy?"

"The private detective I told you about, the one checking up on the students you think made the video. His name is Murphy. He's an old friend who is very discreet and very capable. I think he's the best private detective in Detroit. I want you to talk to him."

It didn't take Jack long to agree to Baxter's plan. He was relieved to be doing something to fight back against his bad fortune. He also was relieved to be done explaining an experience he still had trouble understanding himself. He was especially thankful that Baxter hadn't asked him the name of the person who told him to go back.

He wasn't ready to talk about that, with Baxter or anyone else, even though it had been twenty years since the break-in.

Twenty years since the last time he had seen her alive.

TWENTY-TWO

The Drunken Master

Jack's spirit was not lifted when he opened his front door to meet the private detective Baxter Fineman had recommended.

He had imagined a tough guy in a trench coat. Instead, standing on his porch was a significantly overweight older man wearing an old worn brown sports coat over a white dress shirt spattered with bloodstains. He smelled like last call was on him.

"I'm Murphy."

Jack shook his hand and led him to the office in the back of his home. Murphy addressed one of the many concerns Jack had as they sat down.

"I apologize for looking like shit. I stopped by Slow's before I came here. I should cover myself with a tarp when I eat barbeque."

Jack felt somewhat better about barbeque sauce than blood, but not much.

"This is a nice place," Murphy said.

"Thanks. It's a little piece of Detroit history," Jack said. "It was built by a lumber baron more than 100 years ago."

"I like your Grande Ballroom posters, too" Murphy added. "Also a piece of history."

"I don't know if Baxter told you or not, but I am a big fan of the Sixties."

"He did tell me that. I'm a big fan, too. Some people think I'm stuck in the Sixties. I used to go to the Grande back in the day, saw some great bands there: the MC5, the Stooges, Cream, the Who, John Lee Hooker. I smoked a joint with Chuck Berry in the Men's Room."

"It was before my time, but it sounds like a really cool place."

"It was, but that was then and this is now. It's like Buddha said, 'Do not dwell in the past, do not dream of the future, concentrate the mind on the present. Don't screw around.'"

Jack didn't know much about Buddha, but he was pretty sure he never said, "Don't screw around."

"Are you interested in Buddhism, Mr. Murphy?"

"It's just Murphy, and I'm more than just interested – I'm a Buddhist. Didn't Baxter tell you that?"

Jack wanted to say Baxter didn't tell him a lot of things about the detective he recommended, but he said something more polite instead.

"He didn't tell me much about you, other than you are a very capable private detective. In fact, he said you were the best at what you do."

"I can see by the way you're looking at me you're having doubts about that. My looks are deceiving, that's a plus in my business. You should trust your friend Baxter, he's a great man, I owe him my life. But since he hasn't told you anything about me, how 'bout I give you the highlights?"

"Sure."

"I joined the Army out of high school, they taught me how to sneak around and kill people. I did a couple of tours in 'Nam, when I came back the only place I could apply my job skills was with the Detroit Police department. I joined the force, got a few medals for bravery and a few suspensions for stupidity, retired after 30 years and started my own private investigation business."

"I gotta ask – when did you become a Buddhist?"

"It's a long story. Short version is I learned it from Buddhist monks in Cambodia when I was in the Army."

"I thought you went to Vietnam."

"I was an Army Ranger, what they called a lurp: Long Range Reconnaissance Patrol. Our job was to hump it through the backcountry looking for bad guys. One time they choppered us into Cambodia on a Black Ops mission and we got our asses handed to us. Some monks found me crawling around half dead in the jungle and saved my life. They taught me Khmer swear words and Buddhist wisdom. I've been using both ever since."

"Wow."

"Yeah, wow. That's enough about me. You wanna know what I found out about the three students who you think set you up yet?"

"Yes, of course. I was going to ask about that."

"Bradley Fennimore, Kevin DiNardo, Maxwell Rodner. You call them the Wise Guys, they call themselves Melcher, Casper and Baltimore. You were right about them – they did it. Shot the video on a cell phone, edited it to make you look bad, and put it on the Internet. They used that social media shit to get everyone all riled up and to organize the protest in front of your office building."

"I knew it. You have proof?"

"I got proof. Recordings of them talking about it."

"How did you get that?"

"I put a bug in their couch."

"You broke into someone's home?"

"No. You told Baxter they hang out at the Old Miami on Cass Avenue."

"They used to talk about it in class all the time."

"That worked out pretty good for me – I like to hang out there, too. Before the kids took it over the Old Miami was where all the Vietnam vets hung out. They remembered us when no one else did. They got metal sculptures of an M-16 and a guitar on the front door and a little Vietnam war shrine behind the bar. Some of us vets are too stubborn to go somewhere else. I put a listening device in the couch where they always sit. When they show up I speed dial a number on my phone and I can listen to what they're saying and record it if I want. I hear a lot of things, not just about what they did to you."

"What do you mean?"

"Your Wise Guys are quite the busy beavers. They're into mixed martial arts, ultimate fighting, that sort of stuff. They're also into parkour – you know what that is?"

"Never heard of it."

"Me neither, I had to look it up. It comes from the French word 'parcours' which means 'course.' It's when you run around a city jumping and climbing over everything."

"You mean those idiots who race around campus like demented acrobats?"

"Yeah, those guys. They're also into what they call 'roof and tunnel hacking.' That's where you find ways to sneak onto rooftops or into the utility tunnels under buildings."

"Really? I didn't know that was a thing. I guess I understand the appeal of going on rooftops, but I don't get tunnels. I didn't even know we had them around here."

"Every big building has them for the maintenance people and building engineers to use. Around here we have steam tunnels as an added bonus. There's miles of them in downtown Detroit, they built them more than a hundred years ago to heat buildings. I used them myself one time on a case."

"You went in a steam tunnel?"

"I used an abandoned steam tunnel to sneak up on some bad guys. It's a long story, I'll tell you some other time. I got one more thing to tell you about your students."

"My former students. What is it?"

"I'm not sure exactly what it is, but they are planning something big. It's coming up in a few weeks. They were talking about it and the band started playing, I couldn't hear anything after that. I'm going to try to find out more as soon as I can. In the meantime, I have a question for you."

"Go ahead."

"What do you want all this information for? Obviously you knew these guys did it before you called Baxter and got me involved. Are you going to take them to court and sue them or maybe try to get them thrown in jail?"

"No."

"That's good. I'm not sure how legal or admissible any of the stuff I have is. It might not stand up in court. So what are you going to do, have them beat up? That's not something I normally do, but in this case I might make an exception. I like most of the kids who hang out at the OM but these little shits need to be flushed."

"Thanks, but I don't want them beat up. I thought I had a plan. Once I had proof I was going to organize a protest of my own against them and what they did to me. I was going to get the professors and students who supported me to march and picket, maybe have a sit-in. But I've decided not to do that."

"What made you change your mind?"

"I had a heart attack and died."

"Heart attacks are a bitch. I've had couple myself, but I've never died."

"I wouldn't recommend it, but it wasn't all bad. I'm not sure exactly what's changed, but I feel different now. The idea of getting revenge doesn't have the same appeal to me that it did."

"But you still have some unfinished business. That's why I'm here."

"There were a lot of ugly things written about me on the Internet after that video was posted. I got attacked by a mob in front of my office and sucker punched by the chairman of my department."

"So a lot of people don't like you."

"After that someone gave me an illegal street drug and I died."

"And there's somebody who really doesn't like you."

"I want to find out who drugged me, and if they plan on doing anything else."

"Sounds like a good idea. So tell me what happened, from the start."

Jack took a breath and gathered his thoughts, then told his story straight through: from the class where his lecture was secretly recorded to the protest knockout to the party poisoning to his death and resurrection in the hospital. His near-death experience still felt slightly embarrassing and completely unbelievable to him, so he left that part out.

"I need you to find out who gave me the drug and how they did it, and what happened at the hospital when I died. What do you think?" he asked.

"Let's start with the drug. Someone at your party slipped you a mickey."

"You mean they put a drug in my drink? I thought of that, but it's impossible. I was surrounded by friends and colleagues all night."

"You'd be surprised by what friends and colleagues can do. What about before the party? Did you have anything to drink then?"

"I had an iced tea at lunch and nothing after that. I felt fine all afternoon."

"Who served you the drink?"

"The waitresses at the Traffic Jam. There were two of them that served us drinks during the dinner. They took turns serving our table."

"What were you drinking?"

"What difference does that make?"

"Maybe none. What were you drinking?"

"Moscow Mules."

"You were drinking Moscow Mules at the Traffic Jam?"

"Yes."

"Were you the only one at your party drinking Moscow Mules?"

"Yes."

Murphy leaned back in his chair and smiled, as if the answer they were seeking was too obvious for words. Jack tried to follow his logic, but before he could catch up Murphy was racing off in another direction.

"That's enough about the party for now. Tell me about the hospital."

"Like I said, they took me to Henry Ford Hospital because I was experiencing the symptoms of a heart attack. When I got there they followed protocol and gave me a beta blocker, but that drug interacted with the street drug and caused a real heart attack."

"You want me to confirm all this so you can sue them for malpractice."

"I don't want to sue them for malpractice. I just want to find out what happened."

"Have you asked them?"

"Yes. They wouldn't tell me anything, other than I had a heart attack and died."

"What else is there to know?"

"I want details. I want to know what happened before I died and after I died. What did they say? What did they do?"

Throughout their conversation Murphy had sat back casually in his chair, now he leaned forward and stared straight at Jack. For a moment he seemed to be turning things over in his mind, then he sat back and nodded.

"I can find that out if you want."

"Even if they don't want to talk about it?"

"I've hauled a lot of gunshot victims into the Henry Ford emergency room over the years, myself included. I'm sort of a preferred customer, frequent flyer, whatever. I have contacts there who will tell me what you want to know. My question to you is *why* do you want to know? If you're not going to sue them, what difference does it make?"

Jack had reached a familiar crossroads, one that he was reluctant to move beyond. He was uncomfortable talking about things he didn't understand or believe in. He had told himself beforehand that he wasn't going to mention it to Murphy, and nothing about the private detective's appearance or demeanor had caused him to change his mind.

And yet…

It had happened, of that he had no doubt.

If someone could confirm what he heard and saw that night it would prove that it was real. The man sitting across from him had contacts who could tell him what happened. He claimed to be a Buddhist, which seemed like an indication of open mindedness.

And he clearly had been drinking, which would probably help.

More drinking would probably help even more.

He could use some help himself.

"Would you like a drink?" Jack asked. "I'm going to tell you a story that will be hard to believe."

TWENTY–THREE

Connecting The Dots

It took Luc all of 30 seconds to find Casper at the Old Miami Lounge.

He told the bartender he was looking for a guy named Casper and was directed to a couch in the corner where three young men were sitting. Luc left Jasper sitting at the bar and went over to introduce himself.

"You fellas got a minute? I'd like to talk to you."

The three kept talking among themselves and did not look up.

"I'm a friend of Ajeet."

This time they looked up.

One of the young men motioned for Luc to pull up a nearby chair. There was usually an old fat guy who sat there, but today it was empty.

"How do you know Ajeet?"

"I met him up north. We hung out, partied. He was a nice guy."

"He's dead."

"I know. He killed himself, eh? That's too bad. Like I said, he was a nice guy."

"You met him up north, are you a yooper?"

"Yeah, I'm yooper. I live in Houghton. And you guys are trolls."

"Trolls?"

"You never heard about trolls? A troll is someone who lives under the bridge."

Luc thought it would help to break the ice with a joke.

No one was smiling.

"You know, the Mackinaw Bridge."

Still no smiles.

"So what are you doing here? Why are you talking to us?"

"Before he killed himself, Ajeet told me if anything happened to him I should look up Casper in the Old Miami Lounge. It was like he knew he was going to do it soon. The bartender sent me over here, he said one of you is Casper, I'm not sure which one he was pointing to."

"I'm Casper," said the one in the middle. "This is Baltimore and this is Melch."

"Nice to meet you. I'm Luc."

Luc stuck out his hand but there were no takers.

"So tell me, Luc, why did Ajeet want you to talk to Casper?" asked Melch.

"My friend and I – he's sitting at the bar, his name is Jasper. That's funny, eh, Jasper and Casper."

Once again there were no smiles, so Luc continued.

"Jasper and I are the ones who delivered the party supplies to Ajeet. He said that's what you call them, party supplies. I figured with him being gone I would come down here to pay my condolences and offer my services."

"What kind of services are you offering?"

"I told you, I deliver party supplies."

"I don't know what you're talking about," said Melch. "But why don't you go sit with your friend at the bar for a minute, we have something we want to discuss in private."

Luc went back to the bar and poured himself a beer from the pitcher Jasper had ordered. By the time he finished it the three students sitting on the couch were motioning him back over.

"Before anyone says anything more about party supplies, we have a few questions to ask you," said Melch.

"Ask me anything you want."

For the next ten minutes the three young men questioned Luc about every detail of his relationship to Ajeet – how they met, how they partied, how they made the drug deal. At one point Baltimore couldn't restrain himself any longer, he had to ask.

"Why the fuck did you name it Howdy Doody?"

Luc laughed.

"There's an old guy we work with, a relative of mine. He used to watch a TV show when he was a kid that had a puppet called Howdy Doody. They're white pills with a big smile and red spots, he thought they looked like freckles. It reminded him of Howdy Doody. They're both friendly little guys that make you smile. You can google it, see for yourself."

"We did that already, but we weren't sure about the connection," said Baltimore. "We just thought it was a cool name. We even…"

"Okay, that's enough for now," said Melch. "We only have one more question. Are you a cop?"

"Hell no. I hate cops."

The three looked at each other for a moment and exchanged barely discernable nods before Melch spoke.

"Okay, we're in. Let's do this."

Luc returned to the bar a few minutes later.

"We got a deal," he said.

"Same price?"

"Higher price. I told them the cost of our supplies had gone up, they didn't say a word. They want twice as much as their normal order."

"We only brought what they usually order with us."

"No shit, Sherlock. They're going to go get half the money and call me in two hours, tell us where to meet them. We'll give them what we have with us."

"Then what?"

"They come up north next week with the rest of the money to pick up the rest."

"You think it could be a trap? Maybe they'll try to rip us off or something."

"I'm not worried about that at all. They act tough, but they're college boys. They'd shit their pants if I pulled my piece, but I'm not going to have to. They're not to try anything stupid."

"So we just sit here and wait for the call?"

"We're not going to sit here drinking beer for two hours. We got some work we can do, won't take long."

"What's that?"

"We gotta visit a professor and pick up the package our friend Ajeet sent her."

TWENTY-FOUR

Ghost Story

Baxter had mentioned one other thing about Murphy: he liked Jack Daniels.

To prepare for their meeting Jack had bought a bottle to use for a toast when Murphy took his case. But before they could get to the celebration he found himself pouring them both a generous amount of Old No. 7 over ice to loosen his tongue and to make his story easier for Murphy to swallow.

He spoke between sips as Murphy listened without interruption. When he finished Murphy downed his drink in one tilt of his glass and then spoke.

"So you were a ghost."

"No. It was what they call a near-death experience."

"You left your body and floated around. You could see and hear them, but they couldn't see or hear you. You flew through the roof."

"Yes."

"Then you were a ghost."

"Whatever you call it, I know that it happened. I know it's hard to believe – it's hard for me to believe – but it was real, and you can prove it."

"By finding out what the doctors and nurses did and said when you died."

"Yes. I've told you what happened. If they tell you the same story then what happened to me wasn't a dream or a hallucination – it was real."

"Okay, professor. I'll check my sources and see what happened. I'll even get you up on the roof to see if Howdy Doody is still up there. But I have a question for you – what happens if your story checks out?"

Jack didn't have an answer for that question. He was so focused on finding out if what happened to him was real that he hadn't thought about anything beyond that. If he knew it really happened would it change how he looked at things? Would it bring him peace or drive him crazy? Would he talk about it publicly and risk being ridiculed and ostracized, or had that ship already sailed?

"I don't know what happens if it was real," he said finally. "I hadn't thought that far ahead. I guess it will change things, but I'm not sure how."

Murphy grabbed the bottle and poured them both another generous drink.

"Baxter told me you had two mysteries you needed help with. You've added another, so now you have three," he said.

"Three?"

"Who gave you the street drug that killed you. What the medical team did when you died. And what happened to you when you died."

"Will you help me?"

"I'll help you with the first two. We'll get started tomorrow – you can come with me to Henry Ford Hospital and do a little detective work with me. Cheers."

They clinked their glasses. Jack took a sip and Murphy finished his in one gulp.

"What about the third one?"

Murphy set down his glass and smiled.

"Buddhists believe in an afterlife, that not everything ends with death," he said. "I don't know anything about ghosts, but I should be able to start you down the right path."

"How?"

"I got a gal."

TWENTY-FIVE

A True Genius Appears

Jack surprised himself by agreeing to meet with a physics professor to talk about his death. He was equally surprised when Murphy called her and she agreed to meet him in an hour. His final surprise came when he arrived at her office and found himself sitting opposite a casually dressed woman with cropped blonde hair and a warm smile.

His first thought was that she didn't look like a scientist.

His second thought was he should say something, not just sit there staring at her.

"I was told you are very busy right now, Professor Stollard," he said finally. "Thanks for meeting with me on such short notice."

He silently scolded himself for focusing on appearances and not accomplishments: he'd heard her work was at the leading edge of the boy's club known as physics. But he wasn't just reacting to a shattered stereotype.

Something more was going on.

"Please call me Maggie, and there is no need to thank me. I'm always happy to help out Murphy. I also was curious to meet you."

"Can I ask why?"

"You were dead. That is something I've been interested in professionally for many years… and recently much more personally."

"I suppose it is interesting. I hadn't really thought about it that way."

"And you were viral. That's interesting, too."

"The whole thing with that video…"

"Don't worry, Murphy told me your side of the story, and he said it
checks out – that's good enough for me."

"I'm not the crazy, angry guy you see in that video. I really care about
my students. I try to make a positive difference in their lives."

"I'm sure you do, and I'd love to talk more about it, but I have a lot of
work to do this afternoon. So let's stick to death for now."

"Murphy said you have a theory based on quantum physics that
explains what happens when you die."

"I didn't develop the theory, but I find it logical and compelling. But
first things first – tell me what happened to you."

This was the hard part.

When Jack thought about what had happened to him he was certain
it was real. But when he began explaining it to other people that certainty
slipped away. Saying the words out loud made the whole thing seem impossible; a bad dream not worth sharing. On top of all that, for some reason he
couldn't quite fathom, he had suddenly become concerned about what she
thought of him.

Howdy Doody didn't help.

He decided to stall for time.

"Murphy said you two met at a Buddhist studies group."

"Yes. It's an informal group that meets here on campus, mostly
professors from different disciplines, with Murphy being the most interesting exception."

"Are you a Buddhist?"

"No. Religious beliefs are sort of a hobby of mine, especially as they relate to consciousness and afterlife. I'm intrigued by the Buddhist concept of Dukkha."

The blank look on Jack's face was her signal to continue.

"Dukkha is usually translated as 'suffering' but it really refers to the ultimately unsatisfactory nature of temporary states and things, including pleasant things."

"Like love?"

As soon as the words were out of his mouth, Jack regretted saying it. But Maggie seemed to take it in stride.

"Yes, like love. I hate to rush you, but we're running out of time, and I really do have to get back to work soon. Do you want to tell me what happened?"

For whatever reason Jack was now ready to take the plunge. He told her the entire story straight through, including Howdy Doody. She didn't laugh or roll her eyes as he had feared, but instead became increasingly energized as he told his tale, interrupting several times to ask for more details. She was smiling when he finished, but not in a bad way.

"That's fascinating. Are you familiar with quantum theory?"

"I'm familiar with it, but I don't really understand it."

"No one really understands it, not even those of us who have devoted our lives to studying it. It's based on the simple principle that matter and energy have the properties of both particles and waves. But after that it gets very weird very quickly."

"Like the cat in the box that is dead and not dead."

"Until it is observed – the observation itself affects the outcome. In quantum mechanics you don't have a definite position until you collide with something else. The experiment I'm working on right now involves that principle."

"So I'm like the cat in the box?"

"Not really. At the moment quantum theory has only been proven to apply in subatomic particles. The theory that most directly applies to your experience was first proposed a few years ago by Dr. Robert Lanza. He believes that consciousness exists outside of time and space, and can be anywhere: in the human body and outside of it. In other words, it is non-local in the same sense that quantum objects are non-local."

"So where does it go when you die?'

"Dr. Lanza believes the body receives consciousness in the same way that a cable box receives satellite signals. So it does not end with the death of the physical vehicle."

"It goes back to the cable company?"

Maggie ignored Jack's attempt at humor.

"This is where it gets strange."

Jack said nothing, but in his view the conversation was already way past strange.

"Like many mainstream physicists and astrophysicists, Dr. Lanza believes in the possibility of the existence of parallel worlds and multiple universes. The body can be dead in one universe and continue to exist in another, where it absorbs the consciousness that has migrated. A dead person who travels through a tunnel doesn't end up in heaven or hell, but in a similar world he or she once inhabited."

"But this time alive."

"Yes, exactly."

"And you believe this?"

"It's controversial, but it's not outside the realm of possibility."

Before Jack could ask another question, Maggie glanced up at the clock on the wall and grimaced.

"I'm sorry, I would love to discuss this further, but I really do have work that can't wait," she said. "If you'd like we can continue this discussion some other time."

"I'd like to, but I'm leaving to go up north in a few days, and I won't be coming back for quite a while."

"That's unfortunate. I don't have any time to spare in the next few days. My experiment involves two locations, and the research assistant who was helping me in one of them passed away unexpectedly last week. It's a terrible situation but I have to keep going, the window of opportunity for completing this project is very small."

"I understand. I've enjoyed talking to you, thank you for your time. I'm sorry to hear about your assistant."

Jack stood to leave, hesitated for a moment, then reached across Maggie's desk to shake her hand.

"Thank you again. I hope your experiment goes well."

Jack shook her hand and thanked her again, but for some reason he didn't leave. Fortunately for him, before his failure to move became too obvious or awkward, there was a knock on the door.

"Who is it?" Maggie asked in a loud voice.

The reply was low and muffled, but unmistakable.

"I'm a friend of Ajeet."

TWENTY-SIX

Friend Of Ajeet

On his way out of the office Jack passed by the person who had knocked.

He didn't like what he saw.

The young man standing in the doorway was older and scruffier than most students. He didn't respond to Jack's nod and hello, and barely waited for him to step into the hallway before slipping inside and shutting the door.

Jack felt a growing sense of unease as he walked down the hall. He slowed to a near stop, wanting to turn around but not knowing exactly why. When he reached a bulletin board he stopped completely and pretended to read a poster. He stood there for more than a minute, confused and embarrassed, hoping no one would see him and trying desperately to think of an excuse to return to Maggie's office.

His problem was solved when he heard the shouting.

Jack hurried back down the hall and threw open the door at the same time he knocked on it. The young man was standing in front of Maggie's desk, she was up and out of her chair on the other side.

"Sorry to interrupt, Professor Stollard," Jack said. "I have another question if you have a moment."

"I do have a moment right now, Professor Crost. This young man was just leaving."

Jack stepped forward and held out his hand.

"I'm Jack Crost. And you are?"

The friend of Ajeet started to say something but stopped himself. He looked at Jack for a moment, shook his head, and walked out of the office.

"You have a question?" Maggie asked.

"What?"

"You said you had a question."

"Ah, sure. Why was that student yelling at you?"

"That's your question?"

"It is now."

"He wasn't a student, I'm pretty sure of that. And he wasn't a friend of Ajeet."

"Who's Ajeet?"

"Ajeet Nirmal is the research assistant I told you about, the one who passed away unexpectedly last week. It was shocking and sad – he was up in the U.P. getting ready to help start my experiment, and he committed suicide."

"I'm very sorry."

"I'm very sorry, too. The last time I spoke to him I yelled at him for being late to a meeting. He was a brilliant student, but I was concerned that he was spending too much time partying with his friends. I feel awful. I might have pushed him over the edge."

"So that wasn't a friend of Ajeet. What does it matter to you?"

"Because Ajeet mattered to me, and I had a bad feeling about his so-called friend. Just before he committed suicide, Ajeet sent a Fed Ex package to my office address for pickup by someone named Chemic."

"Was that his first name or last name?"

"It could have been either, or a nickname. There was just that. The young man claimed he was Chemic – he wouldn't tell me his full name –

and said he wanted to pick the package up. He said Ajeet had sent him a text and told him to."

"But you didn't give it to him."

"I asked him if he lived in the Towers residential suites with Ajeet, and he said yes. Ajeet didn't live in the Towers residential suite. He was not a friend of Ajeet, so I didn't give it to him."

"And that's why he started yelling?"

"Yes."

"What's in the package?"

"I don't know. I locked it in my file cabinet as soon as it arrived."

"So what are you going to do now?"

"Ajeet was here to get his doctorate in physics. His family lives in India. They are Hindu, so he was cremated shortly after he died and his body was shipped back home. His friend Robert, who also works for me as a graduate assistant, is gathering his belonging to send to his family. I am going to add the package to that shipment."

"If he sent a Fed Ex package just before he killed himself there could be some kind of suicide note in it."

"Believe me, I've thought about that. If this Chemic person doesn't show up, I'm going to send it to his family and let them sort it out. It's not my package."

They both stood still and silent after that, looking at each other from across Maggie's desk. Before the moment became too awkward she spoke.

"So tell me again why you came back – it wasn't to ask a question. He didn't start yelling for several minutes, you should have been long gone. Why did you wait around?"

"To tell you the truth, I'm not exactly sure why. I had a bad feeling about him, like you did, but there was more to it than that. It felt like a rubber band when I walked away – the farther I got, the stronger the pull backwards."

"There are two things I think I need to point out before we go any further. First, I'm not a damsel in distress, I can take of myself. Second, I don't believe in magical thinking."

"Magical thinking?"

"Irrational beliefs based on emotions. Unfortunately, the hippies I'm told you so admire were great practitioners of magical thinking."

"I'm not sure I'm following you."

"I don't belief a mysterious force pulled you back to me."

"But you do believe a cat in a box can be dead and alive at the same time?"

"Touché, professor. There are many things in this universe that we can't explain. I didn't mean to insult you, I just wanted to be clear that logic is the tool I prefer for unlocking mysteries. Thank you for coming back to my office, for whatever reason."

Maggie reached across the desk and shook Jack's hand, but when he tried to withdraw it she didn't let go. Instead she looked into his eyes and considered an alternative to saying goodbye.

"Are you claustrophobic?" she asked finally.

"Not really. Why?"

"I'm going to spend most of my time in the next few days monitoring equipment underground, in a salt mine under the city. I have to be there for several hours but the work itself doesn't take much time. If you come with me we could continue our conversation."

"I'd like that."

"Then come back here to my office tomorrow at one o'clock."

TWENTY-SEVEN

Back Up On The Roof

Murphy and Jack were barely able to squeeze into the elevator crowded with doctors, nurses and patients going about their business in the Henry Ford Hospital Clinic building. Fortunately, by the time they reached the top floor everyone else was gone.

The business they were going about was best done without witnesses.

The two men walked off the elevator and down the hall with Murphy leading the way. They rounded a corner and walked to the end of that hallway before stopping in front of a door marked "Hospital Staff Only."

Murphy looked around, then tried opening the door.

"It's locked," he said.

"What did you expect?"

"I know a guy who works here, he was supposed to leave it open for us."

"So what now? Should we leave?"

"No. Not a problem. I got this."

Murphy reached into his sport coat and took out a piece of wire and something that looked like a small Swiss army knife. He bent down to the lock and a moment later they were walking through the door into a tall, narrow service corridor crowded with pipes and ductwork. Murphy led the way down the corridor into a small room with a metal ladder built into the wall.

"Up you go," he said. "There's no lock on the hatch, just give it a hard push. And don't close it behind you, it's hard to open from the outside."

"You're really not coming with me?"

"I told you, I have to talk to a few of the people I know here about what happened to you. I'll meet you in the lobby in an hour."

Jack made the mistake of muttering, "it is a long way up there" to himself a little too loudly.

"You think I couldn't climb that ladder?" Murphy asked. "I may be old and fat but I got skills. I could be up and through that hatch before you made the third rung."

"Sorry, Murphy. I'm kind of nervous. I wouldn't mind a little company."

"Buddha said, 'The whole secret of existence is to have no fear. Never fear what will become of you, depend on no one. Only the moment you reject all help are you freed.' My guy assured me no one will bother you. You got this."

"Right. See you in the lobby."

Jack turned and began to climb up the ladder. He had estimated that the hatch was 15 feet above the floor, but when he reached it felt more like a mile. He braced himself on the ladder and pushed up on the hatch. It took more effort than he expected, even with Murphy's instructions, but it finally swung open and Jack climbed out onto the roof.

He stood up and looked around, and felt as if he had been struck by lightning.

This was the spot.

The hatch opened up at the bottom of a two-story structure on the clinic's roof that housed its heating, ventilating and air conditioning systems. Jack stood at the far end of this structure, in front of him was a breathtaking view of downtown Detroit, behind him, painted on its brick wall, was a massive blue and white Henry Ford Hospital logo.

It had been less than a week since Jack had seen Howdy Doody on the roof. He was certain he would find him in the same spot, sitting at the bottom of the Henry Ford sign. When he first looked around his certainty turned into euphoria: he had definitely seen this place before. But when he looked down euphoria crashed into reality.

Howdy Doody was nowhere in sight.

His plan had been to photograph the puppet sitting there, meet up with Murphy afterwards, then notify the authorities. They might claim he put it there himself, but Murphy would back him up as a witness. Whatever anyone else thought or did afterward, the most important thing was proving it to himself.

Jack stood staring at the spot for a long time, certainty and euphoria replaced by disappointment and fear. Had he imagined all of this? Was he losing his mind? After a week of incredible events how could he know what was real anymore?

In desperation his mind finally latched onto a Plan B: he would examine the area where he had seen the puppet sitting for any small trace of its existence. It wasn't much, but it was the only logical way forward.

He left the hatch open as Murphy had instructed and walked over to the spot below the sign, not sure exactly what he was looking for – a length of black string, a piece of checkered cloth, a tiny boot? He looked and saw nothing, just some white specs on the black tar of the roof.

White specs with red dots.

Jack moved closer and saw the specs were a handful of pills scattered in front of the wall where Howdy had been sitting. He knelt down, picked up several and put them his pocket without thinking, logic and purpose giving way to the mindless numbness of shock.

He could think of nothing more to do.

Jack admired the distant skyline for a moment, then turned and walked back to the hatch. He lowered himself down carefully until his feet found a rung, then ducked inside and shut the hatch behind him. Climbing slowly down the ladder he tried and failed to think of what his next steps should be. Maybe Murphy would have a suggestion, or at least have more information to share.

Jack walked back down the service corridor and opened the door to the hallway. As he closed the door behind him, two hospital security guards stepped up to meet him.

"Sir, you are not authorized to be in a service area," the closest one said. "Please come with us."

"This is a little embarrassing, but I can explain what I was doing up there," Jack said. "Believe me, it was totally harmless."

"Sir, come with us," the guard repeated. "You can tell your story to the police."

TWENTY-EIGHT

Overheard In The Diner

"You look like shit, Jack."

"The valet forgot to iron my shirt."

"Let's get some breakfast. I'm buying."

They walked a short distance from the front steps of the jail to Murphy's car. The car's badges were missing – there was no blue oval or gold bow tie – so Jack couldn't figure out its make. All he knew for sure was that it was a gigantic beast from the '70s with a front seat as big as a couch.

It started up with a deep rumble and they sped away.

They rode in silence for several minutes before Murphy spoke.

"Coney Island okay?"

"Sure."

"American or Lafayette?"

Jack hesitated.

In Detroit it was big deal which chili hot dog restaurant you chose – the American, started by a Greek immigrant in 1917, or the Lafayette, started right next store a few years later by his brother after a fight over the ingredients in their chili. You picked one and remained loyal for life, risking the loss of family and friends if you switched.

Jack decided to play it safe.

"Whichever one you like best is fine with me."

They drove on in silence. A few minutes later Murphy executed a tire squealing U-turn, pulled to the curb and exclaimed, "Lafayette – we are here!

When they went inside Murphy was greeted enthusiastically by the staff and customers. They sat at the counter and ordered breakfast. Murphy waited until their food arrived to apologize.

"I'm sorry I got you arrested," he said. "My guy had it all set up for us, there shouldn't have been any problems."

"So what happened?"

"I should have known something was wrong when the door to the service corridor was locked. My guy left unlocked for us, but somebody noticed it was open and locked it up again."

"Was that why they were waiting for me?"

"Yeah. They found the door unlocked a week ago and since then they've been checking it every day. My guy didn't know that. Last night the security guard who relocked it before we got there came back to check it again. When he saw it was unlocked and the hatch was open he went back to the main hallway and radioed for backup."

"And where were you when all this was going on?"

"I told you, I went to talk to my sources. After that I waited in the lobby like we said. By the time I figured out what happened you were at the police station."

"I had to spend to spend the night in jail in Detroit. I wouldn't recommend it."

"You're lucky you got out as fast as you did, on your own recognizance without any bail. I had to call in a lot of favors to make that happen. It usually takes a lot longer to process a suspect, especially someone charged with trespassing and drug possession."

"Those drugs weren't mine!"

Everyone in the diner froze, and Jack realized belatedly that he had protested too loudly. As people began to resume their activities he lowered his voice and continued.

"I found those pills up on the roof right where Howdy Doody was sitting the night I died. I thought they might be some kind of clue, I was going to show them to you later."

"Don't beat yourself up, I would have done the same thing. The problem is you were taken to the same hospital a week ago for a drug overdose. The police are testing the pills right now, if they are an illegal drug that charge will stick."

"So what do I do now?"

"I'd talk to Baxter, get his advice. This is pretty serious stuff. Based on your three trips to the hospital in the last 10 days, your drug overdose and your Internet video, the police think you're some kind of flipped out drug abuser."

"I'm not crazy!"

Once again everyone in the diner stopped what they were doing, and Jack realized for a second time he had used an inappropriate volume. After another moment of silence activity in the diner resumed and Murphy asked a question.

"You want to hear the good news?'

"There's good news? Sure."

"I told you I'd solve two mysteries for you: who gave you the street drug that killed you and what the medical team did to you the night you died."

"Yeah."

"Yesterday while you were getting arrested I found out what the medical team did that night."

"How'd you do that?"

"I told you I know lots of people who work in that hospital. So I asked around and found someone who was right there in the room as part of the medical team."

This time Jack made a conscious effort to keep his voice calm and quiet.

"What happened?"

"Everything you told me checks out. What you said happened is exactly what happened."

Jack's mind began racing, fueled by a combination of joy and fear. He was happy to know he was right about what happened, but afraid of what getting a peak beyond the veil might do to him. Murphy kept talking but it took a few moments before Jack could follow what he was saying.

"So then the two doctors had a big fight. One of them was saying the drug you had taken had a bad reaction with the beta blocker they gave you. The other said you'd had a heart attack and died, straight up. Lucky for you, the first doc ignored him. He gave you six shots of adrenaline, like you said. That brought you back from the dead."

"I remember it clearly. It's like a movie I can rewind and watch any time I want."

"Not bad for a dead guy."

They paused their conversation while the woman behind the counter took their empty plates and refilled their coffees. When she left Jack had a question for Murphy.

"Would your source be willing to make a public statement about what happened?"

"I thought you said you weren't going to sue."

"I'm not. But at some point I might want to prove that what happened to me was real, that it wasn't a hallucination or my imagination."

"That you're not crazy?"

"Yeah, I guess that's it – that I'm not crazy."

"I'm not sure if my source would be willing to go on the record or not. The hospital is very nervous about the whole incident, that's why it's been so hard for you to find out anything. If it comes down to that, I can ask for you. But in the meantime, you and I know you're not crazy, so that's something."

"It is something. It's very important to me. Thanks for making it happen."

"You're welcome. Now I gotta find out more about who gave you the drug in the first place. To me that's even more important, whoever wanted to hurt you is still out there. I have a few leads I'm checking out, it shouldn't take too long. In the meantime I'd suggest you talk to Baxter as soon as possible, see what he says you should do about the charges."

"I will, but first I have to do a little investigating of my own."

"What are you investigating?"

"The third mystery."

"What happened to you when you died? I thought you already talked to Maggie."

"This time we're going to go a lot deeper."

TWENTY-NINE

A Date With Death

"You look like shit, Jack."

"You're the second person who's said that to me today."

"Rough morning?"

"The last 24 hours haven't gone exactly as planned."

"We need to get going, but if you'd like you can tell me about it on the way."

Jack used the 15 minutes it took to drive from Maggie's office to the salt mine to describe the most recent events in his rapidly unraveling life. He emphasized his reluctance to break any rules, Murphy's insistence that there would be no trouble, and his absolute innocence regarding drugs. He then explained that he had arrived at her office straight from a night in jail, stopping only for breakfast.

Her response was not encouraging.

"You thought you'd find a puppet on the roof?"

"Well, yeah."

Maggie stopped the car at a guard shack and was waved through. She parked outside an industrial warehouse and a few minutes later they were huddled in a noisy elevator plunging downward.

"I'm not especially fond of this part of the journey," she said. "I prefer the cargo elevator but they won't let us take it unless we're bringing in equipment."

When the elevator stopped they walked out into a large white chamber and climbed into a golf cart equipped with headlights. As they sped down a tunnel she continued their previous conversation where she left off.

"I should clarify my remark – I have no reason to doubt that you saw a puppet on the roof of Henry Ford Hospital. But I am curious as to why you thought it would still be there a week later."

Jack had no good answer for this.

"There was no logical reason to think it would be there. I just hoped it would."

"Hope is a waking dream."

"Buddha?"

"Aristotle."

They were speeding down a wide tunnel barely lit by bulbs in cages strung along the wall. Maggie clearly had the route memorized, making sudden turns without hesitating. When the string of light bulbs ended she switched on the headlights and drove on without slowing down. After several minutes of riding in silence she pulled to a stop in front of a small side tunnel.

"We have to walk from here, the cart won't fit down this tunnel," she explained. "Again, not my favorite part of the journey."

Maggie grabbed a flashlight, located a panel on the wall, and threw several switches. The side tunnel revealed itself in an uneven patchwork of dim lights and she led the way down it, using the flashlight to help point out obstacles along the way.

"Watch your step around these cables," she cautioned. "And try to keep up, because I go through here in a hurry."

True to her word, she moved quickly through the tunnel. Jack followed as best he could, trying not to trip over the cables that snaked along the floor. When they emerged from the tunnel Jack froze.

It was awesome.

They stood in an immense white room lit by spotlights focused on what appeared to be a metal sewer pipe at least 50 feet long. The cables they had followed through the tunnel split up and ran along the ground to metal boxes on both ends of the pipe. Maggie walked over to a table covered with computers and electronic devices, sat down, and waved Jack over to join her.

"Give me a few minutes to check out these instruments, then we'll talk," she said.

Jack spent the next fifteen minutes watching as she pushed buttons and turned switches. He filled the time by looking around the room and reminding himself this was not a movie set: he really was sitting in a massive underground room next to a science experiment that made less sense to him than the efforts of Dr. Frankenstein.

"Do you want to talk about death now?" Maggie said finally, without looking away from the computer screen in front of her.

"Yes, I would. But before we do that would you mind explaining what this experiment is about?"

Maggie burst into a deep, throaty laugh.

"We're only going to be down here for four hours – that's not enough time. "

"Just give me the CliffsNotes version."

"CliffsNotes?"

"You've never heard of CliffsNotes? They're what my students used to cheat on reading assignments before they had the Internet. The name has become a generic term for a short, easy-to-understand summary."

"Okay, the CliffsNotes version of quantum entanglement is this: In 1964, a physicist named John Bell theorized that two particles can be linked to each other even if they are separated by billions of light-years of space."

"And you're going to prove that's true?"

"Bell's Theorem has been substantiated many times. But most of these efforts come up short of being indisputable proof because it's tough to design and build equipment with the needed sensitivity and performance. They've used fiber optic cables or lasers, I'm going to do it without using any type of physical connection."

"Sounds like a magic trick."

"Not magic, science. Quantum entanglement also postulates that tiny particles can instantaneously affect each other's behavior at a great distance. Einstein called that 'spooky action at a distance.'"

"He was skeptical."

"He was. I am hoping to prove him wrong."

"You're trying to prove Einstein was wrong?"

"About quantum entanglement, yes."

"Good luck with that."

"Thank you. Can we talk about death now?" Maggie asked.

"Sure."

Maggie turned away from the computer and faced Jack. He could see the big pipe over her shoulder, and in the murky distance far beyond it the wall where the room ended. He could not recall ever being in a stranger place, which seemed appropriate for the conversation they were about to have.

"Dr. Lanza…"

"The cable guy?"

"Yes, the cable guy. If you remember, he believed that consciousness was a quantum signal the body receives."

"I remember."

"Drs. Hameroff and Penrose have similar theories that are more specific. They argue that our experience of consciousness is the result of quantum gravity effects in the microtubules of our brain cells. These micro-tubules are the primary sites of quantum processing, which make them the place where consciousness resides. When you die this quantum information is released from your body, and your consciousness goes with it."

"So what *exactly* happened to me?"

"When your heart stopped beating your blood stopped flowing, causing the microtubules in your brain to lose their quantum state. The quantum information – your consciousness – wasn't destroyed, it just dissipated into the universe. When your heart started beating again it returned."

"And if my heart didn't start beating again?"

"They believe this quantum information can exist outside the body, perhaps indefinitely, as a soul."

"That sounds more like religion than science."

"I told you, studying religious beliefs is sort of a hobby of mine. They've been pointing the way for thousands of years using metaphors and allegories. In many ways science is just catching up."

Their conversation continued for hours: life, death, religion, science and a much more detailed explanation of Maggie's experiments. At one point Maggie asked what Jack thought was an odd question.

"Have you noticed anything different about yourself since you died?"

"What do mean?"

"I'm speaking primarily of your emotions. Studies have shown that most people who have a Near Death Experience are profoundly and positively transformed. They are more at peace with themselves and more accepting of others. They live in the moment and are happier and more appreciative of what the moment brings them."

"Since I died I've spent most of my moments being ridiculed, beaten and arrested. So, no, I don't think I'm any happier. But I'll let you know if anything changes."

Toward the end of their discussion Jack switched the subject to literature to demonstrate that he too possessed a degree of expertise in at least one area. As he talked about the themes of death and rebirth in the novels of the mid-twentieth century he realized to his great surprise and embarrassment that he was trying to show off.

He struggled with that thought for a moment, then thought "why the hell not?"

He doubled down with a joke.

"Did Hameroff and Penrose say anything about Howdy Doody?"

Maggie laughed, and for a moment Jack forgot about death. The only thing he could think about was how desperately he wanted to make her laugh again.

"I usually don't talk about death on the first date," he said.

Somehow a completely silent room got quieter.

"Do you really think this is a date?" Maggie asked.

"I was joking. Really."

"I believe you," Maggie said. "First dates usually involve dinner and a movie, not sitting next to a sub-atomic particle chamber in a salt mine talking about death."

It was Jack's turn to laugh.

He was relieved they had moved past his awkwardness inducing joke so easily and delighted to discover she had a sense of humor as well. Before he could begin to worry about what to do next Maggie spoke again.

"You said in my office you were leaving in a few days," she said. "And you'll be gone a long time?"

"Yes. I'm on sabbatical for a year because of that stupid video. I'm going up north to work on a novel."

"Where up north?"

"Hancock. It's in the Upper Peninsula."

"Yes, I know where Hancock is. The other half of my experiment is there."

"The other half?"

"It's the exact same setup as this one, only it's located in an old copper mine."

Jack started to ask another question, but noticed she was staring at him.

"What? What is it?" he asked.

"This is extremely presumptuous, and very spontaneous, which is not like me at all. I wouldn't ask it if I wasn't desperately short of time…"

"Ask what?"

"Will you run my experiment in Hancock for me?"

THIRTY

On The Road

"I was supposed to work at the lumber yard today."

"We needed to stick around for another day and get the package, nothing else was more important than that. When those college boys come up to get the rest of their order next week we'll have a nice pile of cash. Then you can tell those assholes at the lumber yard to go fuck themselves."

"I told you, I like working at the lumber yard."

"And I told you you're an idiot, eh? I'm going to use my share of the money to dump this rust bucket and get myself a new truck with one of them big Boss plows. We can make a lot of money plowing parking lots this winter."

They were headed north on I-75 in Luc's 20-year-old Chevy pickup.

It was getting dark and Luc was tired, but Howdy Doody was keeping him alert.

His plan had worked perfectly.

When Professor Stollard kicked him out of her office he lingered outside the door and listened. He heard her and the guy who had interrupted him – he said his name was Crost – making plans to meet at the office tomorrow and leave together at 1:00 pm. The next day he had Jasper hang around in the hallway and text him when they left. A few minutes later they had picked the lock and were searching the file cabinet she kept glancing at while he was talking to her.

They found the Fed Ex package easily.

Figuring it out was much harder.

"What do you think it means?"

"You keep asking me that, Jasper," Luc said. "And I keep telling you I don't know. But I'm going to figure it out."

"He wrote the note to that guy Chemic, his friend. He wanted him to do two things, but he didn't want to write them down."

"No shit, Sherlock. He was probably afraid someone else might open the box, like that professor bitch. So he wrote down two clues, to two puzzles. The first puzzle is, 'What is this?' It's obvious he's talking about the bottle of pills in the box. That rat bastard Ajeet wanted his friend to figure out the ingredients in our pills."

"So he was only trying to bluff us. He didn't know how to make Howdy Doody."

"No."

"So we didn't have to kill him, Luc."

"I told you, it was an accident, but I'm glad it happened. He was trying to figure it out so he could screw us."

"What about the other puzzle? The note says, 'Here's where the prize is.' What's the prize?"

"I don't know, but I want to find it. It's a prize, so it's gotta be worth something. I'm guessing those three college boys Ajeet was supplying the drugs to have something to do with it."

"The clue that's supposed to tell you where it is doesn't make any sense. Above the immortals and a bunch of numbers. What does it mean?"

Luc didn't say anything.

The light was fading.

They were heading home.

THIRTY-ONE

How Einstein Figured It Out

Maggie tried hard to persuade Jack to help her, but his answer was a polite "no."

Judging by his expression his real answer was "hell no!"

She explained that it would only take a week to run the experiment. She could easily teach him the simple tasks involved on his end. The other graduate students involved in the experiment had classes to attend at Wayne and she had classes to teach – they couldn't go up north to replace Ajeet. Time was running out, and she needed his help desperately.

"I'm sorry, I really would like to help," he said. "But the idea of getting involved in a physics experiment scares the hell out of me. I'm really no good at science, and I would hate to let you down."

She was going to tell him that not helping her was the ultimate letdown, but she changed her mind.

It was time for a different tactic.

It was time to get high.

"I understand," she said. "Do you mind if I light up a joint?"

Of all the sentences in the English language that she could have said to him at that moment, this was easily the least expected.

"A joint? Like a marijuana cigarette?"

"Yes. Don't worry, it's perfectly legal. I have a medical condition – nothing contagious – and a permit to smoke pot. I'm also somewhat claustrophobic, and I find it relaxes me when I'm down here."

While she was talking she had reached into her purse, pulled out a perfectly rolled joint and a lighter, and held them up in front of her.

"Okay?"

"Uh, sure. Why not?"

Maggie pressed the joint to her lips, lit it up, and inhaled deeply.

"Want to try it?" she asked when she finally exhaled.

"Geeze... I don't know."

"I've put you on the spot, I'm sorry. You teach Sixties literature, and I'm told you're quite enthusiastic about all things Sixties. I just assumed..."

"A lot of people assume that about me. The truth is, I haven't smoked pot since I was going to college myself, decades ago."

"I understand. I'll finish it myself, no problem."

While she took another hit off the joint, Jack began to reconsider.

He really did admire the free spirit of the Sixties, their willingness to experiment and try new things, to live life to the fullest. She said it was legal. No one was going to catch them anyway, they were at the farthest end of an enormous salt mine. And if they did get caught, he didn't have to worry about being publicly humiliated and losing his job.

That had already happened.

"I'll have some," he said finally.

"Pardon me?"

"I'll have some, please. Some marijuana."

Maggie laughed and handed him the joint.

"Good for you, Jack. Have some marijuana."

After a few tentative puffs, Jack began inhaling deeply and holding in it. They passed the joint back and forth until it burned down to a stub. Maggie snuffed it out on the salt floor and put it back into her purse.

"For someone who hasn't smoked a joint in decades you did that very nicely."

"My college education served me well."

They both laughed a little louder and longer than seemed appropriate. When they stopped laughing Maggie studied Jack for a moment, gathered her thoughts, and spoke.

"Did you know that the greatest scientific discovery of the 20th century was inspired by a Near Death Experience?"

To Jack it seemed like a lot of big words jumbled together and spoken quickly. By the time he figured out what they meant Maggie had moved on.

"One of Albert Einstein's professors at Zurich Polytechnic Institute was Albert Heim, a distinguished geologist. Heim had fallen while climbing in the Alps and had a Near Death Experience. After that he collected accounts of other people who had similar experiences and became the first person in modern history to publish a collection of what would later be referred to as NDEs."

"Einstein studied geology?" Jack said finally.

"He often took classes outside of his main area of study as electives."

"I hate it when students take my class as an elective. At least when the pre-med and pre-law students take it. They insist on getting A's, and that's what got me into trouble. But I wouldn't mind if Einstein took my course. He seems like a pretty smart guy."

They both laughed loud and long.

"Let me get to my point, Jack."

"There's a point?"

When they finished laughing she continued.

"Heim, and many of the people he interviewed who had fallen, said that time slowed down as they fell toward the ground. Years later that story inspired Einstein's thinking. Among other things, his Theory of Relativity states that as an object hurdles through space, time is altered relative to motion and speed."

Jack used his hands to make the "my head is exploding" gesture and they laughed some more.

Then Maggie got serious.

"I really am quite busy these days, you know. This experiment means everything to me. The only reason I agreed to meet you in the first place was because Murphy told me you'd had an NDE."

"You're interested in death."

"I'm interested in a lot of things that go beyond conventional physics. We don't really understand consciousness and the role it plays in the universe. Physicists are afraid to talk about it, they think it will make them look like philosophers and not scientists. I've been ostracized and shunned professionally just for asking questions about it."

"And that's why you wanted to talk to me?"

"At first. Then I found you interesting for other reasons."

"Oh. Okay."

Jack was dying to ask her what those other reasons were, but he didn't want to appear to be fishing for compliments. Or find out that the reasons she found him interesting were strictly scientific.

"I'm sorry you won't help me, but I'm even sorrier that you are going away. I would have liked to get to know you."

Jack's brain was screaming the same thing.

He thought about it, and what he could do about it. There was only one way to stay in contact with her, to find out more about this fascinating woman, to see where the relationship would go.

It was so simple and easy, he wondered why he hadn't thought of it sooner.

"Maggie, I want to help you with your experiment."

THIRTY-TWO

Who Done It

"I know who killed you."

Jack hadn't thought of Murphy as being a morning person until he opened his front door to confront the idiot who had woken him up.

It was the drunk detective, eager to share his news.

Jack could smell the booze before he opened the door. He was not as enthusiastic about having a meeting as Murphy seemed to be. It was the morning after he got out of jail and got high in a salt mine. He was tired and confused, but it was obvious there was no chance of sending Murphy away. They walked back to Jack's office and sat down to sort things out.

"It's a little early in the morning to be drinking, isn't it?" Jack asked.

"It's not early in the morning, it's late in the evening," Murphy replied. "I been out all night working on your case."

"Let me guess – you went to the Traffic Jam."

"Yeah. Then I closed the Old Miami, then I did a few other things, none of your business. I was killing time until morning."

"And you figured out who put the drug in my drink?"

"It was easy. A smart guy like you should have figured out where I was going with this the first time we talked. When you order a Moscow Mule at the Traffic Jam, what do they take from you?"

"Your driver's license."

"Copper is expensive, and too many people were ripping off the copper mugs. So they keep your license at the bar until you pay up and leave."

"You think somebody saw my driver's license and put a drug in my drink?"

"Not just somebody – Maxwell Rodner, aka Baltimore, aka Wise Guy."

"That little shit drugged me?"

"I checked the work schedule at the Traffic Jam. He was working as a bartender the night of your party."

"Why would he do that? Wasn't getting me fired good enough?"

"I've listened to your Wise Guys talking about you at the Old Miami. Of the three of them, he hates you the most. It's almost an obsession with him. He definitely has the motive, and now we know he had the opportunity."

"To try to kill me."

"I don't think he was trying to kill you. What he put in your drink was what they call a recreational drug. I think he just wanted to mess with you."

"So what do we do now? Can we go to the police?"

"I wouldn't do that right now. The evidence we've got is circumstantial. I'd wait and see how your drug arrest shakes out. You can double check with Baxter, but I would only play the Baltimore card is if the charges stick. If they decide not to prosecute you I wouldn't tip your hand at this point. There's a lot going on, and it's all connected by the drug he gave you."

"But nobody knows what it is, do they? It's just some kind of street drug that acts like meth."

"I know what it is. I heard the Wise Guys talking about it at the Old Miami. They sell it at parties they throw. It's the same white pills with red spots and a happy face stamped into them that you found on the hospital roof."

"You're kidding me."

"I'm not kidding. And it gets even crazier."

"What do you mean?"

"You know what they call this drug?"

"I have no idea."

"Howdy Doody."

THIRTY-THREE

Quantum Entanglement

Learning to run the experiment was as easy as Maggie said it would be.

Understanding it was a much greater challenge.

They had returned to the white room in the salt mine for a crash course in experimental protocol. Maggie handed Jack a clipboard with a list of tasks to be completed in order to run the experiment. His job was to flip the switches and push the buttons that turned on the equipment – a variety of lasers, computers, sensors and other devices. After a couple of dry runs Maggie declared him ready to go.

"The equipment in the Quincy Mine is identical. I'll send you a text message on the first computer when we are ready to begin – that's the only way we can communicate. Any questions?"

"What are we doing?"

"We're teleporting an entangled photon to a distant location."

"I've been reading up on this stuff online, but you've stumped me already. What's an entangled photon?"

"A photon is a particle of light. When you split it in two you call the pair of photons you've created entangled. We're sending one entangled photon from the mine where it was split to the other mine. When it gets there we are going to measure it, which will instantly change the state of its entangled partner at the location that sent it."

"Instantly?"

"Faster than the speed of light."

"I thought nothing was faster than the speed of light."

"That's what Einstein said. That's why he called quantum mechanics spooky action at a distance. He was one of the fathers of quantum theory, but he became estranged from his offspring when it got older."

"Has anyone ever done this before?"

"Many times. There's even an imaginary couple used as a standard reference: Alice and Bob."

"Alice and Bob?"

"Point A and Point B. In quantum teleportation, Alice and Bob share an entangled pair of photons. When Alice performs measurements on her particle, Bob's particle changes to match it."

"So you have Point A and Point B, how do you get the entangled particle from one to the other."

"In the past they've used optic fiber to send an entangled photon 100 kilometers. And they've used lasers to send them even farther, but both ways have their drawbacks. Both ways cause the photons to lose some of their integrity when they travel over fiber cable, and lasers have to be pointed directly at their target, or bounced off something."

"Which method are we using?"

"Neither. That's what makes this experiment interesting and important. I've developed a new way to transmit photons."

"How does it work?"

"It's complicated. And proprietary."

"You don't trust me?"

"I trust you, but I don't have three months to explain it to you. No offence, but even then you wouldn't understand it. Let's just say it's based on the quantum properties of the photons themselves and leave it at that."

"I think you underestimate me."

"Okay. The CliffsNotes version is this: the space between objects isn't empty, it contains mass and energy. Using the dynamical Casimir effect, physicists have been able to extract photons from space. Electro-magnetic fields can be used to interact with this vacuum energy. Scientists in Finland were able to beam a gravitational wave for over one kilometer, it traveled at sixty four times the speed of light. So, if we take..."

"Never mind, you're right. This is going take too long, and I probably wouldn't understand anyway. Can I ask one more question?"

"Of course."

"Why are you doing this?"

"The potential practical uses for what I'm doing are mind-boggling. This could have an incredible impact on computer science and cryptography. I hate to mention it, but perhaps someday even teleportation."

"Like in Star Trek?"

"That's why I hate to mention it. Talking about teleportation sensationalizes what we're trying to do, and gets us way ahead of ourselves. To tell you the truth, I don't really care about the practical applications of what I'm doing. What I'm really interested in is trying to figure out how quantum mechanics works."

"I had the impression we already knew that. Or at least you scientists did."

"We know *what* it does, but not *how* it does it."

"I'm not sure I'm following you."

"Quantum mechanics explains the behavior of matter and energy on the scale of atoms and subatomic particles. It is indispensable to modern electronics – it led to the invention of diodes, transistors, lasers, electron microscopes, and lots more. We know how to use it to make things work, but we really don't understand what's going on at the most basic level."

"And that bothers you."

"It bothers a lot of scientists. Are you familiar with Arthur C. Clarke?"

"Of course, the great science fiction writer."

"And science philosopher. He said, 'Any sufficiently advanced technology is indistinguishable from magic.' Quantum mechanics is magic. I want it to be science."

Jack thought for a moment about what he was going to say next. It was personal and painful, and he knew what that felt like.

He said it anyway.

"Please don't freak out, but I also did some online reading about you. Enough to understand why you think separating science from magic is important."

"I assume you're talking about what happened at Harvard."

"Yes."

"It was unfortunate. Quantum mechanics tells us that observers *create* reality. Human beings are the ultimate observers. I included consciousness in my theories and research, and the scientific establishment was horrified."

"So you were pressured into leaving, like me."

"Yes. I didn't cause a riot or get punched, but they forced me out. Oh, and my husband divorced me as well – I'm not sure if the news stories mentioned that."

"Why would he do that?"

"He's a scientist, and he couldn't stand being married to a heretic."

"I'm sorry. Losing a spouse under any circumstance is a terrible thing."

Jack hesitated for a moment and gathered himself before speaking again.

"I hate to say it, but Wayne State is quite a step down from Harvard."

"Geography isn't destiny, there are smart people everywhere. The smartest ones don't need an institution to validate themselves. I'll be honest with you, one of the main reasons I came to Wayne State was because this salt mine was nearby, and I needed it for my experiment."

"That explains a lot."

"But not everything. The university has been wonderful to me, they've supported my work 100 percent. There are outstanding facility and students here, as well. As far as I'm concerned, it's a great school"

"Ten days ago I would have agreed with you. I'm not so sure anymore. To tell you the truth, I'm not so sure about anything."

"I have to confess, I read about you online, too. Most of it was about the video incident. But there were a couple of stories from twenty years ago."

"About the robbery. About my wife."

"I'm sorry."

"Me too."

The silence that followed was as long as it was awkward. Jack searched his mind frantically for something to say, and was greatly relieved when Maggie finally spoke.

"I knew you were single before I looked online."

"I knew you were single before I looked online, too."

"Murphy?"

"Yes. Apparently he considers himself a matchmaker as well as a detective."

Maggie didn't laugh.

"I'm not much of a match these days," she said.

Jack wanted to disagree, to tell her she was a great match, but he hesitated and the moment was lost. They returned to awkward silence.

"I have a question for you," Maggie said at last.

Jack was hoping the question was 'do you want to smoke a joint?' It wasn't, but what she did ask was equally mind blowing.

"Will you help me find the person who killed Ajeet?"

It took a moment for the question to register in Jack's brain, and another before he could respond.

"I thought he committed suicide."

"I did, too, until that young man stopped by my office the other day. There was something about him that just wasn't right. My suspicions were confirmed when the Fed Ex package was stolen."

"The one that your grad student sent? When did that happen?"

"The day after the young man came to my office and asked for it."

"And you didn't tell me about it until now?"

"To be honest, when we were down here yesterday the only thing I wanted to do was get you to help me with my experiment. I didn't want to scare you off by asking for anything more than that. But the more I thought about it, the more I knew I had to ask. If Ajeet *was* murdered and I didn't do anything about it I could never forgive myself."

"What do you want me to do?"

"I'm certain the man was from the Upper Peninsula. He had that yooper accent – he kept ending his sentences in 'eh?'"

"So?"

"Ajeet spent a lot of his time up north hanging out in bars. So much so that it became a problem. He must have met this guy in a bar. You remember what he looks like, don't you? I want you to go to the bar and see if you can spot him."

"There are a lot of bars up there."

"Ajeet always talked about the Hoist House. It was his favorite hangout. You could start there."

"I know the Hoist House. It's not far from where my house is."

"Then you'll do it?"

"Why don't you just go to the police?"

"And tell them what? That there was a young man who asked about a Fed Ex package who I thought was creepy? I reported the theft to campus security. They wrote a report and said they'd get back to me if anything turned up. It was their polite way of saying 'case closed.'"

"This guy was a creep and may have stolen a Fed Ex package. That doesn't make him a murderer. I'm leaving tomorrow morning, the experiment starts on Monday. I don't have time to chase someone down."

"You don't have to go to every bar in town. Just one."

Jack said nothing.

"I just have a feeling something bad happened to Ajeet," Maggie continued. "It's not scientific or logical, but it's real. Ajeet was brilliant, he had a bright future ahead of him. He was enjoying life, perhaps a little too much, but he was always upbeat and positive about everything. Maybe that creepy guy didn't kill him, but I can't shake the feeling that *somebody* did."

She reached out and squeezed his hand.

"Jack, will you help me?"

In the end, it was a no-brainer in every sense of the word, including literally: he always stopped by the Hoist House for a beer when he stayed in Hancock. Also, his brain was completely blank: he could think of nothing but the touch of her hand.

"Jack?"

"I'm sorry. Of course I'll help you."

The hug that followed those words was payment in advance for any future trouble they might cause him. Then Jack broke the silence, which no longer seemed awkward.

"It's too bad we don't know what was in that package."

"I do know what was in the package. I was so suspicious after he left that I opened it up and looked at what was inside, then put everything back and taped it shut again. I was still going to send it to his family, but I had to know what was in it first."

"So what was in it?"

"A piece of paper and a bottle of pills. Ajeet had written a message on the paper, I recognized his handwriting. I made a copy, let me read it to you."

Maggie pulled a piece of paper out of a drawer.

"It says, 'What is this?' which I assume refers to the bottle of pills. Then it says, 'Look above the immortals for the prize,' and it has some numbers written below it."

The message didn't make any sense to Jack, but he had a gut feeling about the pills.

"What did the pills look like?"

"They were white with red spots. And they had a happy face stamped into them."

"A happy face?"

"You know, two dots for eyes, a dot for the nose, a curved line for a smile."

He would tell her all he knew in a moment, but he first he had a question.

"The line 'Look above the immortals' – what were the numbers below it?"

"I've got them written down in my office. You have to stop by there tomorrow anyway to get a copy of the key to the copper mine lab. The maintenance man promised me he'd make one for you tonight and leave it on my desk. As long as you're coming by we may as well try to crack the code and solve the mystery."

Jack had a thought but didn't share it: like Shaggy and Velma.

THIRTY-FOUR

Case Closed

When he called Murphy that evening, Jack got his first good news in weeks.

It was immediately followed by bad news.

"I talked to a guy I know this afternoon, and the police are going to drop the charges. Whatever those pills are, they aren't illegal. They're too new to have any laws passed against them."

"That's great news."

"Don't get too excited, you're still on their shit list. They think you are involved in making or distributing the pills. Legal or not, that makes you a bad guy."

"Right now I'm on everybody's shit list. I guess I'll have to learn how to live with it. But that's not why I called. I was talking with Maggie yesterday."

"She's pretty smart, huh?"

"More than pretty smart – she's a genius."

"Not too bad on the eyes, either. You like her?"

"Yeah, Murphy, I like her."

"Do you *like* like her?"

"Oh my God, Murphy, I'm a college professor, not a seventh grader. Can we please talk about what Maggie told me?"

"I'm all ears, professor."

Jack proceeded to tell Murphy everything Maggie had told him in the mine: the suspicious young man, the theft of the package, the pills, the puzzles, the plea for help. When he finished there was a long pause before Murphy spoke.

"So you're going to walk into a bar and try to spot a guy who might be a murderer? A guy who can just as easily recognize you?"

"Yeah. I guess so."

"That's the dumbest thing I ever heard. Do me a favor, stay out of that bar."

"The chances of this guy actually being there are close to zero. If he is there, I'm not going to confront him or anything, Maggie insisted that I not do that. It's a simple request, and a bar I usually go to anyways. Why not do it?"

"So you *do* like like her. You want to be her brave hero and solve the crime. I get that. To be honest, I don't think this guy did anything. But if he did, it would mean he is a dangerous individual. Leave him alone, or get a professional to deal with him, okay?"

"How about you? You could come up to the U.P. and help me."

"Sorry, professor, but I'm finished with your case. I told you I'd help you find out what happened at the hospital and who drugged you, and I've done that. I did it as a favor for Baxter, no charge, and now I've got paying clients who need my help."

"That's no problem, I'll pay you."

"I'd like to help you, but I don't have the time to go up north. I'm booked solid. The punk who drugged you is not going to do anything else. You're not in any danger unless you bring it on yourself. Go home, write your book, and stay out of that bar."

"What about the student who was murdered?"

"With all due respect to Professor Stollard, the state police investigated the death of her graduate assistant and said it was suicide. The fact that somebody broke into her office and stole a Fed Ex package doesn't change that."

"But what about the pills that were in the package?"

"Somebody knew they were in there, that's why it got stolen."

"And the puzzle?"

"They're sending drugs in a Fed Ex box, they're going to use some kind of code to communicate. It doesn't mean they killed anybody."

"I guess."

"I'll tell you what, I still hang out in the Old Miami, and so do they. My bug is still in place. I'll keep listening to what they have to say. If anything interesting comes up I'll let you know."

"Thanks, Murphy. I appreciate it."

"In the meantime, do me a favor, let this go. Some kids screwed you over. They're jerks, but they're not murderers. Cut your losses, get on with your life. Stay out of that bar."

"Thanks for your help, Murphy, I really appreciate it."

"Namaste."

THIRTY-FIVE

Love And Other Mysteries

Jack stopped by Maggie's office early Saturday morning to pick up a key. He also was going to try to sort out the numbers puzzle, and perhaps his own feelings.

He admired and espoused the carefree spontaneity of the Sixties, but he was not an active practitioner himself. Outside of telling a few jokes in the classroom, he led an orderly and routine life, especially in matters of the heart. The speed and strength of his growing feelings for Maggie were disturbing to him, and he was determined to slow things down and examine them rationally.

The first step was to get the key.

The second step was to solve the riddle.

The third step was to go far away and think.

"The salt mine here is privately owned, and our experiment is set up in a remote location, so we don't have to lock it up," Maggie explained. "The copper mine has tourists walking around in it, so we built a plywood wall to block off the room and secure our equipment. This key unlocks the door."

"Got it. Now what about those numbers?" Jack asked.

"That's them behind me in the lower corner of the blackboard. I came in early this morning to try to figure them out, but I haven't been able to yet."

Jack looked at the blackboard behind her and saw them in the corner, circled and set apart from the equations that crowded the rest of the board.

9710112195

"I plugged them into a bunch of equations Ajeet would be familiar with," Maggie said. "I checked the periodic table to see if they were chemical elements listed by atomic number. I even ran them through a cryptography app I have on my phone."

Jack was going ask why anyone would have a cryptography app on their phone, but decided against it. He went with the more obvious and relevant question instead.

"Did you solve it?"

"No. Not even close. I got nothing."

Jack racked his brains for something that would sound smart and useful.

"Did you Google it?"

"Yes. That caused a bit of excitement – it pulled up phone numbers in India, near where Ajeet is from. I actually called the number, it has nothing to do with Ajeet."

"You talked to somebody in India?"

"Before you got here, yes. It's late afternoon there. I spoke to an older gentleman. He was lovely, but he had absolutely no idea what I was talking about."

"Could he have been lying?"

"He could of, but I'm sure he wasn't. No one could have faked that level of surprise and confusion, and graciousness. He was sincere in his ignorance."

"So what do we do now?"

"Carry on, I suppose. Why don't you write the numbers down and take them with you. We can both keep trying to figure it out. Maybe you could share it with Murphy."

"I already have. He couldn't figure it out, either. He's off the case, by the way."

"Off the case?"

"He's solved the two mysteries I asked him to – who put the drug in my drink at my party, and what happened in the hospital. So he's done with the case."

"You sound like you're not happy with that decision."

"I wish he'd stay on and help us. I told him that."

"What did he say to that?"

Jack hesitated.

"What did he say?"

"He thinks the Wise Guys are harmless, that they won't come after me anymore."

"And what about Ajeet?"

"Murphy is an ex-cop. A crazy-ass ex-cop, but still an ex-cop. The State Police say it was suicide, so that's what Murphy believes."

"And what do you believe?"

"I'm not sure what to think about anything anymore, but I want to find out."

THIRTY-SIX

Helltown

Jack started the 10-hour drive to Hancock early Saturday morning. Despite his promise to Murphy, he wanted to arrive by the afternoon to give himself options. His destination was his family's home just outside of Hancock in Michigan's Upper Peninsula.

It was a bittersweet journey.

He had grown up spending summers in Hancock after school got out in Detroit. One place had failed and one was failing, but their flaws and faded glory only made him love them more. He admired their toughness and resilience, their grim and ironic gallows humor, their sisu.

He loved the idea of coming back to Hancock, but not as a failure himself.

As he told friends and colleagues who asked where he was going to spend his sabbatical: "On a map the U.P. looks like a shark about to have its tail grabbed by the Lower Peninsula's big mitten hand. The shark's top fin is the Keweenaw Peninsula. That's where I'll be."

Those who asked for more details got this: Keweenaw is surrounded on three sides by Lake Superior, and cut through at the base by the Portage

Lake Canal. On the canal's south bank is the city of Houghton, clinging to the steep north bank is Hancock, Michigan's northernmost city. Hancock's main street, Highway 41, runs north up the hill and out of town.

Just outside the city limits is Quincy Mine.

Not far from the mine is Helltown.

One of many small shanty towns built by the mine operators to house their employees in the early 20th century, Helltown got its name from the fierce drunken fights that took place there every Saturday night. Over time the mines shut down, the fighting stopped, and with few exceptions the houses fell apart.

Jack's home in Helltown was one of the exceptions.

It stood alone in a field, a two-story wood frame home covered in sandy brown tarpaper. The summer kitchen, a separate building used for cooking in hot weather, stood nearby. Out back was the wood-burning sauna, a fixture for the thousands of Finnish families who came to the Keweenaw to pursue the American dream.

Six years before the gold rush in California, America's first mineral rush took place there and gave the region its nickname: Copper Country. The copper boom lasted nearly a century, then ended almost as quickly as it began.

Jack's mother's family were Finns who came to America to work in the copper mines, his father's family were English mining engineers from Cornwall who came to supervise the work. When his parents passed on the house became Jack's.

Now he was coming to stay for a year.

He hated to admit it, even to himself, but the events of the last few weeks had shaken him terribly. Violence had impacted his life before, but not in the form of a sucker punch to the head. Death had also impacted his life in the past, but he had never experienced it for himself until now. And he had never even been given a speeding ticket before, let alone spent a night in jail.

While all of that was happening his public persona had mutated from well-liked weirdo and campus cult favorite to universally despised hatemonger. Not to mention the scary sensation of having feelings for someone growing at a speed and strength he had only experienced once before in his life.

He needed this time alone in a place that would help him heal and reflect on his life.

As always, his spirit soared when he turned off the gravel road onto the dirt driveway. As a boy he had spent his summers here, visiting his grandparents and collecting quarters from his great aunts and uncles for promising to stop swearing in Finnish. As a man he visited as often as he could, to take care of his parents when they moved there to retire, and to reconnect with his roots after they passed.

A chorus of crickets greeted him as he stepped out of his car and carried his suitcases, food supplies and laptop into the house. After he put everything away he opened a warm beer and went out on the front porch to wait for nightfall.

He had plenty of time to make his decision.

Murphy had told him he shouldn't go looking the killer by himself, but he'd told Maggie that he would. One option was logical, the other emotional. He could keep himself out of danger, or keep the undying gratitude of a fascinating woman.

In the end it was an easy decision.

He ate the pasties he had bought in town, had a long hot sauna and an ice cold shower, and headed north on Highway 41.

He would honor the traditions of Helltown: on Saturday night you went to the bar.

THIRTY-SEVEN

Road House Blues

Jack was fairly certain his visit to the Hoist House would not put him in danger.

He was wrong.

His reasoning: Just because someone says "eh?" doesn't mean they are from the U.P. – maybe Maggie's young visitor was from Canada. Even if he was from the U.P., and perhaps even somewhere around Hancock, the chances of him being in one particular bar on a given night were extremely small. And if he was in that bar, the chances of spotting him in a crowd were even smaller.

But there he was.

Jack saw Ajeet's friend sitting at a table in the corner the moment he stepped inside the Hoist House. He looked away before the young man could see him, made his way to the bar and ordered a beer.

He had no idea what to do next.

His plan had been to go to the Hoist House and have beer, look around and not see the young man anywhere, then tell Maggie he had done his best to help her. The plan was more focused on endearing himself to Maggie than finding a murder suspect. Actually seeing him had messed up Jack's plan, now he had to figure out what to do next.

He went over his options, which ranged from doing nothing and just telling Maggie her hunch was right to confronting the young man about the missing Fed Ex package. He finally settled on something in between.

"See those two guys sitting over in the corner?" he asked the bartender, nodding his head slightly to the left.

"Yeah."

"The guy facing toward us, what's his name?"

"Are you a cop or something?"

"No, I'm a college professor. I was introduced to him last week but I can't remember his name. I'll be terribly embarrassed if I talk to him and can't recall it."

"Lucian Novikov, goes by Luc. He's a regular here."

"That's it – Luc Novikov. Thank you."

Jack's new plan had worked perfectly. Now all he had to do was finish his beer, leave the bar, and let Murphy take it from there. He drank slowly, savoring his second lucky break in as many days. When the pint was gone he motioned the bartender over, paid for his beer, and left a generous tip on the bar.

The tap on his shoulder was not part of his plan.

"You're that crazy professor who hates his students, aren't you?'

Jack turned in his bar stool to face a man in his early twenties with shiny black hair and a reluctant goatee. He was wearing a black tee shirt with the word "Jenius" on it.

Under different circumstances Jack might have found that funny.

"No, I'm not that person," he said.

"I think you are, and you're a liar for saying you're not."

Jack turned back around.

"I'm sorry, you've been fooled by a clever hoax."

The man tapped his shoulder again, this time much harder.

"Turn around when I'm talking to you."

Jack turned slowly in his seat.

"We don't like crazy professors around here, and we don't like liars."

"That's good to know. If I see any I will tell them to leave."

"You're a smartass too, eh? If I were you I'd get out of town right now and not come back. Someone like you stays around here too long, they could get hurt."

"Is that a threat?'

Jack turned around completely and stood up. It had been more than 30 years since he'd been in a bar fight, but he knew how the dance went – he'd learned it well up here in the summer nights of his youth. If he didn't step up this punk would keep harassing him, and probably hit him from behind. If he faced him and stood his ground it might not come to that, and if it did at least he would see the punch coming.

His moved worked, at least temporarily. The kid stepped back to rethink his strategy. Jack glanced over to see if Luc Novikov had spotted him yet, and for the first time tonight was afraid. Luc was sitting alone at his table, staring straight at him. The person who had been sitting with Luc was no longer there.

He was standing in front of Jack.

"It's not a threat, it's a promise, eh?" he said.

It was clear to Jack now that there was no way this would end well. Luc had seen him at the bar and sent his friend over to threaten him, pick a fight, and beat him up. The Jenius was decades younger than Jack and looked pretty strong.

The only thing Jack had going for him was the element of surprise.

He lunged forward and swung as hard as he could. The Jenius was caught off guard but managed to partially block the punch before it smacked the side of his head. He punched back but Jack's forward momentum sent them both tumbling to the ground. They grabbed onto each and Jack waited with great relief for the next phase of the fight – the bouncers arriving to pull them apart.

They didn't come.

Instead he felt an explosion of pain in his back as someone began kicking him. He twisted and pushed but the Jenius held him in place while the second attacker continued kicking. He was beginning to drift into unconsciousness when he heard someone yelling "break it up and get the hell out of here."

The kicking stopped and the Jenius let him go.

Jack lay face down on the floor trying to catch his breath and figure out how badly he was hurt. He heard footsteps and shouting and chairs screeching across the wooden floor. Then he felt someone grabbing him around the shoulders and turning him over. He looked up to see a police officer standing over him.

"Are you okay to walk?"

"I think so."

"Then come with me, you're under arrest."

THIRTY-EIGHT

Fight And Flight

Murphy figured it would be easy to honor his commitment to keep track of the Wise Guys. He would just keep going to his favorite bar, the Old Miami, for his usual nightly meditation session. Order a Jack on the rocks, plug earphones into his iPhone, and wait for the three young men to arrive.

If you drink it, they will come, he mused.

They didn't disappoint.

They arrived earlier than usual, and he switched on the listening device with his phone as they sat down on their couch and ordered beer. To the Wise Guys and everyone else in the bar Murphy was an old drunk who was zoned out listening to music on his phone – no doubt some kind of classic dinosaur rock. He had heard them say as much when he listened in on their conversations.

This evening they began with the usual frat boy banter – boasts, put-downs, crude jokes. Murphy had almost tuned them out, focusing instead on the Tiger's game playing on the TV above the far corner of the bar.

Then he heard it.

The Wise Guys had a new plan.

At first it wasn't clear to him what they were discussing, just that it was different than their usual trash talking. But as he listened it became obvious that were planning something. As they went over what they were going to do – repeating objectives, assigning responsibilities, arguing details – Murphy's understanding grew, and so did his concern.

He had to warn Jack.

There was no need to rush out and draw attention to himself. He would finish his drink, pay his bill and casually walk away. It was good plan, but like a lot of good plans it didn't work out.

Before he could finish his drink three men walked into the bar and straight toward the Wise Guys. Murphy heard one of the Wise Guys say "It's the Grand Marquis dude" and another one say "And he brought some friends with him." From the tone of their voices it was obvious this was not going to be a friendly get-together.

When the newcomers reached the couch the Wise Guy called Melcher spoke. Murphy pulled out his earphones; he wouldn't need a listening device to hear this conversation. Neither would anyone else in the bar.

"Gentlemen, what can we do for you?" Melcher asked loudly.

"You guys are the assholes who run down the street jumping on cars."

"We prefer to think of ourselves as parkour enthusiasts."

"I don't know what the hell you're talking about. All I know is that you dented the hood of my Grand Marquis and sucker punched me from behind."

"We didn't like being yelled at," Melcher said. "And here you are, doing it again."

"You're not going to like getting your ass kicked, either."

"Are you threatening us?"

"I'm telling you what's going to happen when we go outside."

"This place has a great patio area out back, it's wide open. Why don't we go out there and see if we can settle this disagreement?"

The Wise Guys left the couch and headed out the back door, followed by the three angry men and half the bar. Murphy finished his drink and joined the crowd.

The patio of the Old Miami was a large open space surrounded by an eight-foot-high wooden fence. Against the back wall of the building was a slightly raised wooden deck that served as a stage. To the right of the stage there was an outdoor bar, and beyond that a large grass yard scattered with outdoor chairs and tables. A tall cement statue of an angry dog with dragon wings stood facing the stage from thirty feet away.

It was a great space for a concert or a fight.

The Wise Guys walked to the middle of the yard before turning around to confront their three visitors. The six men squared off across from each other while the bar crowd continued to gather around them. Murphy noticed a waitress who had followed them outside had turned and headed back, no doubt to call the cops.

Whatever was going to happen would be over quickly.

The angry man and his friends were older, bigger and more solidly built than the Wise Guys. Murphy figured them to be construction workers or tradesmen who did physical labor for a living. He wouldn't have given the Wise Guys much of chance except he knew from his background check they had studied martial arts.

It looked like he was going to find out if they had paid better attention in those classes than they had in Jack Crost's class.

"So what now?" Melcher asked.

"Now you're going to pay for what you did in one of two ways. Either you give me money to fix my car or we beat the shit out of you."

"There is a third option," Melcher said.

"What's that?"

"We beat the shit out of you. Do you know karate?"

"No."

"Well, we do."

The instant Melcher said those words Baltimore and Casper delivered vicious roundhouse kicks to the heads of the men opposite them. As the aggrieved car owner turned to look at his fallen friends Melcher lunged forward and landed a full force punch to his midsection. When the man doubled over Melcher came down hard on the back of his head with an elbow.

Murphy was at the back of crowd and couldn't see what happened next, but he could tell what was going on from the sounds he heard. The fight was over after the first blows, but the Wise Guys were kicking and punching their fallen opponents. Murphy pushed forward through the crowd to intervene, but before he could reach them he heard the waitress yelling from the back door.

"We called the cops, they're on their way."

The crowd began to vanish immediately, turning around and heading back inside. Murphy and a few other regulars who were too old and battle-scarred to be concerned about the police were the only spectators who stayed behind.

All of the participants stayed.

The Wise Guys were breathing hard but smiling, standing over the three men they had attacked and beaten. One of the regulars who Murphy knew had been a medic in Vietnam began helping the men on the ground. The Wise Guys did nothing to interfere with him, which saved Murphy the trouble of kicking their ass.

Instead they stepped back and began high fiving and recounting the details of their victory. Before they could get too far into their stories they were interrupted by the wailing siren of an approaching police car.

"You fellas is fucked," one of the old timers said. "The only way out of here is back through the bar."

"You got it wrong, old man," Melcher replied. "These guys are fucked. We're outta here."

With that the Wise Guys turned and began running toward the back fence. Without slowing down they jumped up and kicked off the fence, vaulting over it. In a moment they appeared again, climbing up a gutter pipe on the building across the alley. When they reached the roof they ran down the length of the building, leaped across another alley to the building next door, and disappeared from sight.

As they ran out of view one of the remaining old timers spoke to Murphy

"Those kids are smart-ass punks, but they're damn good fighters."

"Pretty good at fighting," Murphy replied. "World-class at getting away."

THIRTY-NINE

Good Cop / Bad Cop

The Hancock police station was quiet at midnight.

Jack sat in a small room facing across a table from the cop who arrested him. He ignored the throbbing pain in his back and left rib cage and tried to focus his thoughts as the officer read him his rights. To his dismay he realized his many recent encounters with the police made the words very familiar to him.

"Why am I here?" he asked.

"Are you waving your right to legal counsel?"

"I'll let you know when I know why I'm here."

"Disorderly conduct. Maybe assault."

"I didn't do anything. I was attacked in the bar by two guys, one held me down and the other kicked the shit out of me."

"That's not what I heard. I heard you sucker punched someone who was talking to you at the bar."

"Some kid was harassing me."

"So you punched him?"

"Maybe I will ask for that attorney."

The cop sat back in his chair and smiled.

"Unless you have a twenty-four hour attorney service you can call that means you're spending the night in jail. It doesn't have to be that way."

"What do you mean?"

"You seem like a nice guy. I don't want to go through all the hassle of writing you up any more than you want to spend the night in jail and face serious charges. All they told me at the bar was you punched some kid. So why don't you tell me your side of the story and maybe we can both get out of here."

Jack was familiar with the good cop/bad cop technique from watching countless movies and TV shows. This cop seemed to be playing both roles himself, and there was no reason to trust him. But the thought of spending another night in jail was enough motivation to give it a try.

"I was sitting at the bar and this guy came up behind me and started poking me in the back and yelling at me. I tried to ignore him, but he wouldn't go away. It was clear to me he was going to fight no matter what I did."

"Why was he so mad at you?'

"It's a long story. I'm a professor at Wayne State University in Detroit. A few of my students thought it would be funny to make a video of me and edit it to make it look like I'm saying horrible things to my class. This kid must have seen the video."

"You're from Detroit, what are doing up here?"

The logical thing to do was tell him about his encounter with the young man in Maggie's office, and the missing Fed Ex package, and the dead graduate assistant. But something told him not to do that, at least not right now.

"I'm on sabbatical for a year because of the video. I came up here to work on my novel and not get harassed by angry students."

The cop laughed.

"That didn't work out to well for you, eh?"

"No."

"What were you doing in the Hoist House?"

"My grandfather worked in Quincy Mine back in the day. I inherited his house in Helltown, that's where I'm staying. Hoist House is the closest bar, I go there all the time when I'm up here."

"I got two pieces of advice for you professor. The first is stay away from the Hoist House. The second is go back to Detroit."

"You think I'll be safer there?"

"I think you won't freeze your ass off in the winter time there. There's not a lot of houses left standing in Helltown. Your name is Crost, I'm gonna you're you staying in the old Crost place. An old tar shack with a wood stove, and the snow will be over your head by Thanksgiving."

"I've been trying to finish my novel for twenty years. If I get snowed in I'll have nothing else to do but write."

"Your funeral. If you do stay keep away from the Hoist House. I'm serious."

"Why should I stay away? Why don't you arrest the guys who beat me up?"

"What guys? When I got there you were lying on the floor and whoever you were fighting with was gone. The witnesses I talked to said you threw the first punch."

"And nobody knew the names of the guys who attacked me?"

"No. Nobody knew who they were."

Jack started to say he knew the name of one of them, and so did the bartender, but stopped himself. For starters, he hadn't seen the guy who kicked him. He couldn't prove it was Luc Novikov, although he had no doubt that it was. But there was something else going on, a growing feeling that things weren't quite right.

The cop's next question made it even stronger.

"Did you get a good look at the guys you say attacked you?"

Jack had a vague memory of the cop breaking up the fight, which meant he had seen the guys who attacked him. Why was he asking him what they looked like? More importantly, why didn't he arrest them?

"One had a black tee shirt with the word 'Jenius' on it spelled with a J. Dark hair, kind of a scraggly goat tee. I didn't see the other guy."

There were other odd things happening here: when they got to the police station the cop had walked him straight back to this room without getting fingerprints or mug shots. And this cop seemed more interested in his background than what happened at the bar.

Jack decided to keep his mouth shut and let Murphy sort things out later.

"So what do we do now?" he asked.

"I'll walk you out front and get somebody to drive you back. You're free to go."

Jack was puzzled but relieved, and was not going to risk his freedom by asking dumb questions. But on their way out of they encountered another cop who did.

"I thought you were on desk duty tonight," he asked.

"I am. Everybody on patrol was busy, so I had to go break up a bar fight. This guy threw a punch at somebody."

"Since when have we started bringing in guys for throwing a punch in a bar? Half the town would be in jail."

"You've been here a year? And you're telling me how to do my job? Fuck you."

As they pushed past him and walked on the young cop called after them.

"Sorry, Vladdie."

FORTY

Portage Canal

Luc wanted to have the follow-up discussion with his uncle by phone, but when Vladdie finished his shift he insisted Luc come by the house. It was past midnight when they sat down on the back porch in the moonlight and cracked open beers.

Luc looked out over the dark water of the canal and wondered if his uncle would slap him again, and what he would do in return. He had gone over endless scenarios in him mind, but what happened next caught him completely off guard.

"You did good," Vladdie said.

"What?"

"You were smart to call me. How'd you know who the guy was?"

"He was in that bitch's office when I went to get the package. When Jasper turned around to check him out he recognized him, too – he was in this video online going crazy and yelling at his class."

"Since when has Jasper ever looked at anything online?"

"The kid from Detroit showed it to him the week before we took him to the bridge."

"This time you called me before you did anything, that was smart. And you waited until I pulled up outside like I told you. But you weren't supposed to get involved in the fight."

Luc braced for a slap in the dark that didn't come.

Still, it was never a good idea to get too comfortable around Vladdie.

"Jasper started to get his ass kicked. I went over to help him until you got inside."

"You're lucky – he didn't see it was you kicking him. But tell that idiot Jasper to lose the Jenius tee shirt and shave that ugly ass beard of his."

"I will. What'd you find out about the guy? Did he come here looking for me?"

"He says he's here to finish writing a book. He owns the old Crost place up there in Helltown."

"That makes sense, eh? Jasper said he got fired from his teaching job 'cause of that video."

"It seems okay, but I dunno. I gotta work tomorrow, I'm going to use the computer database at the station look up a few things, see if his story checks out."

"What if it doesn't?"

"If it doesn't you don't do shit until I tell you."

"Then what?"

"Then we make him wish he'd never come back to Helltown."

FORTY-ONE

Electro-Magnetic Wave Communication

In the morning Jack called Maggie on his cell phone.

It took him awhile to work up the nerve: he was eager to tell her he had found her man, but reluctant to share the messy details. He decided if he started with the good news the bad news might not come up.

He was wrong.

"I found your young man," he said immediately when she answered his call.

"Jack? You found him? Where?"

"Right where you said he would be, in the Hoist House bar."

"Did you talk to him?"

"No. I stayed away like you told me."

"Good. Did you talk to the police?"

Jack hesitated, then told the truth.

"Yes."

"What did they say?"

"It's a long story," he said.

"I have all day," she replied.

He explained the events of the previous evening as nonchalantly as possible for someone who was assaulted and arrested. He emphasized that he got the young man's name and mentioned his distrust of the police officer who arrested him.

Her rebuttal was less nonchalant.

"Dammit, Jack, I asked you not to confront him. You could have been killed!"

"I didn't confront him. His buddy confronted me."

"And you got into a fight with him."

"I had no choice, he was going to start the fight with or without me."

There was a long pause of silence before Maggie spoke again.

"So in the last two weeks you've been beaten up twice and arrested twice."

"Actually, I was questioned by the police in the hospital after I was poisoned and died. But they didn't arrest me, so I guess that doesn't count as a third time."

Jack had taken a chance with his low-key joke, and was rewarded with laughter.

"I've forgotten my manners," she said. "You've done me a tremendous favor at great danger to yourself. Thank you so much."

"You're welcome."

"You got his name, that's a great start. But if you don't trust the police then we have a problem: what do we do next?"

Despite his aching ribs and strong sense of foreboding, Jack was thrilled that she said "we" and not "I."

"I'm not sure what we should do next," he said. "It seems like could use a little of the special magic they were very fond of in the Sixties right about now."

"What are you talking about?"

"Serendipity."

FORTY-TWO

Two Wrongs

"It's Murphy. I'm back in."

Jack had just finished talking to Maggie when he got the call from Detroit. He was surprised to hear from Murphy, relieved to hear he was back on the case, reluctant to tell him about his fight.

Unlike Maggie there was no heroic upside to telling Murphy the Hoist House story. Better to focus on Murphy's good news.

"What made you decide to take up the case again?" Jack asked.

"First things first – you gotta pay me. What I did before was a favor for Baxter."

"I'll pay you whatever you want, but you haven't answered my question."

"There're two reasons I'm coming back," Murphy said. "But it's a long story."

"I've got all day."

Murphy proceeded to tell Jack about the incident at the Old Miami. He was grudgingly respectful of the Wise Guy's fighting skills, but in complete awe of their ability to escape.

"I haven't seen anything like it since my Ranger training," he said. "They went over an eight-foot fence like it wasn't there, climbed a up a two-story building and jumped over to the next one. By the time the cops got there they were long gone."

"Did the cops get their names? Are they going to go after them?"

"No one told them their names, including me. There's a certain code of conduct at the Old Miami, turning people in to the cops is frowned upon. The bad news is I won't be getting any more inside information from their couch conversations – I doubt they will coming back any time soon."

"But you're a retired police officer, you know they're bad guys, you saw what they did. Why didn't you turn them in?"

"That's one of the reasons I'm back on the case – I want to take them down myself. The cops would give them a slap on the wrist, I want to hit them harder than that. What they did to those guys – sucker punching, beating a man when he's down – that's unacceptable behavior. I didn't like them before, I really don't like them now. They may have martial arts skills but they fought a dishonorable fight."

It was as good an opening as any for Jack to bring Murphy up to date.

"Speaking of fights, I was kind of was in one of my own."

Murphy listened as Jack told him the Hoist House story using the same order and emphasis as he had with Maggie: he had located the bad guy and cleverly figured a way to find out his name. Oh and also: after that he was beaten up and taken to jail.

Murphy was surprisingly serene.

"I'm glad you're okay."

"You're not angry?"

"Buddha said holding onto anger is like holding onto a hot coal – it only hurts you. I try to live in the moment and not dwell on the past. My hope is that you have learned something from your suffering."

"Don't get in a bar fight with someone half my age?"

Murphy didn't laugh.

"I told you it would be dangerous to go there. Next time you should listen to me."

"Don't worry, I will."

"I have to admit I totally misread you, Jack. That doesn't happen very often. I'm in the business of figuring out what makes people tick."

"How did you misread me?"

"First of all, I wasn't really worried about you going to the bar, especially after I warned you not to. No offense, but I didn't think you had the cojones for it."

"No offense taken. It was a pretty dumb thing to do."

"And even if you did go, I was sure you wouldn't fight anybody. I thought you were all about peace and love."

"I am, or at least I try very hard to be. Old habits are hard to break."

"You were a tough guy growing up?"

"I was angry. I did what angry young men do."

"So what changed you?"

"It's a long story, I'll tell you about it sometime. I'm just glad you called, I'll let you do all the follow-up."

"Follow up?"

"You know, figure out if this Luc kid murdered her graduate assistant. Check out the cop who arrested me, see why he was acting so suspiciously."

This time Murphy did laugh.

"I love Maggie, and obviously she's very smart. But just because some kid tried to pick up a package and was rude to her doesn't make him a murderer."

"What about the cop? I told you all the strange things he did."

"Did you get his name?"

"No. He didn't tell me and I forgot to ask. Somebody called him Laddie when I was leaving, maybe that's it. Whatever his name is, doesn't the way he handled things seem suspicious to you?"

"No, it doesn't. To me it seems like a veteran officer trying to keep the peace in a small town."

"What do you mean?"

"A couple of locals get in a bar fight with an older guy from out of town. The officer shows up, recognizes the locals, knows they're not usually troublemakers, and tells them to get lost. He takes the out-of-towner back to the station to get him out of harm's way and see if he has any prior arrests or outstanding warrants. When the out-of-towner checks out as an upright citizen, the officer lets him go."

"You think that's what happened?"

"It's a lot more likely than the conspiracy theory you and Maggie have cooked up. I don't know anything for sure, but I'm going to check it out when I get up there."

"You're coming up here?"

"I'm coming up right away. I'll be there tonight."

"That's great. I'll text you my address, you can stay here with me if you want."

"I was planning on staying with you even if you didn't invite me."

"What do you mean?"

"I'm coming to check things out and make sure you're safe."

"You said you don't believe my theory."

"I said I doubt it, but I'm going to check it out. There are some interesting connections I've found out about, I'll explain them when I get up there. In the meantime, you've been beat up and arrested – those are facts, not theory. I don't know if it's related or not – hell, it might just be karma – but I'm gonna keep you safe while I figure it out."

"I'm not hiring you to be a body guard."

"I'm throwing it in at no extra charge. It's the other reason I'm back on the case."

"What do you mean?"

"Before the Wise Guys got involved in that cowardly beat down I heard them planning something new that made me want to get involved again."

"What's that?"

"They're coming your way."

FORTY-THREE

No Names

"It's me, shut up and listen."

Luc started to say 'Vladdie?' but his uncle cut him off.

"No names."

The anger in Vladdie's voice made Luc happy it was a phone call and not a personal visit.

"Where you at?" he asked.

"I'm on a break, calling from a pay phone. I did some checking at work and found out more about your crazy professor."

"Yeah?"

"He's more than just crazy. He was arrested in Detroit last week for possession of drugs. They didn't press charges because the pills he had on him weren't illegal."

"So?"

"So they were white happy face pills with red spots, you dumbass."

"Howdy Doody's?"

"I said no names."

"That's not somebody's name, it's a puppet."

"Will you just shut up and listen, and quit arguing with me? He was caught carrying white happy face pills with red spots, which means the odds of him being at the bar by coincidence just went down a whole shitload. That means we gotta rethink everything."

"Okay."

"You said the Fed Ex package had pills in it."

"Yeah. He was sending it to somebody named Chemic to analyze. There was a note with the bottle that said, 'What is this?' He wanted to figure out how to make his own."

"You told me he already knew how to make it."

There was a long pause before Luc spoke again.

"He did, for sure, eh? I'm guessing he was just double checking the formula with this Chemic guy."

"Was there anything else in the package you haven't told me about?"

"There was one other thing on the note. It said, 'Here's where the prize is' and had a bunch of numbers under it."

"What numbers?"

"I dunno. I got them written down, I'll text them to you."

"Do *not* text them to me, you idiot. Bring them by my place when I get off work."

"Okay. Anything else?"

"Yeah. I checked, there's nobody in the Detroit area named Chemic, so I'm assuming it's an alias or a nickname. You said you ran into this guy when you went to pick up the package. Maybe he's Chemic, maybe he got some of the pills out of the package before you stole it."

"No way. The package was locked in a file cabinet it took forever to break into. The package was sealed with tape. The bottle of pills was full. No way he took any."

"Well, he got them somewhere and then he came looking for you. I'm not sure what the connection is, but I don't want to wait to find out, 'cause by then it might be too late. We need to do something fast."

"You want me to take care of him?"

"What, you mean like you did before?"

"Not the same way, but the same result."

Luc moved the phone away from his ear while his Uncle unloaded a string of expletives as loud as it was long. When he finally finished he resumed talking in a low, flat voice stripped of all emotion.

"You do nothing, do you understand?"

"Yeah."

"Yeah, what?"

"Yeah, I understand, eh?"

"I will take care of this mess, like I always do. And I will take care of you, like I always do."

Vladdie hung up before Luc could respond.

Luc would have said 'thank you' but that wasn't what he was thinking.

He was thinking you *should* take care of me, asshole.

My dad took care of you – he took the rap for the 'cat you were cooking in his hunting shack and went to prison instead of you.

He was killed because of you.

The good news in all the bullshit Vladdie had talked about was that the cops said Howdy Doody wasn't illegal. That meant it had to be safe or they wouldn't say that. He'd been taking it fairly often to stay sharp while all this shit was going down.

It was good to know he could keep doing that, maybe even do more.

He reached in his pocket, worked up some saliva, and swallowed another one.

FORTY-FOUR

The Delvecchio Code

The first of many surprises Murphy brought to Helltown was the late-model car he arrived in.

"Why aren't you driving your tank?" Jack asked from the steps at the side door.

"I wasn't sure it would make it," Murphy replied, pulling a battered leather suitcase out of the trunk. "And I need to be inconspicuous for the work I have to do, so I rented this incredibly unspectacular sedan."

It wasn't until they went inside and sat down at the kitchen table and Jack poured a generous dose of Old No. 7 that Murphy explained himself.

"I listened in on your Wise Guys at the bar and they talked about their plans. They're throwing a big party in a few weeks, an after party for the Movement festival."

"The electronic dance music thing?"

"Movement is in Hart Plaza on Memorial Day weekend every year. These guys are having a party after the show on Sunday night, they're charging money to get in and selling Howdy Doody's to the people who come."

"Where's the party?"

"I don't know yet. It's semi-private, you have to know the right people or the right things to get in. I'm still figuring it out, that's one of the reasons I'm here."

"How are you going to find out about it up here?"

"They're coming up next Saturday to buy drugs for the party. I know the exact time and location of the deal, they talked about all this stuff before the fight."

"They're buying drugs in the U.P? From who?"

"This is where it gets interesting. They're buying them from Luc Novikov."

"The punk who kicked me when I was down?"

"And the guy Maggie says stole the Fed Ex package and murdered her assistant."

"Why come all the way up here to buy drugs? Can't they get them in Detroit?"

"Not Howdy Doody's. It's a special new kind of meth. As far as I know, they only make it up here."

"You're telling me Yoopers invented a new drug?"

"You sound surprised, but you shouldn't be. You're from around here, you don't know the history the U.P. has with meth?"

"I know a lot of people used it back in the day. Most of them ended up in rehab or prison, a lot of them died."

"They didn't just use it, they practically invented it. The U.P. was the birthplace of methcathinone in the United States. The only other place it was popular was Russia."

"Methcathinone? Is that what they used to call 'cat'?"

"Yeah. It's a form of methamphetamine. There was a chemistry student from the University of Michigan who worked part-time at Parke-Davis in the late 80s. He found the formula in their archives and gave it to a friend in the U.P. who started making the stuff. It spread like wildfire and turned into an epidemic up here in the 90s."

"Like I said, I remember it very well. It was like the Walking Dead."

"Here's another fun fact for you. I did a background check on your buddy Luc. His record was clean, but it turns out he is Luc Novikov, Junior. His father was arrested for having a cat lab in a hunting cabin in the woods. He went to prison in Marquette and was killed in a fight with another prisoner."

"So what does all this mean? What are we going to do?"

Murphy picked up the bottle of Jack Daniels sitting on the table between them, refilled his glass and topped off Jack's. He set the bottle down and took a long drink before he spoke again.

"You don't do anything. I'm going to be here all week keeping your ass safe and checking things out. The Wise Guys are coming up Saturday night. They're picking up the drugs and heading right back home."

"They're not coming after me?"

"One of them talked about coming by your house and doing something while they were up here, but the other two talked him out of it. As long as you don't go back to the Hoist House you'll be fine. They're going straight back to Detroit after the deal to stash the drugs where the party is going to be. I'm going to follow them and see where that is."

"You're going to follow them all the way back to Detroit?"

"Yeah."

"Won't they see you?"

"It will be night for most of the trip. All they'll see is a pair of headlights. After that, don't worry – I got skills."

"How are you going to protect me? I'll be down in the mine helping Maggie run her experiment."

"I'll be in the mine with you most of the time. And in case something happens when I'm not around I'm going to show you four moves to use in a fight."

"You're going to teach me how to fight?"

"From what you've told me, you already know how to fight, you just don't do it very well. I'm going to teach you how to *win* a fight."

"No offense, Murphy, but…"

Murphy held up his hand to stop Jack in mid-sentence.

"You've been in a few bar fights, you know how to trade punches with drunks. I was an Army Ranger and a Detroit cop. I'm going to teach you what to do when your *life* depends on winning a fight. If something serious *is* going on here, it might come in handy."

Jack was genuinely touched and suddenly very afraid.

"Thanks, Murphy. I appreciate it."

They sat in the tiny kitchen sipping their drinks without speaking for several minutes. Jack opened the window a crack to let in the cool night air, and the army of chirping crickets seemed to grow closer and louder.

"There's a couple things you should know about," Murphy said finally. "First off, just for the hell of it I checked with the DIA to see if anything out of the ordinary had happened with their Howdy Doody puppet."

"And?"

"There was something. The morning after your party at the Traffic Jam the security guard reported that Howdy Doody was missing from his showcase."

"Somebody stole him?"

"That's what they thought at first. But later that day they found him in a back room where they do routine cleaning and repairs for their puppet collection."

"So it wasn't a big deal."

"No. Except he wasn't scheduled to be taken back there for several months. And they couldn't find anyone who said they did it – curators, security guards, janitors – no one came forward."

It wasn't much, but it was a slim ray of hope that Jack wasn't crazy, or tripping, or dreaming on the night that he died.

Maybe he just saw Howdy Doody.

"You said there were a couple of things I should know about. What else?"

"You know that clue on the note in the Fed Ex package? The one about finding the prize?' I figured it out."

Jack bolted upright in his chair and nearly spilled his drink.

"You figured it out?"

"I don't why I didn't think of it right away. It's really pretty obvious, especially if you're a big hockey fan like I am."

"What do you mean?"

"9710112195 is not *one* number, it's *seven* numbers: 9 – Gordie Howe, 7 – Ted Lindsay, 10 – Alex Delvecchio, 1 – Terry Sawchuck, 12 – Sid Abel, 19 – Steve Yzerman, 5 – Nick Lidstrom."

"What do the Red Wings have to do with it?"

"Those are all players whose numbers are retired. Their jerseys hang from the rafters in Joe Louis Arena in that order. So if you're looking for a prize 'Above the Immortals' you should look on the roof of the Joe."

"Baxter was right, you really are great at what you do, Murphy. I have to raise a toast for that one."

They clinked their glasses and drank. When they set them down Jack started to speak again but once again Murphy raised his hand to stop him.

"Quiet," he said in a whisper. "Did you hear that?"

Jack shook his head no.

"Crickets stopped chirping. Someone's out there. How many ways out of here?"

"There's a front door on the porch and the side door you came in. There's also a fruit cellar door on the other side of the house."

"Is it locked?"

"From the inside. They're double doors with a two-by-four crossbar you take out to open them."

"How do you get down to the cellar?"

"Take a right out of here and go all the way to the end of the hall. The steps are behind the last door on the right."

"Stay here in the kitchen, but move away from the window. I'll be right back."

"Where are you going?"

"I'm going to go welcome our visitor."

FORTY–FIVE

Bump In The Night

Jack sat in the kitchen and waited.

Outside it was dark and silent. Inside the light bulb hanging down from a wire glared like the noon day sun and he could hear his heart racing. He had moved his chair back from the window and closer to the wall so he couldn't be seen by anyone standing in the field behind the house.

Other than that, he had no idea what to do next.

So he waited.

His mind raced off in a thousand different directions but always landed back in the same place: what the hell had happened to him? The life that he had carefully carved out over the last two decades had been blown apart in the last two weeks. He had been physically assaulted and arrested, his reputation was ruined, and the one thing in life that he loved doing and was good at had been taken away from him.

And yet…

As badly as he had been shaken, he had also been stirred.

First of all, dying wasn't as bad as he thought it would be. Despite all the setbacks he had faced since then, for some reason he was feeling more at peace with himself and more grateful for what he had – the things that Maggie had told him might happen. He was ready to face whatever was coming, and confident he would be up to the challenge.

The Finns had a word they used to describe a quality they deeply admired and typically possessed: sisu. Translated into English sisu means determination, perseverance, guts – an inner strength or crazy recklessness that inspires a person to take on something in the face of incredible odds. Jack grew up knowing what sisu meant, but despite being half Finnish he never felt he possessed it.

Until now.

He had begun his quest to uncover the truth about what had happened to him with a great deal of anger and fear: mad at the students who had punked him and afraid he would be ridiculed about his Near Death Experience. But those emotions were fading, slowly replaced by simple curiosity and a growing certainty. He wanted to know how the things happening to him were connected, and he was sure he would figure it out.

Or at least fail in a spectacular and satisfying way.

Whatever the outcome, he was looking forward to the journey.

There was something else going on as well, something that he had raced up north to get away from, something that needed to be named and confronted: he was falling in love.

That was a path on his journey that he did not want to take.

Love was a feeling he hadn't experienced in decades, one that he was convinced would never come his way again. Maggie was changing that.

She was smart and beautiful, with enough rough edges and eccentricities to make her even more desirable. Looking back, he was sure it began the moment he met her, but he had been slow to acknowledge what was going on. It wasn't until he found himself driving to the Hoist House that it hit him fully: the only reason he would be doing something this stupid was if he was in love.

The idea of being in love scared him more than all the other dangerous things going on in his life. It had been so long he had forgotten how good love could feel, but the pain of losing it had never receded. Not to mention the guilt he was already beginning to feel. He wasn't sure if he was ready to give it a try.

Or if she was.

He spent the next several minutes trying to figure out if Maggie shared his feelings. It was a futile exercise that made him feel like a Junior High student. But he couldn't keep himself from reviewing her words, body language and facial expressions over and over in his mind, searching for signs of affection.

He had just decided the evidence was inconclusive for a third time and begun going over it again when he heard the loud crash outside. He ran out of the kitchen and down the hall to the side door, pulled aside the curtain and stared out into the night.

He was fairly certain the crash had come from inside the summer kitchen, which was about 50 feet away on the other side of the dirt driveway. But there was nothing to see except darkness, and no further noise to hear. He stood staring out the window into the black night trying to decide what to do next.

His problem was solved when the flashing lights of a police car appeared suddenly on the dirt road in front of his house. He watched as it raced down the road and slid into his gravel driveway, clouds of dust swirling in the headlights.

The cop who had arrested him at the Hoist House stepped out of the car.

Jack turned back the dead bolt and walked out onto the small side porch. The instructions he received were as simple as they were alarming.

"Keep your hands were I can see them and step off of the porch."

"What's going on?"

"Step off of the porch."

Jack did as he was told then repeated his question.

"What's going on?"

"Do you have the key to this outbuilding?"

"The summer kitchen? It doesn't have a lock on the door."

The cop pulled up a flashlight that was hanging from his belt and pointed it toward the small wooden shack.

"Let's go take a look inside," he said. "You first."

Jack crossed the driveway and walked down the path to the kitchen. He opened the door and stepped inside, then called out to the cop waiting outside behind him.

"You want me to turn the light on?"

"Yeah. Then step back outside."

Jack reached behind him in the dark and felt along the wall for the switch. Nothing in his entire life or recent death had prepared him for what the light revealed.

A young man dressed in black with a large pack strapped to his back was lying on the floor. Sitting behind him on an old crate smiling broadly was Murphy.

"Hey Jack," he said. "I see you brought reinforcements."

FORTY-SIX

The Lurp And The Perp

As the initial shock of the strange scene in front of him receded Jack recognized the man lying on the ground.

It was the Jenius who started the fight at the Hoist House.

His hair was shorter and he didn't have a beard, but it was him.

Jack started to say something but Murphy shook his head no. Then the cop behind him took over, telling him to move aside and crowding past him into the narrow room.

"Officer, I'd like to report a breaking and entering," Murphy said.

"Who the hell are you?"

"My name's Murphy. I'm a retired Detroit police officer and a friend of Professor Crost. I heard a noise and came outside to see what it was. I found this young man hiding in here and when I asked him what he was doing he assaulted me."

"Why is he lying on the ground? What did you do to him?"

"He took a swing at me so I gave him a light tap to calm him down. He'll be fine, he's already coming around."

The cop moved down the narrow hallway to where the young man was lying.

"You all right, Jasper?"

The young man sat up slowly and nodded his head yes.

"What the hell are you doing here?"

Jasper looked puzzled. He started to say something but the cop cut him off.

"I'll bet you were listening to your police band radio again, weren't you? You heard me get the call to come here and came to see the drug bust, didn't you?"

Jasper still looked puzzled, but nodded his head yes again.

"What drug bust?" Jack asked. "What are you talking about?"

"We got a tip someone was cooking meth in this shack. I was on patrol and I got a radio call to go check it out."

"Like I told you, this shack is a summer kitchen," Jack said. "But nobody's cooked anything in here in years, and especially not meth. That's crazy."

"We'll see. Jasper, go wait in my car. You two step outside."

Jasper stood up and walked slowly out, looking back at Murphy the entire time. Jack turned to follow him but stopped when Murphy stood up and spoke.

"If you don't mind officer we'd like to stay here while you conduct your search. This is Professor Crost's property, that is his right. I won't even ask you about your search warrant, I'm sure you have one."

The cop said something about probable cause and began opening and closing cupboards filled with old tools, car parts and miscellaneous junk. He made his way down the length of the kitchen, then turned around and walked back to the door.

"There's nothing here, it must have been a bad tip. Sorry for the inconvenience."

He turned to walk out but Murphy called after him.

"I didn't catch your name officer."

"That's right, you didn't."

"What about the breaking and entering?"

"Jasper is an idiot, not a burglar. I'll take care of him."

With that he was gone, leaving only a cloud of dust from his spinning tires.

"What the hell just happened?" Jack asked as the squad car raced into the night.

"I went out through the cellar door. When I got outside I looked around and saw him going into this building. I followed him inside and he took a swing at me so I put him out of commission. Nothing that could really hurt him, just one punch."

"It's pitch black out here. How could you see him? Then you got into the summer kitchen without him hearing you and knocked him out with one punch? What are you, some kind of ninja guy?"

"I told you, I was a lurp in Vietnam. I've lost a little speed since then but I can still sneak around in the dark with the best of them. And those idiots weren't the best of them."

"There was more than one?"

"After I knocked out the perp I heard someone sneaking around outside. Probably a lookout. He whispered Jasper a few times, then took off when the cop showed up."

"I know the punk you knocked out. He got a haircut and shaved off his beard, but he's the one who started the fight in the bar."

"I figured you recognized him, but I didn't want you to say anything. There's something funny going on here, no sense tipping our hand until we know more."

"Something funny?"

"Your friend didn't have camping supplies in his backpack, he had some beat up lab equipment and baggies filled with white powder."

"Like meth lab stuff?"

"You were being set up. I'm sure he was going to spread it around in here for the cop to find."

Jack took a moment to process all this new and disturbing information.

"That was the same cop who broke up the fight and took me to the police station. We still don't know his name."

"No matter. I'll put it on my list of things to find out. That list is getting long – I don't know what is going on here, but I don't like it."

"I'll bet anything the other guy you heard sneaking around was Luc, the one who was kicking me in the bar, the one Maggie thinks killed her graduate assistant."

"No doubt."

"So what do we do next?"

"We go back inside the house and have a drink."

"Then what?"

"Then we start your lessons."

FORTY-SEVEN

Plans, Puzzles, Prizes

"So what do we do next?"

Luc was back on his Uncle's porch trying to understand what had just happened and figure out a new plan.

"What's next is you do nothing until I tell you," Vladdie said.

"Okay, but while I'm doing nothing what are you going to do?"

"I'm going to find out who this Murphy guy is and what he's doing up here."

"He already told you, he's a retired Detroit cop. A friend of the crazy professor."

"The crazy professor who came all the way up here from Detroit looking for you. The one you kicked the shit out of."

"Maybe the professor brought the cop up here to be his body guard."

"I don't know what he's here for, but it can't be good. He's not some college kid or old geezer professor. This guy knows what he's doing."

"Jasper says he didn't see or hear him until he was right in front of him."

"Jasper's an idiot. He wasn't paying attention. You guys didn't smoke any pot before you got there, did you?"

"Hell, no, we didn't smoke. It's not Jasper's fault, like you said this guy's good."

Luc wanted to say more, but didn't want to get smacked. It was Vladdie's idea to plant the meth in the summer kitchen. He said another drug bust, even if it didn't stick, would take away whatever credibility the crazy professor had left if he tried to make any accusations against Luc. And if he was just straight up trying to muscle in on their Detroit connection it would slow things down for now and make it easier to deal with him later.

The truth was he and Jasper had taken Howdy Doody before they headed up to Helltown so they would be super alert. It was Vladdie's plan that sucked, not them.

"He knows the law and he can throw a punch 'cause he used to be a cop. But he's no ninja warrior, he's a fat old man. There's no way he could have snuck up like that unless Jasper had his head up his ass. My plan was good."

It was a perfect opportunity for Luc to tell his Uncle what he really thought about his plan, and who was to blame for the disaster at Helltown. But it was obvious from what Vladdie just said that he was being dared to disagree.

Luc let it go.

"The college kids from Detroit are coming up next Saturday to pick up their stuff," he said. "It would be nice if we knew what was going on with the professor and the cop before then, eh?"

"Are you being a smartass with me?"

"No."

"Good. You take care of your own business, I'll take care of what I gotta do."

Vladdie paused for effect before he shared his next bit of information.

"I figured out your secret code, by the way."

"The numbers in the Fed Ex package?"

"Yeah. I seen on the news where they're getting ready to demolish Joe Louis Arena. Gonna blow it up."

"What's that got to do with the numbers I gave you?"

"You don't know nuttin' do you? When they retire the jersey of one of the Red Wings stars they hang it in the rafters. That's what those numbers are, Gordie Howe and all them guys. They showed their jerseys hanging up there when they were talking about blowing up the Joe on the news. Hell, I seen 'em play at the old Olympia, I can't believe they're going to another new arena already."

"The message said look for the prize above the immortals," Luc said quietly.

"Yeah, the immortal hockey players."

"That's good work, Vladdie. Thanks, eh?"

Luc still didn't know what the prize was, but now he knew where it was

And now he really wanted it.

FORTY-EIGHT

The Light At The End Of The Tunnel

There was something about Quincy Mine that made Jack uneasy.

He had taken the tour many times growing up, and it had never bothered him before – if anything, he found it boring. He wasn't claustrophobic and he wasn't afraid of cave-ins. For most of the time during the weeklong experiment Murphy would be with him in the mine as a bodyguard and self-defense instructor.

Still.

On the short drive over in Murphy's rental car he felt a rising sense of dread he couldn't shake. Fortunately, when they arrived at the mine the process of getting to where the experiment would take place helped him ignore the feeling temporarily. They met Tim – the employee Maggie told him to contact – in the parking lot outside of the #2 shaft house, then boarded a cog rail tram for the ride down Quincy Hill.

When they got to the bottom of the hill and walked toward the mine entrance Tim explained what Jack already knew from his previous trips.

"Quincy is a horizontal mine that goes straight back into the side of the hill. It's approximately 15 feet high and 15 feet wide. The entrance to a horizontal mine is called an adit. If you'll follow me inside the adit I'll drive you to your location."

Jack and Murphy followed Tim inside and climbed onto a wagon lined with bench seats on either side. Tim started up a small diesel tractor and they began the trip into the mine. The mine was dimly lit by the occasional light bulb hanging overhead, and as they moved deeper inside the brightly sunlit entrance behind them shrank into a dot.

That was it.

In the dream he had a few weeks ago this was where he had stood talking to the ghost of his deceased wife. He was looking at the distant light of the entrance when she told him he would be joining her soon. Then and now, he assumed she meant he was going to die.

As much as he stilled loved her that was not something he looked forward to.

Knowing the source of his unease helped relieve some of it, but opened up a number of troubling questions. Jack had seen his wife briefly the night he died at Henry Ford Hospital, standing in front of a bright light coming from a tunnel, she was the one who told him to go back… did that count as joining her? If it didn't, and he was going to die again, would it be for keeps?

She said it would be soon.

The wagon kept rolling, the tunnel darkening and brightening as they passed beneath the lights. Jack's mood did the same as he kept wrestling with his thoughts.

Obviously he was going to die someday, so his wife wouldn't have told him he was going to be joining her if it wasn't going to happen in the near future. Unless his near-death experience was what she was talking about. But almost dying wasn't dying – or was it? What good was having a premonition in a dream if you didn't know what it was warning you about?

Soon.

Suddenly Jack had another source of apprehension – in addition to dying, which was no small thing, he was now one of those weirdoes who had premonitions. He had never believed in them, and had never had one until now. But there was no doubt that what he had seen – the dot of light that was now almost faded from view – matched the scene in his dream perfectly. Of course, he had visited the mine before, but that was decades ago.

Oh shit… did he just have a déjà vu?

That was another crazy thing he didn't believe in.

Jack had just finished deciding it wasn't a déjà vu when Tim called back to them.

"We're passing the half mile mark. This is where the tours stop. Not much farther."

It seemed like they went a lot farther before the tractor stopped by a side tunnel. Jack and Murphy climbed out of the wagon and got their final instructions.

"If you go about 100 yards down that tunnel it runs into the room where all your equipment is set up. We put a Porta Potty in there, too, in case you need it. I'll be back to pick you up in six hours."

As Tim turned around and headed back they walked in silence down the narrow side tunnel. When they reached the plywood wall installed to safeguard their lab equipment Jack unlocked the door and they stepped inside. Murphy was the first to speak.

"Holy shit!"

The room was much smaller than the one in the salt mine in Detroit, but the equipment set-up was identical. Jack started to explain the experimental protocol to Murphy but noticed he was staring blankly at the room.

"Murphy, you okay?"

"Not a big fan of tunnels. I went in more than my share in Vietnam. The Viet Cong built regular cities underground. They didn't like it when you came in looking for them."

"Are you going to be alright? We'll be down here all day every day for a week."

"Don't worry about me, I'll be fine. Remember I told you I went through a steam tunnel in Detroit one time to sneak up on some bad guys?"

"Yeah, but you didn't finish the story. You want to tell me about it now?"

"Not much to tell. There's this preservation group in Detroit called the POEs."

"I've heard of them. They threw rotten eggs at a developer's press conference."

"That's them. A movie company was going to build a studio in Detroit, they got a bunch tax breaks to do it. But they were going to knock down a bunch of houses and buildings to do it. The POES helped stop that. They're a little crazy, but their heart is the right place. They want to preserve the old buildings in Detroit, quit knocking things down."

"How did you get involved with them?"

"Long story short, I needed to get into a restricted area, and they showed me how to get there through the old steam tunnels that run under the city."

"And the tunnels reminded you of your time in Vietnam."

"More than reminded me – I had a major flashback, hadn't had one in years until then. Halfway through the tunnel I froze."

"What'd you do then?"

"I used my Zen training, the stuff that helped me move past Vietnam in the first place. Sat down in the tunnel and meditated. It worked, which was good – I had a client one the other end of the tunnel who might have been killed if I didn't get there."

"You had Zen training?"

"That's a story for another time. We have work to do."

Jack looked closely at Murphy, he seemed calm enough.

"Okay, let's get to work," Jack said. "I don't know a lot, but while we're down here I can teach you a little bit about physics and how to help with the experiment."

"And I'll teach you how to kill someone with your bare hands."

FORTY-NINE

Spooky Actions And Deadly Force

The week underground together went by quickly for Jack and Murphy, and in the end changed everything the world has ever known.

It started simply enough: every hour for four straight hours Jack would either send a light particle to Maggie or observe and record a particle she sent to him. That took all of 15 minutes an hour, leaving the rest of the time free for Jack to teach physics to Murphy, and Murphy to teach fighting to Jack.

They sat and talked in metal folding chairs in front of a table stacked with lap top computers and lab equipment next to a long grey tube. Murphy knew much more about fighting than Jack did about physics.

"What I'm doing is splitting a particle of light, which makes a pair that is what they call entangled," Jack explained. "I send one from this mine to the salt mine where Maggie is. When she measures it, it supposed to change the state of its partner, the one I kept here. Then the next hour we reverse the process, and she sends me one."

"How will you know if it's working?"

"She's keeping track on her end. By the end of the week she should have enough data to see if what's supposed to happen has happened."

"What's supposed to happen?"

"When you do something to one partner, like measure it, it's supposed to change the other one instantly."

"And if it does?"

"I'm not sure. It has some practical applications that will make computers faster or smarter or something. And maybe someday send objects from one place to another."

"What, like Star Trek? A transporter?"

"Yeah, but don't say that to Maggie, it pisses her off. It also will prove that Einstein was wrong about quantum physics."

"Einstein was a pretty smart dude. I'm guessing it would be tough to prove he was wrong about anything, but especially about physics. What's the argument about?"

This part of the explanation was slightly embarrassing to Jack. What was in dispute was something called quantum nonlocality. He really didn't understand it, but he had memorized the words and could recite it – just like the Wise Guys did in his class.

"Quantum nonlocality says two or more light particles can act in a coordinated way, no matter how far apart they are – without sending out a sound wave, beaming a radio signal or communicating across the gap that separates them. They behave as though they aren't separated."

"How can that happen?"

"No one knows. Einstein called it 'spooky action at a distance.' He said that if the theory was correct then the world would be crazy."

"So you're trying to prove that the world is crazy."

"I guess we are."

"Hell, I could have told you that, saved you a lot of time and effort."

"There is one possible explanation that Maggie talks about. She says maybe the light particles are rooted in a deeper level of reality where distance has no meaning."

"That sounds like something Buddha would say."

"It does. I think that's gotten her into trouble in the past – this stuff is so weird that science starts sounding like religion. That makes scientists nervous."

"She told me about the trouble she got into at Harvard. It sucks."

"No doubt about it, somebody was really out to get her."

Murphy turned toward Jack with and looked him over carefully, as if making an assessment in his head. He didn't seem overly excited about what he saw.

"Somebody is out to get you, too," he said. "We need to start your lessons."

Murphy began the training that first Monday morning by explaining the fighting moves he was going to teach Jack.

"These moves aren't in the Marquess of Queensberry rules. They're not something you use when a guy spills his beer on you in the bar. They're for saving your life when someone is out to do you real harm."

"Like the punks at the Hoist House?"

"Yeah, but it's important you use them in the order I tell you. There's four of them, and they go from the most effective to the most deadly. The last one can kill someone. You have to promise me you will use them the way I tell you to."

"I'll make that promise without even knowing what they are, Murphy. But what are they?"

"The number one best fighting move is to run away."

Jack laughed and Murphy looked at him sharply.

"I'm not kidding here. The best way to win a fight is to avoid it. You have to promise me that's what you'll do."

"I promise."

"If for some reason you can't run, then you go to number two: the groin kick."

"Classic bar fight move."

"Yeah, but I'm going to teach you how to do safely and effectively. Too many guys swing their leg like they're getting ready to kick a football. Your opponent can see it coming a mile away and grab your leg, now he's got you standing on one foot with your balls hanging out for him to kick."

"So how do you do it?"

"An upper cut with your knee. Hard to see coming, hard to block."

"Then what?"

"Number three is a throat punch. Very painful and potentially deadly. Number four is an eye gouge."

"Those are serious moves."

"That's why I want you to use them in order. Best thing always is to run away."

They spent the rest of the week practicing moves two, three and four whenever Jack wasn't running the experiment. The only break in this routine came on Wednesday, when Maggie send a text asking that Murphy take the measurements on their end. Jack showed him how, and he did it with no problems. On Thursday, when Murphy left early to "check things out" as he put it, Jack continued to practice the moves by himself.

On Friday Murphy declared him pretty damn good, but still insisted the number one move was his best option. When they finished their last training session Jack checked a laptop to see if Maggie had any final instructions for him before they wrapped up.

There were no instructions, just a cryptic and ominous message:

"I'm coming up. We have to talk."

FIFTY

The Perfect Problem

Maggie arrived at Jack's house late in the afternoon looking agitated.

He had called her as she made the drive up, but she wouldn't tell him what she was coming up to talk to him about. It was no small consolation, however, that she agreed to stay at his house instead of the Copper Crown Hotel in Hancock.

He had insisted.

When she arrived Jack carried her suitcase to one of small upstairs bedrooms, then gave her a quick tour of the house, summer kitchen and sauna. When the tour ended he threw some pasties in the oven, grabbed two beers and led her out to the hanging swing on the front porch. They sipped and swung, looking out over open fields, dirt roads and the occasional still-standing house. In the distance the empty chairlifts of Ripley ski hill marked the spot where the land dropped down steeply to the Portage Canal.

"So what is it you had to come up the way up here to tell me?" Jack said finally.

"First let's talk about Ajeet. Are there any new developments?"

"Murphy's been checking around town all week, that's where he is right now. I've discovered he likes to get all his ducks in a row before he tells you anything. If he has anything new he hasn't shared it with me yet."

"How about you, Jack? Have you been staying out of trouble like I asked you?"

It was the moment of truth for the truth.

He didn't want to alarm her, but he needed her to trust him. If he wanted their relationship to move forward he would have to tell her about the phony police drug raid. Their relationship – whatever it was at this point – made him feel guilty and scared, but now he desperately wanted it to move forward.

She took it as well as could be expected.

"The cops are working with the killer? They tried to frame you for having drugs?"

"Actually, it would have probably been for making drugs."

"Like on Breaking Bad?"

"Yes, like on Breaking Bad. But only one cop was involved. I told you, it was the same one who picked me after the bar fight. I don't think the whole force is after me."

"Well now I feel better," she said.

They both started laughing in spite of themselves. Then Maggie got serious again.

"I'm sorry I asked you to get involved in this. I've put you in danger."

"It was my choice, and I'm glad I made it."

"Do you know who this cop is?"

"We don't know anything about him yet, not even his name. Murphy has been following up on Luc Novikov and his buddy in his spare time, when he wasn't babysitting me in the mine. He was going check out the cop today."

"But he stayed with you in the mine the whole time, right?"

"I hope you don't mind. He wanted to make sure I was safe."

"Not at all, I'm glad he was there, he even helped out with the experiment. I just wish I hadn't gotten you into this mess."

"Well, I'm all in now. It's too late to back out, and I don't want to. Don't worry, we're going to figure out what's going on."

"Speaking of which, I've been working on the numbers puzzle, but I still haven't figured it out. Have you had any luck?"

"I'm sorry, I forgot I haven't told you yet. Murphy solved the puzzle. I would have told you sooner but I didn't want to send the message in a text from the mine. I could have called, but…"

"Murphy solved it? What is it?"

"It's not one number, it's seven numbers. The numbers of Detroit Red Wing players that are retired. They hang their jerseys from the rafter in Joe Louis Arena."

"The numbers are hockey jerseys?"

"Yeah."

"The note said to look for the prize 'Above the Immortals.'"

"Whatever it is, we think it must be somewhere on the roof the arena."

"Of course. What do we do next?"

"For now let's wait for Murphy. He should be here pretty soon, we can figure out what our next step is then. In the meantime, why don't you tell me what you came all this way to tell me."

Maggie slowed the swing down to a stop with her feet and took a big gulp of beer before she turned to Jack and spoke.

"The experiment was a success. You remember I explained that photons lose some of their integrity when they travel over fiber cable, or even through laser light. The new method I used achieved a substantial reduction in signal loss."

"That sounds like a good thing."

"It is. It has great practical application, and the potential to help us understand what is going on with quantum mechanics."

"So what's the problem?"

"You are."

"What do you mean?"

"I noticed something different right away. I wouldn't normally change up the variables once an experiment started, but I wanted to see if I could get different results with different observers, so I asked my graduate assistants Donna and Robert to take measurements."

"I'm not sure I'm following you."

"On our end, it didn't make any difference who did the measuring, the noise to signal ratio stayed the same. When I had Murphy take the measurements on your end his results matched the rest of us exactly."

"What about me?"

"That's the problem."

"What's the problem?"

"You were perfect."

FIFTY-ONE

The Enemy

"What do you mean I was perfect?"

"When you observed the entangled photon there was absolutely no noise in the signal. The results on our end matched perfectly."

"I really don't understand all this, but isn't that a good thing?"

"It's good in the sense that it helps prove my hypothesis, and makes my method of sending entangled photons the most accurate and reliable."

"But…"

"But it also suggests that it's not just the act of observing that has an impact on the photon, it's the observer. Different observers can get different results – that makes them another variable in the experiment."

"So it complicates things – that's the problem."

Maggie laughed.

"I can't think of anything more complicated than quantum physics. Adding another variable is like dropping another grain of sand on the beach."

"So what is the problem?"

"The problem, as always, is us. If there is anything more complicated than quantum physics, it's people. Scientists get nervous when you add us into the equation."

"We have met the enemy, and he is us."

"What?"

"It's a famous line from an old comic strip. Never mind. I still don't see why this is a problem."

"The scientific establishment gets upset when you try to add human consciousness into a physics experiment. I know this first hand, it's what got me into trouble at Harvard."

"I thought scientists were supposed to be logical and rational observers who followed the facts wherever they led."

"'Supposed to be' is the operative statement. They're not. They have preferences, biases and blind spots just like all of us. Physicists in particular tend to lose it any time you bring the human element into the discussion."

"You're talking about me now."

"Yes. I'd have to try the experiment with a lot more people to come to any firm conclusion. But I believe the fact that your results were different is significant."

"Do you have any ideas about why I was different?"

"I do. And that's what upsets me the most."

In the distance to their right, the sun was beginning to drop down behind Shaft House #2 at Quincy Mine. Jack drank down the last of his beer. He thought about taking hold of her hand, but chickened out.

"It's because I died, isn't it?" he said. "You think that's what made my results different."

"Not just different, better. Perfect. Yes, I think it's because you died. I have absolutely no logical reason to believe it, but I do."

"Is there any way you can prove it?"

"That's the problem. In a perfect world, I would publish my results, then run the experiment again using a 50/50 mix of people who've had Near

Death Experiences and people who haven't. But if I publish my results I will be mocked and marginalized even worse than before. No one will give me any funding to continue the experiment. I don't have tenure, I'll be lucky if I keep my job."

"I'm sorry I caused all this trouble for you."

"It's not your fault. That's just how the experiment came out."

"Is there anything I can do?"

"You're doing it. The reason I waited until I got here to tell you all this is because, quite frankly, it has me rattled. I was going to come up here to dismantle the equipment in a few weeks, but I couldn't wait that long. I needed to talk to someone I could share my feelings with, someone who would understand what I'm going through."

"I'm flattered you thought of me."

She looked at him in the fading light and smiled. His mind began racing, the implications of what she was saying both exhilarating and terrifying him. He tried to think of next steps, considering and rejecting everything from holding her hand and delivering a clever line to kissing her and declaring his love.

His thoughts were interrupted by the distant rumbling of tires on a dirt road.

Someone was coming, driving way too fast to be a lost tourist or a friendly visitor.

Jack's thoughts turned from love to war.

He began reviewing the various places they could retreat to in case these visitors weren't friendly, and cursed himself for not thinking about this earlier. There weren't a lot of safe places to go if someone showed up wanting to do them harm, especially if they brought a gun. He remembered Murphy's training, but it would be useless against a gun.

Except Number One.

It took Jack a moment to remember where he had left his car keys, after which he began calculating how long it would take to get them, run to the car, and leave. He had just finished his estimate when a late model sedan did a controlled slide around the corner and came barreling down the road towards them.

It was Murphy.

FIFTY-TWO

How Bad It Seems

Murphy wasn't as agitated as Maggie had been when she arrived, but he was definitely in a hurry.

"You got anything to eat?"

"I have some pasties heating up in the oven."

"Great. I don't have a lot of time. Let's eat and I'll tell you what I know."

They sat down at the kitchen table, Jack served up the Finnish meat pies, and Murphy served up the Jack.

"What about me?" Maggie asked when she wasn't included in his generous pour.

"Sorry, I didn't know you drank whiskey."

"Normally I don't. But there hasn't been a whole lot of normal lately."

"I'll drink to that," Jack said.

After Murphy filled a glass for Maggie, they clinked and drank and started eating.

"I found out a lot, and most of it isn't good," Murphy said between bites.

"Before you tell us about it, I have a question," Jack said. "Are you still planning to follow the Wise Guys back to Detroit tonight?"

"Yeah, that's the plan. That's why I have to eat and run – they're picking up the drugs at eight o'clock at the Hoist House, as soon as they have them they're heading right back to Detroit. I want to be there waiting for them."

"The Wise Guys? Jack, are those the three students you told me about? The ones that got you fired?"

"I'm actually on a sabbatical, at least that's what they tell me. But yes. Murphy can explain what's going on, maybe tell us what else he's found out."

Murphy summarized everything they knew so far: the Wise Guys threw parties where they sold Howdy Doody drugs. Their supplier was Luc Novikov, the punk who asked about – and most likely stole – the Fed Ex package. It was highly probably that the graduate assistant Ajeet was involved as the middleman between the two groups. Whether he killed himself or was murdered was still to be determined.

"If we know all this, why don't why just go to the police?" Maggie asked.

"It's not that simple," Murphy said. "The police here in town are in on it, at least one of them, maybe more."

"What about the Detroit police?"

"They're overworked and underpaid, and struggling to keep their heads above water with real crimes. They don't have time to investigate theories and speculation."

"But you have friends in the police department," she said.

"I have enemies, too. Some cops don't like it when I get involved, they think I'm interfering in police business. Our boy Jack here isn't too popular, either – the Detroit police think he might be making or dealing drugs. If we went to them with a theory about a possible murder that took place 300 miles away they'd laugh us out of the building."

"What if you called and told them students were bringing drugs into the city?"

"They'd laugh even harder. Might as well tell them that the sun is going to rise tomorrow while we're at it."

"So what do we do?" Maggie asked finally.

"First let me tell what I've found out this week," Murphy said. "Luc Novikov's buddy, the guy who picked a fight with Jack in the bar, is Jasper Peltonen. He and Luc do odd jobs around town – lawn mowing, snow plowing, construction. They have a reputation for being bad apples, but other than bar fights and a few incidents of drunken vandalism nobody has pinned anything specific on them. No one would be surprised if they were dealing drugs, but nobody has any proof."

"What about the cop?" Jack asked.

"That's where it gets interesting. His name is Vladimir Novikov. He's Luc's uncle."

Maggie and Jack both swore softly to themselves and Murphy continued.

"I'm pretty sure he's the only cop involved, but I can't be certain at this point. He came under suspicion years ago when Luc's father went to prison for making meth, but nothing came of it. He's now a respected, veteran police officer."

"I have to ask Murphy," Maggie said. "How do find all this stuff out?"

"You haven't figured it out by now? I turned my hobby into a full-time job: I do most of my best detective work in bars."

"How does that work?"

"This is a small town, everybody knows everybody. You sit at the bar for a while, buy a few drinks, you can find out anything you want to know."

When they finished eating Murphy topped off their drinks. They sipped in silence for a few minutes, then Jack asked the toughest question once again.

"So what do we do next?"

"I'm going to the Hoist House to follow the Wise Guys back to Detroit. They didn't want to keep the drugs in their apartment so they're going straight to where the party will be to drop them off. I want to see where that is."

"What about me?" Jack asked.

"Stay here and lay low, you'll be safe enough. They won't try to frame you again after failing so badly. And they won't fight you unless you go looking for them in bars."

"What about Ajeet? What about the murder?" Maggie asked.

"I haven't forgotten about that. I'm looking into some things. You might be able to help me out, I'll let you know."

"I wasn't going to stay here long, I have to get back to Detroit and figure out what to do with the results of the experiment. But if there's something I can do here do I'll stay."

"I don't like the idea of putting Maggie at risk," Jack said. "If there's something that needs to be done up here I can do it."

"I would never put her at risk," Murphy replied. "There's things she can check out that you can't."

"What things?" Jack asked.

"I'll let you know when the time is right. Trust me, nobody will be in danger."

Jack was going to point out he'd been told the same thing about going up on the roof of Henry Ford Hospital, but he didn't want to alarm Maggie or piss off Murphy. Instead he raised his glass for a toast.

"Safe travels."

They finished their drinks and Murphy rose to leave, but turned back in the doorway to share a final thought.

"I know you've had it pretty rough lately, Jack. You too, Maggie. But the Buddha says 'Every experience, no matter how bad it seems, holds within it a blessing of some kind. The goal is to find it.'"

With that said he was gone.

FIFTY-THREE

Hoist House

The buyers from Detroit looked a little nervous, so Luc tried to put them at ease.

"Relax, fellas. No one in this place gives a shit about drug deals, eh?"

That didn't help.

"Are you crazy?" Melch snapped. "Keep your voice down."

The three Wise Guys were sitting with Luc and Jasper at Luc's usual table in the corner of the bar. They had arrived a few minutes earlier talking tough but looking scared. That wasn't a problem for Luc: the three Howdy Doodys he had taken and the large amount of cash he was about to receive had turned him into a gracious host.

"I know you're in a hurry but I insist on buying you a beer before you go," he said. "Besides, I have a present I want to give you."

Melch, Casper and Baltimore exchanged glances before Melch replied.

"Okay, we'll have one beer. Then we gotta go."

While they waited for the beer to arrive Luc decided to do a little fishing.

"So what's the prize?" he asked.

The Three Wise Guys looked even more nervous.

"What are you talking about?" Melch asked.

"You know, the prize. The prize that's being given away."

"How do you know about the prize?"

Luc had a fish on the line. He started reeling him in.

"Ajeet told me all about it. Sounds really great."

"We give out a prize at every rave, it's sort of like a scavenger hunt," Casper said. "You have to follow the clues to find it."

The other two Wise Guys looked at him sharply but said nothing.

"Yeah, that's what Ajeet told me," Luc said. "But he didn't know what the prize was going to be this time. What is it?"

"It's a surprise," Melch said. "We hide it the afternoon before the rave, but we never say what it is in advance. We always wait until the night of the party at midnight, then we tell people what the prize is and give them the first clue."

"I can tell you the prizes are always cool and worth a lot of money," Casper added.

"That's what Ajeet said," Luc lied. "He told me when the party was, but I forgot."

"Sunday night on Memorial weekend," Baltimore said.

It was catch and release time: Luc had enough information, so he let it go.

The beer arrived and the Wise Guys drank it down quickly. But before they went outside to conduct their transaction in the parking lot Luc had one more surprise for them.

"Wait a minute. Let me give you your present before you go. Check this out."

Luc pulled out his phone and the Wise Guys watched a short video of Professor Crost punching someone and knocking him down in a bar. It looked vaguely like the guy sitting at the table with them and definitely like the bar they were in. They all laughed, then Melcher had serious questions for Luc.

"How did you get this video? Do you know who this guy is?"

"Jasper seen him on the Internet on one of them viral videos. So the guy comes in the bar one night and Jasper recognizes him and decides to have some fun. I was recording it on my phone, but I didn't see that punch coming. Neither did Jasper, eh?"

Luc laughed long and hard, but the Wise Guys sat stone-faced and Japser glared.

"That guy's nuts, he's the Crazy Professor from Wayne State, right?" Luc continued. "You guys are from Wayne State, I don't know if know him but I thought you'd get a kick out of it."

The three looked at each other and nodded.

"Thanks, that's some funny shit," said Melcher. "I'd like a copy for myself – can you send it to my phone? Then let's go do this."

The exchange didn't take long. Luc carried a large cardboard box from his truck and set it down in the trunk of their car. They opened the box and looked inside quickly, then handed him a grocery bag. He looked inside the bag, shook their hands, and took it back to his truck.

A minute later Luc was peeling out of the parking lot.

The Wise Guys left next, driving at a much slower speed.

The next car to leave the lot was a late model sedan.

FIFTY-FOUR

Eyes On The Prize

As they headed down Highway 41 toward Hancock Jasper counted the money while Luc dreamed of the prize.

"What do you think it is?" Luc asked.

"What do I think what is?"

"The prize."

"The prize is a grocery bag full of money," Jasper replied. "I got it right here."

"No, not that. I mean the prize up on the roof at Joe Louis Arena."

"Who gives a damn about that, eh? We got a shitload of money from them college boys. I can't believe they agreed to pay what we charged them."

"That's great, Jasper. I'm digging the money, eh? But I kinda want to go after that prize, too. We solved the clue, all we gotta do is go up on the roof of Joe Louis Arena and find it. They said it was valuable."

"Are you nuts? You're going to drive all the way to Detroit and climb up on a roof you're not supposed to be on to look for a prize that you even know what it is?"

"Maybe."

"That's crazy. Somebody will see you, and the cops will throw your ass in jail. You don't want to go to jail in Detroit, man."

"Don't worry about me. I know how to sneak around cops."

"What about all those college kids? They'll be up there looking, too."

"I don't give a shit about them. If they hassle me I'll pull out my piece."

"You *are* crazy, Luc."

"Is all the money there? They didn't short us?"

"Looks like it's all here."

"Then I'm crazy rich, Jasper."

Luc's long, loud laugh did little to reassure Jasper about his friend. And there was something else bothering him.

"What'd you have to give them that video for?" Jasper asked. "I'm the one getting knocked down by an old guy. Ever think maybe I don't want people seeing that?"

"Don't get a bug up your ass, eh? You don't even look like that anymore, and nobody cares if it was you, anyway."

"I care if it was me."

"I was just trying to make them relax a little bit, they looked like they were ready to shit their pants they were so scared. If we're going to be doing business with these guys they can't be too afraid to come pick the stuff up."

They rode on in silence, rounding the sweeping downhill curve that led into town. As they raced along the edge of the hill fighting the centrifugal force of the turn Luc reached over with one hand and tried to open the glove box.

"What the hell are you doing, man? Keep your hands on the wheel."

"Reach in there and get me a Howdy Doody, would you?"

"How many of those things have you had tonight?"

"What are you, my uncle? Give me one of those fuckers."

Jasper grabbed a pill out of the glove box and gave it to Luc with a reminder.

"They said they hid it the afternoon before their party," he said.

"Then I better get down there before the party starts, eh?"

FIFTY-FIVE

The Blessing

The beer and the whiskey had something to do with it, but it was mostly Murphy's parting words that had Jack thinking about love.

Not the pure and simple universal love for all people he'd taught with mixed results for nearly two decades, but the messy, complicated one-on-one love he'd avoided during that time. Maggie might be the blessing in all the bad experiences he'd had lately.

It was time to find out.

"What should we do next?" he asked.

"I've never had a sauna, can we do that?"

Jack hadn't actually met God when he died, but he must have come close – it seemed his prayers were being answered at last.

"Of course. It's an authentic wood-burning Finnish sauna, so I'll go start the fire and get it heated up."

"Oh wait, I don't have a bathing suit."

For a moment he considered telling her truth – Finns took their saunas naked and beat each other with birch branches – but he didn't want to freak her out.

"No problem. I'll get us towels to wear."

Jack's sauna didn't look like much from the outside – not much bigger than a garden shed, with a weathered wood exterior ar.d a shingled roof. When the temperature inside rose above 150 degrees they walked out to it carrying their towels. Jack went first into the small, unheated outer changing room, took off his clothes, wrapped himself in a beach towel and went inside to the sauna. He called out to Maggie and she did the same.

"This is really nice," she said. "Really hot, too."

The inner room was a traditional sauna made of cedar boards, two rows of stacked benches and a wood-burning stove topped with a metal basket filled with rocks. A wooden bucket and ladle sat under a faucet in one corner, a pile of birch wood in the other. Jack had also stocked the sauna with a small cooler filled with beers.

They opened two cans, cheered and drank.

"To Finns a sauna is a cultural ritual," Jack said. "Almost a form of meditation."

"Do they fool around in their saunas?"

Jack laughed but this time told the truth.

"No. It's almost a holy place to a lot of Finns."

"Sorry. I'm really not a drinker. I didn't mean to be so forward."

Jack was sorry she was sorry – he was enjoying their forward momentum.

"That's okay. I was talking about traditional sauna culture. Who knows what goes on in saunas these days."

"Do you think they smoke marijuana in them?"

He turned to see her smiling wickedly.

"I'm not sure, but I think we're about to find out."

Maggie climbed down from the top bench and disappeared into the outer room. She returned holding what looked like a small cigar. Jack knew from years of studying Sixties literature at the college level that it was what they called a "big fat doobie." She lit it on the stove fire and they passed it between them until its effects were noticeable. He then confirmed the marijuana was working by saying something utterly stupid.

"Now things are really going to get steamy."

Jack carried the bucket over to the stove and ladled out water onto the rocks while quietly repeating the word "loyly."

"Did you say lovely?" Maggie asked.

"Loyly. The Finnish word for steam."

"Well that's lovely," Maggie replied, and the laughter began.

Jack remembered reading what Einstein had said about time being relative – put your hand on a hot stove for a minute and it seems like an hour, sit with a pretty girl for an hour and it seems like a minute. He had no idea how long he had sat by the hot stove with a pretty girl, joking and laughing, but he hoped it would go on to infinity.

The only thing he knew for sure right now in the moment was that it was time to kiss Maggie. He had been thinking about it ever since she got here, maybe since he first met her. Part of him felt guilty, as if it were a betrayal of the love of his life. Another part was terrified, because the stakes were higher now than they were for all the casual dates and minor flings he'd had through the years.

This was it.

He moved closer to her on the bench. She turned to him – smiling, sweating, beautiful. Then she doused him with a giant verbal splash of cold water.

"Tell me about your wife," she said.

Jack froze for a moment, then slumped back on the bench and sighed.

"There's not much to tell," he said.

"I think there is."

He sat in the wet, the beads of sweat slowly making their way down his body, and tried to think of a polite way to say 'no.'

He didn't want to talk about her.

He never talked about her.

He started talking about her and couldn't stop.

"Her name was Cassandra. She was beautiful, inside and out. A real free spirit who for some reason decided to hang out with a cranky, self-absorbed English professor. I'm still not sure why she married me."

"She loved you."

"I guess. She made me a better person, or at least she tried to."

"How did she die?"

This was the hard part.

"When I got the job at Wayne we were living in an apartment in the suburbs. She wanted to live near the university, to do something positive to help turn around the city."

"And you?"

"This was before the whole area was gentrified. There was a lot of crime, a lot of bad guys doing bad things. I didn't think it was safe."

"She talked you into moving."

"Yes. But it turned out I was right. Terribly right."

"What happened?"

Jack sat for a moment before he spoke, feeling the heat press against his skin and his sweat roll down the path of least resistance.

"I was teaching a night class, she was home alone. Someone broke into the house, the police thought it was a couple guys, they weren't sure, they never caught them. Whoever it was took our stereo and TV. And killed my wife."

"I'm so sorry."

"We didn't have a lot of money. There was no jewelry, nothing of value in the house. They shot her in the head so they could have our stereo and TV."

Jack couldn't tell if it was sweat or tears rolling down his face.

It was awful hot.

"What did you do after that," she asked softly.

"For a while I went to a very dark place. Almost quit my job, and nearly got fired. Tried to sell the house so I could move back to the suburbs."

"You're not in that place anymore. What happened?"

"I finally snapped out of it and decided to do something positive for the city and the world. I took my house off the market – there wasn't a lot of demand for murder scene Victorian houses back then anyway. I joined Neighborhood Watch and became a volunteer at Children's Aid Society. It was the oldest child welfare agency in the state, and nearby."

"What brought you back?"

This was the impossible part.

Impossible for him to tell or for anyone to believe. Except maybe Maggie. He thought about it briefly, then decided to go all in on crazy.

"I started having dreams."

"About her?"

"They weren't just *about* her. She'd talk to me, tell me things, give me advice."

"What kind of advice?"

"Mostly to let go of the hate and anger I had. To not feel guilty about what happened. To bring some love into the world, make it a better place."

"Is that why you started helping out in the community."

"Yeah. I also changed the classes I taught. I quit teaching formal, struc-tured courses about the standard classics of literature and focused on the writing of the Sixties."

"Why the Sixties?"

"It seemed to capture her spirit and attitude the best. She was a hippie at heart, unfortunately one who lived in the wrong place at the wrong time."

"I've heard about your class. I understand it is quite popular."

"The English Department fought the idea of teaching Sixties literature at first, but they finally gave in and let me teach a seminar for six students just to shut me up. The classes kept getting bigger after that, which really pissed off the head of the department. He kept saying I was teaching sociology or psychology, not literature. I guess I shouldn't have been surprised to see him leading the protestors at the demonstration."

"If they didn't like what you were teaching why did they let you continue?"

"They jumped on the bandwagon because it was a cash cow for the university. They ended up moving me into a 200-seat auditorium."

"Having a class that was that popular must have been very satisfying."

"It sounds corny, but it was even more satisfying when it felt like I made a difference in a student's life. The truth is, in the last few years I think the course became too popular. Especially with students from other disciplines who heard it was fun and took it as an elective. These days too many of my students are more concerned about their grades than about learning anything."

"I'm sure that's disappointing to you."

"I want to do more than fill their heads with knowledge – I want to change their lives. I tell a few jokes, goof around a little, try to have some fun. But my goal is quite serious. I want them to be better people. We need more love and acceptance in the world."

"It that a tribute to her?"

"Yes. But it's something I want very much, too."

"You teach peace and love. Are you at peace? Have you found love?"

"Funny you should ask. Up until a little while ago I would have said no. But lately I've felt different. This last week I realized that when I wasn't getting beaten up, arrested or dying, I've felt a sort of quiet optimism lately. If I didn't know better I'd say I was happy."

"I told you when we were down in the salt mine, people who experience Near Death are positively transformed. They appreciate life, and what the moment brings them."

Jack was going to say he appreciated what this moment had brought him but decided it sounded too much like a stupid pick-up line. So instead he slid across the bench and leaned in toward Maggie.

And heard his phone ringing.

"I'm sorry, it's Murphy. It could be important."

He went back into the outer room and fished his cell phone out of his pants pocket. After a few uh huhs he put the phone back in his pants and returned to the sauna.

"Is everything okay?"

"Yeah. It was Murphy, letting me know that the drug deal was done and he was on the road following my former students."

"I can't believe he's going to follow them all the way back to Detroit."

"If Murphy says he can do it I believe him," Jack said. "He's pretty remarkable."

"He's not the only one," Maggie replied. "Don't you think it's strange how the Wise Guys and my graduate assistant brought us together. It's like we're…"

"Entangled?"

Maggie smiled and nodded. Once again Jack moved over to kiss her.

He hoped and prayed the third time would be the charm.

Maggie jumped down from the bench and went back into the outer room.

"We need protection," she said.

Jack started to call after her that Murphy had assured him again on the call that they would be safe. He stopped before he embarrassed himself.

"Oh," he said instead, and then more quietly: "Duh."

Maggie returned holding a small foil packet in her hand.

She had left her towel in the outer room.

FIFTY-SIX

Alice And Bob

Maggie wasn't smiling in the morning.

She came downstairs to find Jack in the kitchen humming softly and cooking breakfast. To her alarm she realized the song was "Something" by the Beatles. She poured herself a cup of coffee from the pot on the stove and sat down at the table.

"Watch out, it's hot," Jack said. "Finns love coffee, they always keep a pot going."

"Jack, we have to talk."

It was not the morning after greeting he had hoped for.

"Okay. Sit down, we'll talk over breakfast. It's almost ready."

Maggie took a seat at the kitchen table, grimaced, and spoke.

"Last night was fun, but I'm afraid I may have given you the wrong impression."

"What do you mean?"

"I like you a lot, Jack. But I want to make it clear that I'm not interested in starting any kind of relationship. Not with you, not with anyone."

Jack paused for a moment too long before responding.

"That's cool, that's fine. I'm not either."

"You're a terrible liar, Jack. You have feelings for me, I can tell"

"Is that so bad?"

"Yes. For many reasons I can't get into."

"What reasons?"

"I told you, I don't want to discuss them. You have to trust me."

"Was it the sex? It wasn't good?"

"Why do men always go there first?" she asked. "The sex was good, better than good – what we did last night could win us the Nobel Prize for Chemistry *and* Physics."

Jack laughed in spite of himself, then thought: she makes me laugh.

"Okay, then what's the problem?"

Jack brought two plates loaded with eggs, bacon and pancakes to the table and sat down. Maggie said nothing and they both began to eat.

"You talked about us being entangled last night," she said at last. "But we're really still just Point A and Point B. We're at different places, far apart."

"What do you mean by that? Give me an example."

"You're a man of principle, and I'm a coward. I came up here hoping some of your moral courage would rub off on me, but it hasn't. I'm afraid to publish my results and face the consequences, because most likely it will be professional suicide."

"Do you think I care about that? If I was a man of principle I would've stayed and fought the university, instead I let them bribe me with a paid vacation."

"There's more. I'm obsessed with my work, to the point where I have no qualms about manipulating people. I took advantage of your feelings so you'd help me run my experiment and find out what happened to Ajeet, even when it meant putting you at risk."

"You're obsessed with your work. I get that – I am, too. Whatever brought us together is irrelevant. I know how I feel, and I'm pretty sure you felt the same last night"

"Jack, I lied to you about the experiment," she yelled.

"What do you mean?"

"There was a chance, a very small theoretical chance, but still a chance, that my experiment could have been deadly. One theory says entangled photons are connected by wormholes – shortcuts through time and space. No one has found one yet but they could be deadly. That's one of the reasons I wanted everything underground."

"I thought being underground protected the photons from outside interference."

"It did. But it also would have protected the people in the area if anything went wrong. Everyone but you. I told my graduate assistants about the possibility because they could understand the mathematical risk. I didn't tell you because you wouldn't understand, and I didn't want to scare you away. I'm not a nice person, Jack. I'm a mad scientist."

Jack got up from the table, grabbed the pot of coffee and refilled their cups. He sat back down determined not to leave any cards unplayed.

"Back in the salt mine you said people who've had Near Death Experiences are profoundly and positively transformed. At peace with themselves, accepting of others, living in the moment. I've had all those feelings lately, and more. But I don't think it was because I died, at least not all of it…"

"Jack, don't."

"It was because I met you. I love you Maggie."

Maggie struggled but managed to keep her composure. A range of emotions from joy to despair flickered across her face before it hardened into a grim neutral.

"It doesn't matter what you or I feel, Jack. This won't work, it can't last."

"Why not?"

"Do you think I smoke pot because I'm some kind of hippie? I told you, I smoke it because I have a medical condition."

"You never told me what it is."

"I have cancer, Jack. I'm dying."

FIFTY-SEVEN

Vanishing Acts

Murphy sounded sober and confused on the phone, which frightened Jack.

"Tell me again – what happened with the Wise Guys?" he asked.

"I lost them."

"You lost track of the car?"

"I didn't lose the car, I lost them."

"Okay, this is getting a little too Zen for me. Just tell me what happened."

"I followed them all the way to Detroit, no problem. They ended up at the old Packard Plant."

"Isn't that like old ruins or something?"

"Yeah, it closed in 1953. Some real estate developer from Spain is trying to renovate the place, but it's still pretty messed up."

"So what happened when you got there?"

"They pulled their car into one of the buildings."

"One of the buildings?"

"There's lot of them, the place covers 40 acres. The main plant alone is 3.5 million square feet."

"They drove into one of them, what did you do?"

"They pulled into a loading dock area of what must have been a warehouse back in the day. I was pretty far away at that point so they wouldn't spot me, but I turned up a side street and raced around to the back of the building. I snuck up on foot and saw their car, but they were gone."

"They must have seen your car or heard you coming."

"Weren't you listening when I told you my life story? The Detroit Police department taught me how to follow somebody in a car without being spotted. The United States Army taught me how to sneak around without being seen or heard. Those kids didn't know I was following them."

"So where'd they go?"

"I don't know. I looked around in the warehouse and all the buildings that were nearby. They weren't in any of them, and when I circled back their car was gone."

"You missed them."

"I didn't miss them, I don't miss people I'm tracking. If they were on the grounds somewhere I would have found them. They just disappeared."

Jack wanted to argue that people don't just disappear, and that Murphy needed to accept his failure, but he thought better of it. It would only piss him off and prolong the argument, and they needed to move on.

"So what do we do now?"

"I'm heading back to the Old Miami to see if I can find out anything new. You and Maggie should be safe for now, but stay close to home and watch each other's backs."

"That might be a bit of a problem."

"Why?"

"Maggie left. She's staying at the Copper Crown until she finishes packing up the experiment. She'll be back in Detroit in a few days. She doesn't want to see me again."

"What'd you do?"

"Nothing. We were getting along good, maybe too good. I think she got scared we were getting too close too fast."

"Maggie doesn't scare very easily. I'm guessing she was trying to protect you."

Jack paused to consider his reply. He didn't want to betray a confidence, but Murphy was no relationship expert. He didn't deal in subtleties, he had to know.

"You mean because of her illness?" Jack asked.

This time Murphy paused before he replied.

"Yeah. She told you about it?"

"This morning. We made this incredible connection last night, and this morning she was cold as hell and didn't want to have anything to do with me. How'd you know about her having cancer?"

"She talked about it in our Buddhist group. She uses meditation to help her get through the chemo."

"She's had chemotherapy?"

"One round so far. There's another one coming up."

"Damn."

"Yeah, damn."

There was another long pause before Murphy broke the silence.

"So that's it? You're not going to see her anymore?"

Jack's reply was swift and sure.

"Oh I'm going to see her again. I'm going to marry her."

FIFTY-EIGHT

Help!

Shit.

The last thing on Earth Maggie wanted to do was call Jack Crost. Actually, that was the second-to-the-last thing: the *last* thing she wanted to do was ask him for help.

Then Robert stopped by her office for a final debriefing on the experiment.

In the days following Ajeet's death Robert had seemed worried and distracted. That was understandable: the two were colleagues and friends, close enough for Ajeet's family to ask Robert to coordinate the gathering and return of his possessions. But when he sat down across from her she was shocked to see how much further he had unraveled.

"How long was I up north?" she asked.

"Four days, why?"

"Because you look like you either had the worst sleep or the best party of your life while I was gone."

"Sorry, professor. I've had a lot on my mind."

"I'm sorry, a joke wasn't appropriate. It's just that I'm concerned about you. We all miss Ajeet, and I know he was friend of yours. It must be very hard."

Robert nodded but said nothing.

"If there's anything I can do, please let me know. We have some excellent therapists and grief counselors right here on campus; I've gotten to know some of them personally in the past six months. I'd be happy to…"

"Thank you professor, but I'm fine. I just want to wrap things up if that's okay."

"Of course, Robert. The offer stands, but let's get started."

They spent most of the next twenty minutes discussing the logistics of shutting down the experiment. While Maggie was up north supervising the dismantling and removal of the equipment in the copper mine, Robert was doing the same in the salt mine. He had e-mailed her copies of his invoices and inventory lists, which they reviewed. The computers and electronic equipment were sent back to the physics department, the rest was shipped to a warehouse in Detroit to await the decision on further experiments.

When they got to that point in the discussion it was Robert's turn to broach a painful subject.

"Are you going to repeat the experiment?" he asked.

"I'm not sure. I'd have to publish the results of this experiment before anyone would underwrite another one. I don't know if I want to do that or not."

"Because of the anomaly?"

"Yes."

"We did everything exactly as it should have been done. There were no mistakes – the data is solid."

"I agree. But that's what makes this so hard. The only variable in the experiment was that one of the participants had a near-death experience."

"It could have been something else, we don't know."

"What else could it be? The color of his hair? How much pressure he used when he touched the computer keyboard? There are a million variables, but I have a strong hunch that near-death is what created the difference in the results. Hunches might not be logical or rational, but they have a proud tradition in the history of science."

"I agree. But how would you follow up on your hunch?"

"If I repeated the experiment it would be to find out if a near-death experience in the observer has a real and measurable impact on the accuracy of the signal. If it does that has profound implications, not just for science but for religion, philosophy, the humanities – for everything involved in how we view ourselves in the universe."

"So why not repeat it?"

"Because if I tell people that's what I want to test for, they will laugh me out of the room, perhaps out of the profession."

"You don't know…"

"I do know, Robert. It's happened to me before, it almost ended my career. We want to believe we are seekers of the truth, noble and unbiased, but at the end of the day we are human beings like everyone else, trapped in a narrow mindset of instincts and prejudice. When someone upsets our preconceptions we get angry and lash out at them."

"Sometimes it takes great courage to do science. Look at Copernicus… Galileo… climatologists…"

"As it turns out, I'm using up a lot of my courage on another project I've got going right now. I'm not sure I have the time or energy to take on anything else. I'll let you know when I decide."

"If you do repeat the experiment, I want to be involved, okay?"

"Of course. You've been a great help all the way through, especially after what happened."

As the words left her mouth she found herself struggling to hold back tears.

"You alright, professor?" he asked.

"I'm fine. It just struck me that three weeks ago to the day Ajeet was sitting right there in the same chair you are. I was mad because he was late to our meeting. We ended up hugging it out, but I said some things I regret."

"Ajeet was a huge fan of yours, professor. I'm sure whatever you said rolled right off his back. I'm sure he deserved it, too. We all have regrets…"

It was Robert's turn to stop and try to compose himself. He appeared to be struggling with a thought, but said nothing. They went back to discussing business and quickly wrapped things up. It wasn't until Robert got up to leave that Maggie remembered one last piece of unfinished business.

"Robert, wait. I almost forgot."

She reached into her desk and pulled out a pink Fed Ex receipt.

"Do you know anybody named Chemic? Ajeet sent a Fed Ex package to my office right before he died, he wanted someone named Chemic to pick it up for him. Whoever that is never showed up. I was going to give it to you to give to his family, but someone stole it. Probably just as well, because… never mind, that's not important now."

As Maggie talked, Robert turned around and sat back down. When she finished he put his head down and covered his eyes. After a moment she realized he was crying.

"Are you okay?" she asked softly.

"I'm okay," he said without looking up. "I'm a coward and a hypocrite, giving lectures about courage, but I'm okay."

"What are you talking about, Robert?"

"I'm Chemic. The package was for me."

FIFTY-NINE

Hi Jack

Wow.

Jack had spent the last few days sending texts and leaving phone messages for Maggie without getting a response. He was approaching the point where determined pursuit crossed the line into harassment when suddenly her number was flashing on his phone.

"Hi Jack, it's Maggie. Have you got a minute?"

"Of course I do, I've been trying to get ahold of you."

"I know you have, and I apologize for not getting back to you. But I knew what you wanted to talk about and I didn't have anything to say."

"And now you do?"

"Yes, but it's not what you want to talk about… it's not about us. Is that okay?"

Jack weighed his options for a split second. Talking with Maggie about anything was better than being ignored and twisting in the wind.

"It's okay."

"Promise?"

"Yes, I promise. What do you want to talk about?"

"I know who Chemic is."

"Who?"

"Chemic. The guy Ajeet sent the Fed Ex package to right before he was killed. It's Robert, the graduate assistant I introduced you to who helped with the experiment."

"Who told you that?"

"Robert did. He came by my office yesterday to do the final inventory of the equipment we used in the experiment. He seemed worried and distracted, and he looked he hadn't slept in a week. As he was leaving I asked him if he knew who Chemic was, and he broke down crying and said it was him."

"Why was he crying?"

"He was crying because he's been freaked out ever since he heard about Ajeet. He thought he was going to be kicked out of school, or thrown in jail, or worse."

"Worse?"

"He thinks the same thing I do – that Ajeet was killed. That's one of the reasons he didn't pick up the package. He knew what was in it and why Ajeet sent it."

"How did he know what was in it?"

"Ajeet called him the night before he died and told him he what he was going to send him. He sent him a text the next morning to confirm that he sent the package."

"Why did he send it?"

"Robert is a chemical physicist. He understands physics, but he also knows chemistry. He was supposed to analyze the pills in the package and figure out how they were made."

"What for?"

"Robert confirmed what Murphy suspected, Ajeet was the middle man who handled the drugs deals between Luc Novikov and your Wise Guys. He was trying to bluff Luc into lowering his price by telling him he had figured out the formula for Howdy Doody so he could keep the difference for himself."

"I don't know anything about dealing drugs, but screwing over the partners on both ends of the deal sounds like a dumb thing to do."

"Ajeet wasn't dumb, he was brilliant."

Maggie's voice had a sharp angry edge.

"I'm sorry. I didn't mean to speak ill of him. It's just that, for someone with such a promising future, he was involved in some very risky business."

"Robert says Ajeet was drinking too much, and taking a lot Howdy Doody himself. He needed the money."

"And Robert was going to help him?"

"Before he went to meet with the drug dealers Ajeet made a last-minute decision to go beyond bluffing and actually figure out the formula. He wanted Robert to do that, and to help him figure out what that message meant – apparently it's a clue for some sort of scavenger hunt prize your students are having. Robert swears he was just going to analyze the pills, he wasn't going to help Ajeet make drugs."

"You believe him?"

"He was spilling his heart out to me, I know he wasn't lying. He says he was just buying time until the experiment was over and Ajeet was back in town. He thought maybe if knew what was in the drug he could show Ajeet how bad it was for him."

"So why was the package addressed to Chemic? Is that an alias or some kind of code name or something?"

"It's a nickname they gave him because of his background in chemistry. He didn't want to use his real name in case someone opened the package up and found the pills. He had Ajeet send it to my office address for the same reason. If the package arrived without any problems Robert was going to tell me he was Chemic and take it. If anything suspicious happened, he was going to steal it. He was in and out of my office all the time, it would have been easy for him to take the package when no one was looking."

"But he got scared when Ajeet died, so he didn't do anything."

"Yes. But there was something else later, something that scared him even more."

"What?"

"I told you the family had asked Robert to gather Ajeet's possessions and send them home. He found a list of passwords in a desk and went on Ajeet's laptop to see if he could transfer the money in his bank account to a bank in India. That's when he saw it."

"Saw what?"

"Ajeet's laptop had an app that locates your electronic devices if you lose them. Robert opened it up to see if he was missing anything and it showed the location of Ajeet's cell phone."

"So?"

"Ajeet's phone has been missing since he died. The police assumed it was lost in the lake when he hit the water. But Robert says it's on land."

"Where?"

"In Hancock. Not far from you."

SIXTY

The Observer Effect

Jack knew he was really in love when he pulled out onto Highway 41.

Not that he had doubted it before, but driving into town to catch a killer was undisputable evidence.

Of course, Maggie had given him a long list of cautions and precautions and made him swear to stick to all of them. Don't get too close, don't stick around, don't send the signal if you see anyone, be sure to set your phone to silent mode so it doesn't ring and give you away. And, of course, he had promised to follow all of her rules.

Like that would make it safe.

When they finished their conversation he typed the address she had given him into a phone app to get directions. Robert had figured out the address by cross-referencing the locator map with a more detailed Google map. As it turned out, it looked like it was easy to get there and not too far away. He tried not to give it too much thought beyond that, because when he did he a dark, cold fear welled up inside him.

As he drove down Highway 41 that fear came bursting out, and he knew he was in love. The mission he was on was a chance to please her and an excuse to talk to her again. There were no other reasons in the world he could think of for doing what he was about to do. Meanwhile, the reasons for not doing it were lined up around the block.

The plan, for what it was worth, was for him to drive by the address and check it out. Was it a house, an office building, some kind of store? Then, depending on the circumstances, he would park his car and try to get close to whatever building matched the address. If was able to do that, he would text her a "thumbs up" emoji. That was the signal to launch the *really* stupid part of the plan: Maggie would call Ajeet's cell phone.

He had tried to talk her out of it, suggested they discuss it with Murphy first, urged her to go to the police, but she was determined.

"The police will ignore us and Murphy will tell us not to do it," she said. "I don't want to go to them until we know for sure the phone is there. If you can get close enough to hear the phone ring, we'll know."

"But if someone does have the phone won't it tip them off?"

"We could set off a remote alarm signal if we wanted, but that would definitely tip them off. A phone call won't be as suspicious."

"Won't they be able to see who called?"

"I'll be calling from a university phone. They all show up on ID as the same generic number."

"What if someone answers?"

"No one's going to answer, but if they do I'll say I'm calling about overdue parking permit fees. Like I said, nothing we're doing will make them suspicious."

After a few more what-ifs Jack gave up. He wasn't sure if she was confident in his abilities or indifferent to his fate. The only thing he knew for certain was that she was obsessed with finding this piece of the puzzle, and he was obsessed with her.

The fact that she was dying didn't matter.

He followed the highway into town, turning right at a crossroad just before the sharp left curve that led downtown. One more turn and he was driving slowly down a street lined with houses; two blocks down it was there on the left. When he reached the end of that block he turned left and parked on the side street.

To his dismay there was an obvious and easy way to get closer.

It was an old neighborhood with a layout to match: a narrow alley ran behind the houses, bisecting the rectangular block. The entrance to the alley that led back to the house he had spotted was right across from where he was parked. Other than the fact that he was terrified – and tired of beating beaten up, arrested or killed – there was no reason not to continue with the plan.

Jack got out of his car, looked around, crossed the street and started walking down the alley. It was lined on both sides with a tall wooden fence. Behind each house was a one-car garage with a wide double door that opened onto the alley. He was looking for a faded barn red house about a third of the way down, the only one that color on the block. He found a garage that matched the color, peered over the fence, and there it was.

It was a quiet neighborhood and the house was close to where he was standing. If a phone did ring inside it there was good chance he would hear it. He waited a moment, looking and listening for any indication that someone was home.

There was nothing.

His thoughts flashed back to the end of their phone call, when he ignored his promise and started to talk about his feelings for Maggie. She cut him off with a quick, "Jack, not now." In the time-honored tradition of lovesick fools, he interpreted this as meaning, "I'd love to talk after you finish doing the crazy shit I just asked you to do."

With that thought he found the courage to send her a thumbs up emoji.

A moment later, he heard it: a phone was ringing inside the house. It was muted and soft, but unmistakable, a kind of electronic pinging sound that repeated at short intervals. Jack squeezed against the fence and waited for it to stop. It took a while and felt like forever before it did, but that was a good thing – no one had answered it.

After waiting a moment longer he began walking back toward his car in a way that he hoped looked casual. He was beginning to think that he had gotten away with this crazy shit when he heard a vehicle pulling in behind him at the far end of the alley. He glanced back and saw it was a pickup truck, and even from this distance he recognized the two men in it immediately. He turned and started walking again, and after a few steps dared to hope that they hadn't recognized him.

Then he heard the tires squeal.

SIXTY-ONE

Highway 41 Revisited

As the pickup truck raced down the alley toward him, Jack employed the first of Murphy's four fighting moves.

Run.

He wasn't sure if Luc and Jasper were trying to hit him with their truck or not, but he didn't want to find out the hard way. They definitely weren't slowing down, as he neared the end of the alley they were closing on him fast.

When he reached the alley entrance he cut to his right, a second later the truck went flying past him. It made a hard left and screeched to a stop while Jack kept running straight to his car. He got in and started it as the truck backed slowly toward where he was parked. The truck swerved toward him and skidded to a stop with only a few inches separating its tailgate from the front of his car.

Luc and Jasper stepped out.

"Why the hell are you sneaking around our house?" Luc yelled.

Jack had a quick decision to make: get out of the car and explain what he was doing to two angry young men who had already beat the shit out of him once, or continue with fight move number one.

He put the car in reverse and gunned it.

Luc and Jasper started to run after him on foot, then stopped and ran back to their truck. That gave Jack time to back out onto the cross street, slam to a stop, throw it in drive and race back toward the main highway. He looked in his rear view mirror and saw their truck round the corner and come after him.

By the time he turned back onto Highway 41 they were right behind him. Jack sped up to what he thought was a dangerously reckless speed. They stayed close, and began closing the short distance that remained between them. The road was straight for now, but he knew it took a slight jog to the left ahead before straightening out again. He accelerated, hoping to lose them in the curve.

He hit the curve going too fast and cut across the center line to minimize the amount he had to turn. His tires screamed and the car slid to the right but he stayed on the road. But before he could congratulate himself on making it to the next stretch of straight road he heard a thump and his car sprang forward.

They had rammed the back of his car with their truck.

He sped up and they rammed him again.

Jack did a quick calculation on how much longer it would be before they reached the tight left curve where the road turned toward Quincy Mine. The answer was not long.

They rammed him again.

Running had suddenly become the most dangerous option.

Even if he made it to the curve without being run off the highway he was pretty sure they would push him through the flimsy wooden guardrail at that point. He would have to turn off the highway and take his chances before then, and there was only one road left to do it on. It was not a great place to hold a last stand, but it would have to do: Scenic Lookout Road.

By the time he thought of it he was almost there – a gravel road turnout that allowed tourists to pull over to the edge of the hill and admire the view. At the last second he yanked the wheel to the right and slid into the entrance, kicking up rocks and dust. As the dust settled he pulled to a stop by the guardrail and stepped out of the car.

Not too far away a group of people taking pictures by their cars turned to stare angrily at Jack. These tourists had stopped to see the two cities spread out below them: Hancock on this side of Portage Canal, and Houghton on the far side. Jack was pretty sure they were about to see something even more spectacular.

"Get your cameras ready," he shouted. "In a minute two guys are going to try to kill me."

It was a nervous joke and a desperate plan – maybe having tourists with cameras around would prevent Luc and Jasper from doing their worst.

He was about to find out.

Their truck had slowed down and turned into the far entrance where the scenic turnoff road reconnected to the highway. It rolled slowly past the tourists and parked a short distance away from where Jack stood by his car. Luc and Jasper got out and walked over, splitting up so that they flanked him, his car blocking any escape route behind him.

"I'll ask you again: why were you sneaking around our house?" Luc said.

"I just stopped by to say Howdy Doody," Jack replied.

Luc and Jasper looked at each other but said nothing.

"Jasper, why don't you encourage our friend to explain himself."

Jasper looked at Luc and shook his head slowly, but still advanced on Jack.

Jack quickly went over fight move number two in his mind. Murphy said he was great at it, but that was practice. He was about to find how good he was in real life.

Jasper stepped forward and threw everything he had into a roundhouse punch. Jack ducked under Jasper's arm, leaned into his body, and drove his knee upward into his groin. His knee slammed into its target and Jasper collapsed to the ground with a grunt.

Jack was thrilled with the results of the move, but worried that Jasper might recover in time to help Luc double team him like they did at the bar. As Jasper rolled on the ground he decided to finish him off with an adlibbed fight move of his own: a quick kick to the face. When he finished he turned back to Luc.

"I'm going to go home now, I don't want to see you again," he said.

"Like hell you are. I'm going to kick your ass like I did before."

Luc put up his fists and began moving from side to side, giving Jack time to consider his options. He assumed Luc would be looking for the knee to the groin, which meant it was time for fight move three. He noticed Luc was keeping his right hand low to protect his crotch, it was the opening he needed.

Jack angled to his left, lunged forward and threw a straight hard jab at Luc's Adam's apple. The punch landed with a sharp crack and Luc fell to his knees clutching his throat. As he slumped to the ground gasping for air Jack stopped to consider his next move.

Jasper had recovered enough to raise himself on one elbow; Luc was down on all fours breathing slowly and deeply. Jack's work was done, no need for an adlib kick or the gruesome fourth move. He had the information he needed and the revenge he wanted.

It was time to go.

"I'm going to go home now, I don't want to see you again," Jack said again.

He got back into his car and drove slowly toward the far exit, waving at the tourists as he passed by them.

SIXTY-TWO

Angry Birds

By the time Luc and Jasper stumbled back to their truck the tourists were gone.

They climbed inside but didn't start the engine, sitting in silence for a minute before Luc spoke in a raspy whisper.

"Why the hell was he sneaking around our house?"

"Why are asking me? How should I know?"

Jasper spoke quickly and loudly, with an edge of irritation in his voice. When he finished, he shifted in his seat in obvious discomfort.

"What's the matter with you?" Luc asked.

"I got kicked in the nuts, okay?" Jasper replied. "I don't know why he came. And I don't know how he found out about Howdy Doody."

"That part's easy. He got arrested in Detroit a couple weeks ago for possession, he was holding Howdy Doodys. My guess is he got them from our college buddies, or from someone they sold them to. They were sure interested in the video we showed them, eh?"

"Maybe he was coming by our place to buy some more."

"We kicked the shit of him, then he caught you trying to frame him for running a meth lab. You think he would come to us to buy drugs?"

"I guess not."

Luc started the truck, put it into reverse and backed up, then put it back into park.

"So why did he come to our house?" he asked.

"Why do you keep asking me that?" Jasper yelled. "I told you I didn't know."

Luc looked over at his friend with a puzzled expression.

"Okay, man. Calm down. I get it, you don't know why he came to our house. So here's another question – how did he know where we live? We sublet that shithole from a guy who rents it from the owner. There's no way he could connect us to it. "

"Maybe he followed us around."

"You think I don't keep my eyes open for people following us? How stupid do you think I am?"

Jasper said nothing and Luc continue to stare at him.

"You can't lie worth shit, Jasper," he said finally. "You never could."

"What do you mean?"

"I mean you know something, more than you're telling me."

"Bullshit."

"Don't bullshit me. You must have done something that tipped him off, and you're too chicken shit to tell me what it was."

"I'm not chicken shit. There was one thing, but there's no way it would have helped him find us."

"What?"

"When you dropped that kid off the bridge, I still had his cell phone."

"I know. I told you to wipe it down for prints and put it back in his car."

"Yeah."

"Oh shit – you didn't put it in his car, did you?"

"No."

"You kept the fucking phone?"

"It's not a big deal. You can't trace a cell phone unless you make a call and stay on the line a long time, like on the cop shows."

"Yes you can you moron. You can track it with another phone, or a computer or just about fucking anything. Tell me you weren't using it to make calls."

"I'm not stupid. I didn't make any calls with it."

"Then what the hell did you keep it for?"

Jasper looked straight ahead for a long time before he replied.

"I play Angry Birds with it."

It was Luc's turn to yell.

"You do what?"

"Play Angry Birds. I've got an old Nokia phone that barely works. This guy had an iPhone with a bunch of different Angry Bird games on it. I bought a charger for ten bucks. I keep them in the desk in my room and play it at night."

Luc shook his head and put the truck in drive.

"What are you going to do?" Jasper asked.

"Two things. First, we're going back home, you're going to get the phone, and we're going to get rid of it. Then we're going to take care of the professor."

"What do you mean? What are we going to do?"

Luc slammed his foot down on the gas pedal as he replied.

"He's a dead man."

SIXTY-THREE

The Scientist
And The Philosopher

Jack had two phone calls to make.

He made the easier one first.

It wasn't so easy.

"Thank goodness you called," Maggie said. "I didn't want to call you in case you were still near Ajeet's phone. I got your signal and called, did you hear it?"

"Yes."

"Fantastic. Where was it?"

"In a house."

"Great. We can let the police figure out who lives there. Whoever it is must be connected to Ajeet's death in some way, probably his killer. No one saw you, did they?"

Jack didn't respond.

"Jack, I told you not to send the signal if anyone was around."

"There was no one around when I sent the signal."

"Good. Then no one saw you."

Once again there was no response from Jack.

"Jack, quit messing around with me. Please just tell me what happened."

Using what he hoped was his most nonchalant voice Jack outlined what happened in the simplest terms so he wouldn't alarm Maggie. He left out being almost run over in the alley and rammed on the road. It worked until he got to the end of the story.

"They followed you in their truck?"

"Yes. So I pulled into a scenic turnoff to see what they wanted."

"You stopped to ask them what they wanted? That phone ties them directly to Ajeet's death. They are killers, Jack."

"It would certainly seem that way."

"But you stopped to talk to them. What did they say?"

"They wanted to know what I was doing at their house."

"They called it that? They called it their house?"

"Yes."

"What did you tell them?"

"I told them I stopped by to say Howdy Doody."

It was Maggie's turn to not respond.

"C'mon, that's pretty funny, isn't it?" Jack asked.

"No, it's not. You have no idea how guilty I felt about putting you in danger before, and how reluctant I was to do it again. I only did it because I might not have much time left, and I want justice done for Ajeet."

"Sorry."

"No need to apologize, you've been helpful and brave beyond anything I could have hoped for. You've found Ajeet's killers, I'm sure of that. Now please just be careful, this should be over soon."

"Are you going to call the cops now?"

"I don't trust the police in Hancock after the things they did with you."

"That was one guy, they can't all be bad."

"I have a better plan. The State Police were also involved in the investigation of Ajeet's death. Murphy gave me the name and phone number of their lead detective in case I remembered anything else I could tell them. I'm going to call him."

"That sounds good. I'll call Murphy, fill him in on everything."

After Maggie thanked him profusely again, they ended the call. Jack phoned Murphy reluctantly, assuming that despite his embrace of Buddhism he would be pissed. This time he did not leave out the details of his encounter with Luc and Jasper.

Murphy was surprisingly philosophical about what happened.

"I'm not angry, Jack, I'm disappointed. Sneaking around is what I do best. You should have called me first."

"I told Maggie that, but she wanted to find out where the phone was right away. She didn't want to wait for you to drive up, and didn't want you to talk her out of it."

"And you didn't want to disappoint her. You *do* like-like her."

Jack laughed.

"I do, Murphy. I told you, I'm going to marry her."

"If you don't get killed first doing the stupid shit she asks you to do."

"I didn't get killed, thanks to what you taught me."

There was a long pause before Murphy replied.

"I'm glad it worked, but don't get comfortable. I've dealt with punks like them my whole career. They don't like fair fights, especially when they lose. Next time they won't be throwing punches, they'll be firing bullets."

"There won't be a next time, I'm going anywhere near them again."

"You won't have to, they'll be coming for you."

"You think so?"

"You know where they live. You know what they do – you told them that when you made the joke about Howdy Doody."

"I wasn't thinking, it just came out."

"They know where *you* live. They already tried to plant some stuff on you. Next time they won't be trying to harm your reputation, they'll be trying to harm you."

"Maggie's calling the state police as we speak, she's going to talk to the detective you told her about. I'm going to hunker down in my house and hope he follows up on this lead right away."

"I've worked with him a few times, he's a good man. He'll follow up in a hurry, I just hope it's fast enough."

"What do you mean?"

"These guys were stupid enough to keep Ajeet's phone after they killed him. But nobody is stupid enough to keep that kind of evidence around after someone comes looking for it."

"They don't know that I was there to find the phone."

"They don't have to know for sure. If they have any brains at all they won't take any chances – they'll smash it to pieces and throw it in the lake."

"Back up a minute. You said they killed Ajeet. You believe that now?"

"Yeah, I'm pretty sure of that. Ajeet used his phone to post a suicide note on Facebook just before he jumped off the bridge. If he puts it back in his pocket it's gone, if he leaves it in his car the cops find it. These guys end up with Ajeet's phone in their house. Most likely they threw him off the bridge and made the post themselves. The only thing I can't figure out is why they would keep the phone."

"So what do you think I should do?"

"Are you at home now?"

"Yeah."

"When we're done talking get in your car and drive back to Detroit."

"I'm tired of people running me out of town, Murphy. I can't do that again."

"Then lock your doors, close your curtains, and do what you said – hunker down. And hope the police get to them before they get to you."

When he ended the call Jack did what Murphy suggested, walking through the house closing curtains and locking doors. He had just sat down with his laptop at the kitchen table to try to work on his novel when Maggie called. She spoke before he even said hello.

"We lost the signal, Jack."

"What?"

"The phone is gone."

SIXTY-FOUR

Gimme Shelter

Jack fell into an uneasy sleep shortly after midnight.

He did not dream.

He slept in a small room next to the kitchen that had been converted into a bedroom many years ago. It had started out as a dining room, evolved into a family room, and decades ago finally succumbed to overcrowding and simple convenience and became a place to sleep. Jack lived alone in Helltown house, but like many in his family before him he used it as a bedroom to avoid the steep stair climb to the upstairs bedrooms.

As it turned out, that was a life and death decision.

The explosion that rocked the house in the night jolted him awake. He sat up in bed, half-asleep and fully terrified, and tried to figure out what had just happened. There was a propane tank at the side of the house, right outside his room: it could have exploded. But the sound of flames crackling was coming from the kitchen, which was on opposite side of the house – on the other side of the wall from where he sat in bed.

He jumped out of bed and threw open the bedroom door, then jumped back – the hallway was on fire. He slammed the door shut and started thinking fast. There were no windows in the room, and only one door out. He would have to break through a wall, but the question was which one?

There were two interior walls, one shared with the kitchen and the other with the hallway. These interior walls would be easier to break through; they were only thin wood slats covered in plaster. But the kitchen and the hallway were on fire; breaking through to them would most likely lead to a painful burning death.

As if to emphasize this point, smoke began curling in under the bedroom door. He grabbed a blanket off the bed and stuffed it in the crack, then stepped back to think again.

The two exterior walls would be a safer choice; he would end up outside, away from the fire. But they would be harder to break through – plaster, wood slats, insulation, exterior wood, tarpaper – and time was a factor. A big factor, to judge from the steadily rising roar of the fire outside his room.

He needed to come up with an answer quickly.

For a moment he tried to calm and amuse himself with classroom humor: will this question be on the final? A loud cracking sound right outside the door brought him back to the moment, and a darker thought: will this be the final question?

He was about to give up and try to punch his way through the thick exterior wall when remembered something important he had overlooked. This was a trick question – there were actually three interior walls.

One exterior wall was a double wall – interior and exterior. Half the space behind the interior wall was taken up by a closet with a curtain for a door. The other half provided headroom for the staircase to the cellar. He could break through that wall, jump down onto the stairs and escape through the cellar door.

The second he thought of it he flew at the wall and landed a heavy kick with his heel. It produced a hole big enough to give him hope, so he repeated the kick several more times. Gradually a hole nearly big enough for him to get through took shape, and he could see the stairs leading down into the darkness below.

Jack quickly grabbed another blanket off a shelf in the closet and wrapped himself in it, then grabbed his phone, wallet and keys off a side table. He hesitated for a second before reaching under the bed and pulling out a briefcase. He tucked the briefcase under his arm, backed up against the far wall and threw himself at the hole shoulder first. He crashed through and slammed against the wall on the other side, fell backwards and rolled down the stairs into darkness.

He lay on the dirt floor for a moment, checking himself for damage and cursing. When he was certain nothing was broken or bleeding, he felt around in the dark until he had gathered up his valuables, then turned on his cell phone light.

The cellar was not quite six feet high, with shelves along the walls and floor-to-ceiling wooden support beams crisscrossing the space at eight-foot intervals. Decades of detritus – rusty garden tools, broken lamps, old toys, worn out tires – lined the shelves where food was once stored. The door to the outside was just ahead along the dirt wall.

Jack stood and up rewrapped himself in the blanket – he was in his underwear and it would be cold outside. He walked slowly to the doorway, a short set of stairs dug into the wall by the corner. He set his briefcase down, took the two-by-four that barred the double doors out of its metal bracket, then reached up over his head to push them open.

The double doors didn't move.

He stepped up and pushed again and nothing happened. There was something heavy on top of the doors. He couldn't tell what it was but it was obvious it wasn't going to move – he couldn't use this door. At the top of the stairs he had just tumbled down there was a door to a hallway – which was engulfed in flames.

It was at this point Jack realized this wasn't an accident.

Someone was trying to kill him.

In the past few weeks he had been drugged, framed, beaten up, arrested and nearly killed. But his previous death was an unintended accident. This was a whole new level: someone was deliberately trying to end his worldly existence. Jack sat down in the stairwell to think about what this meant and what to do next.

The first order of business was staying alive.

He dialed 911 and got a busy signal. After several more attempts with the same result, he tried the Hancock police and fire departments, and in both cases got a recorded message. He was about to try 911 again when he heard the faint sound of a siren.

For a moment he was filled with joy, then he realized his night wasn't over. Flames began flickering through the bottom crack of the hallway door. And he recalled with alarm that the propane tank was right outside the double doors above his head.

It would ruin their rescue if he died before they got here.

He swept the light from his cell phone around the room, looking for something that would save his life. The unlikely saviors he settled on weren't much – a shovel, a rusty panel of corrugated steel, and two old tires – but he didn't have time to be choosy.

He started digging a shallow hole the size of a man in the cellar floor.

It had to be fairly close to the outside doors so he would be able to get out, or they would be able to find him. But not too close in case the propane tank exploded.

Jack turned over dirt frantically and pushed it to the sides of the hole, which made it deeper faster. When it looked like it was deep enough to offer some protection, he put the tires on top of the panel, lay down in the hole, and pulled the panel over him. Then he remembered his briefcase.

He pushed the panel off, crawled over to where he had left it, and pulled it back with him. Lying back down in the hole, he put the briefcase on his back and pulled the panel over him again. He was face down in damp dirt, the blanket around him and covering his mouth in case of smoke.

He hoped that the panel and tires would protect him from falling objects. He hoped the dirt would keep the flames from reaching him. He hoped they got here soon.

As the sirens got closer he began to allow himself the luxury of belief.

Then everything roared and stopped.

Part Two

When The Going Gets Weird

"When the going gets weird, the weird turn pro."

—Hunter S. Thompson

SIXTY-FIVE

As I Lay Dying

Am I dead or just dreaming?

No response.

Let's back up and figure this out.

My focus on Sixties literature started as a tribute to my late wife's free spirit. Before that I had specialized in classic American literature – Melville, Twain, Hemingway. I was familiar with the works of the Sixties, but for the most part dismissed it as second-rate pop culture. It certainly wasn't the path to follow if you wanted to stay on the tenure track.

That was made painfully clear to me by the head of my department.

But as I studied them more closely these works began to resonate with me, both as literature and as lessons for living a good life. Over time I became increasingly preoccupied with teaching them from both perspectives: as art to admire and examples to emulate. And as the world around me turned increasingly hateful, my avocation turned into obsession.

When I first reviewed the literature I came to believe that most of the great issues of our time were resolved in the Sixties. The path to progress was still a rugged trail of peaks and valleys, but a consensus had been reached: Peace was better than war, love was better than hate. Non-violence was the path to progress. The natural world was good; racism and sexism were bad. People should be free to be who they wanted to be, without judgment or condemnation.

For decades afterward it seemed like everyone was in agreement.

Then they weren't.

I didn't know how it happened or who was to blame. All I knew was that my mission had become more critically important than ever before.

Then they took away my job.

Then my house exploded.

Then I dug a shallow grave.

SIXTY-SIX

Wake Up Call

A phone was ringing.

Jack opened his eyes and realized it was his phone. He was holding it in his hand, lying face down in the dirt underneath a rusty panel of corrugated sheet metal. Something wet and warm was rolling down the back of his ear and dripping off his chin. He needed to figure out what the hell just happened, what to do next, what had spilled on his head.

First things first.

"Hello?"

"I'm sorry I'm calling so early in the morning, but I'm worried about you, Jack."

"Maggie?"

"Yes. Are you alright, Jack? You sound funny."

"Yeah, I'm fine. It takes me a long time to wake up."

"I didn't wake you, did I? I'm sorry, I had to call. I tried to call Murphy after I talked to you last night but he didn't return my call until just now. When I told him we lost the signal for the phone he said you were already in danger and that would make it worse. He wants you to come to back to Detroit immediately, and so do I."

"Did you call the State Police?"

"I was going to, but Murphy told me not to. He said without the signal we don't have any evidence. Even if they believed our story, the house is cleaned up by now, they won't find anything. He wants you come back so we can figure out what to do next."

"And so I'll be safe."

"Of course. Is that so bad? I'm this horrible person who keeps putting you in danger, and it's got to stop. I'll never forgive myself if anything happens to you."

Guilt wasn't love, but it was a start. He could work with it.

"I don't want you to feel bad about any of this. Everything I've done was because I wanted to. Besides, I'm not in any danger right now."

"Are you sure?'

Actually, he wasn't. He assumed the two punks he beat up had tried to burn his house down and kill him. No doubt they took off when they heard the sirens coming. But it wouldn't hurt to take a quiet look around.

Keeping the phone in his hand Jack did a pushup to raise the briefcase and sheet metal that lay on top of him, then sat up and pushed them off. When he did a number of metal objects slid off and thumped to the floor, and the panel crashed down loudly on top of them. Some of the shelves had fallen over and dumped an assortment of old junk on him.

"Jack, what happened? Are you alright?"

"I'm fine Maggie," he lied.

In the dim light of his phone he could see blood on his hand.

"I'm actually in the middle of something right now," he added. "I'm moving some old junk around in the cellar, can I call you back?"

He hit the disconnect button as she was saying "sure."

There were sounds coming from outside.

He heard someone yelling and heavy running footsteps, then a scraping sound.

The cellar doors flew open, a beam of light blinded him, and the person holding the flashlight gave his assessment of the situation.

"Holy shit, he's alive."

SIXTY-SEVEN

Roll Away The Stone

The two policemen walked Jack around the smoldering ruins of his house to their squad car and sat him down in the back seat.

He sat sideways in the open doorway with his feet on the ground as one officer circled his head with gauze and taped it in place. The other sat in the front seat radioing the news to the police station and asking them to call for an ambulance. When the two finished their tasks they both listened intently as Jack told his story.

"The hallway was on fire, so I broke through the wall to the cellar stairs," he said. "I couldn't open the cellar door, so I dug a hole and covered myself with sheet metal."

"There was a rock," one of the officers said.

"What?"

"There was a big rock on top of the cellar doors."

"What was it doing there?"

"We don't know. We figured you put it there."

"There was a big rock by the side of the house. Whoever started the fire must have rolled it over and put it on top of the doors. They didn't want me getting out."

"So you're saying someone started the fire – it wasn't an accident."

"Of course," Jack replied. "What do you think happened?"

The two officers looked at each other and said nothing until the one in the front seat shrugged his shoulders. Then the one who had bandaged Jack's head spoke.

"We really shouldn't tell you anything, but you seem like a nice guy. Henry and I – that's him in the front seat – we were the first ones here. We pulled up right when the propane tank exploded, the fire department was right behind us. They saved a lot of the house, but as you can see the kitchen and the whole lower back end were destroyed."

"I'm surprised the house is still standing."

"It's probably a total tear down, there's too much structural damage. After the fire department put out the fire we searched the parts of the house that hadn't burned. The doors were jammed shut, the heat must have warped them."

"You searched the house? What for?"

"We were looking for you – well, your body anyway. Your car was still here, so we figured you must have been killed in the fire. We were waiting for the rest of the house to cool down so we could search there when the call came, told us to wait."

"Why?"

"One of our detectives was off duty, but he heard about what happened. He said this place was a suspected meth lab, and told us to stay out of the damaged part of the house. All of sudden it's a crime scene, and we have to stay here and guard it."

"A crime scene?"

"They're sending the State Police arson unit and some guys from their Narcotics Task Force up to see if you were cooking meth here."

"Detective Vladdie Novikov, he's the one who told you that, right?"

"Yeah, how do you know him?"

"He came up here a little while ago looking for a meth lab. He didn't find anything. I don't have anything to do with drugs, that guy is out to get me."

"Why do you say that?"

"It's a long story."

"Well, if you're not cooking drugs you have nothing to worry about. Henry and I already checked the parts of the house that weren't damaged, there's nothing there. If the State Police don't find anything where the fire was you're off the hook."

"How long before they get here?"

"Shouldn't be too long. They called them a couple of hours ago, they're coming from District Eight Headquarters in Marquette, which is a two-hour drive."

With the mention of time Jack became confused and alarmed.

"What a minute, how long have you guys been here?" he asked.

"A little over three hours."

"And you got here right when the propane tank exploded?"

"Yeah, why?"

"The last thing remember is a tremendous boom, it must have been the tank exploding. A bunch of stuff fell on the sheet metal that was on top of me."

"That sheet metal saved your life."

"Yeah, but it must have hit my head when everything fell on it. I was unconscious until just before you found me. That means I was knocked out for three hours."

"I guess so. Good thing we got an ambulance coming, should be here soon."

While they waited the two policemen reluctantly agreed to let Jack go inside and exchange the dirty blanket and underwear he had on for clean clothes. When he came back outside someone was pulling into the driveway, but it wasn't an ambulance.

It was Vladdie.

Jack sat back down in the open doorway of the squad car and watched as Vladdie walked up and waved the two policemen away.

"I need to talk to him alone," he said.

"Okay, Vladdie. We'll keep an eye out for the ambulance, wave 'em in."

The two walked down the driveway and stood in the road waiting.

"You should have gone back to Detroit like I told you to," Vladdie said. "You're lucky to be alive."

"I know who did this."

"What?"

"Let's stop playing around. A few weeks ago your nephew and his friend killed Ajeet Nirmal, a student from Wayne State University, which is where I taught. They know that I know that, so last night they set my house on fire and tried to kill me, too. I'm going to assume you were in on their plan."

Vladdie stared at Jack for a long time before he spoke.

"I didn't try to kill you."

"I really don't care either way."

"So what's next? You going to tell your story to these two idiots?"

"A wildly improbable story from a suspected drug dealer against the word of a long-time dedicated police officer? I don't like those odds."

"So what are you going to do?"

"I'm not sure yet, I haven't figured it out. But I am sure about one thing."

"What's that?"

"This is going to end badly for one of us."

"Yeah?"

"It won't be me."

SIXTY-EIGHT

Change Of Plans

"He's fucking nuts, man."

Jasper had spent most of the last half hour trying to prove to Vladdie that he was an innocent accomplice to a prank that Luc took too far.

Vladdie wasn't buying it.

He had raced over from Helltown to the rented house Luc and Jasper shared, only to find Luc gone and Jasper covering his ass. They sat talking in the small dark living room, Jasper rationalizing and Vladdie fighting the urge to break something.

"You say he's crazy but you went along with what he did."

"He said we were just going to start a little fire in the kitchen. The plan was leave the meth lab stuff we tried to put in the summer kitchen, light the fire, and call the cops."

"That was no little fire, you almost killed him. What happened?"

"I told you, he's nuts. When we got there he changed the plan. He found a caulk gun in the back of the truck and took it with us. He caulked the doors shut, then made me help put a rock the cellar doors. He said wanted it to be hard for that asshole to get out."

"Caulk isn't going to hold a door shut."

"I told him that, he didn't believe me. He wasn't making any sense."

"At that point you still didn't think you were trying to kill this guy?"

"No. Like I said, I thought it was just going to be a little fire. We pried open the kitchen window and put a bunch of stuff on the table. I was carrying the equipment in my backpack like before, Luc had the chemicals in his."

"What chemicals? We didn't bring any chemicals to put in the summer kitchen."

"Acetone, ether, sodium hydroxide, hydrochloric acid, like that. He was just supposed to pour rubbing alcohol in through the window on top of all the funnels and clamps and beakers, the stuff I brought. But he added all those chemicals."

"You know that shit explodes. You didn't try to stop him?"

"I asked him what he was doing but he just kept shushing me. He didn't want to wake the guy up."

"So you lit the fire and ran, but you didn't call the police. Don't lie about it – I checked the log. Nobody called the station, a neighbor saw the flames and called the fire department. The two officers who showed up were on patrol nearby when they heard the sirens. They radioed the fire department to get the address and got there first."

Jasper took a long time before he replied.

"Like I said, Luc changed the plan. I ask him when he was going to call the cops and he said never. He did send a text later on, but I don't know to who."

"He sent the text to me, it was two words: 'Problem solved.' I called him but he didn't answer, so I called the station, asked if there was anything unusual going on. They told me about the fire, lucky for you they did. I thought you idiots killed him, but I was hoping you had planted something first. That's the only thing that might save your ass."

"So we did good?"

Vladdie sprang from his chair, lifted Jasper off the couch by the front of his shirt and slammed him against the wall.

"No, you dumb shit, you did not do good. This guy knows you killed that college kid and that you tried to kill him. He told the Hancock police you and Luc set his house on fire. He's coming after you, and if he gets you he gets me."

Vladdie threw Jasper back down on the couch.

"You better back up and start telling the truth. Why did you try to kill him? Because he found out about the kid? Why didn't you call me before you did anything?"

Jasper was scared to tell the truth, but even more scared not to. He told Vladdie about spotting Jack outside their house, the chase and the fight. He said they didn't let Vladdie know what they were up to because they didn't want to involve him in another crime – and Luc was worried he would try to stop them.

He insisted the original plan was a good one, and it would have worked.

"We knew the fat guy wasn't around, so we could take our time and do it right. The crazy professor slept like a log the whole time. He was snoring so loud we could hear him walking up the driveway."

At the risk of more violence Jasper stuck to his story about the change in plans, mainly because it was true. He explained how he talked Luc out of killing the guy and into just framing him – but that Luc went back to his original plan when they got there.

At that point Vladdie asked the hard question.

"What was the professor doing sneaking around your house?"

Jasper reluctantly told him the story of the Angry Birds phone, emphasizing the part where they smashed it to pieces and threw it into Lake Superior right after the fight. He expected a punch, but got none. Instead he got an even harder question.

"What the hell is going on with Luc? Is he messing around with that Howdy Doody shit?"

Jasper braced himself, then told the truth one more time.

"I told you, he's fucking nuts. He's eating those pills like candy, and it's making him crazy. I've tried to stop him, but he just laughs and says I'm a pussy, that they're safe. He thinks they make him smarter, that he sees things better when he takes them."

Vladdie sat in silence for a long time before asking the next question.

"Where is he now?"

"I don't know. I told you, when I woke up he had taken the truck and was gone. I called and left a message on his phone. Then you came."

"I'm here on official police business. The professor told the police you set his house on fire, and I volunteered to come out here and get your side of the story. Your side of the story is that you and Luc were here all night, you got that?"

"Yes."

"Lucky for you he didn't say anything about the college kid. My guess is he doesn't have evidence enough to prove anything. Make sure you keep it that way."

Vladdie stood up slowly and walked toward the door.

"Stay here, don't talk to anyone, don't do anything. If Luc calls, let me know, and tell him to call me."

"What are you going to do?"

"I'm going to try to sail through this shit storm and find us a safe harbor."

SIXTY-NINE

Eat, Drink

Jack used an old family trick to get home from the hospital: he walked over to Gino's, ordered a pizza for delivery, and rode along with it to what was left of his house.

For a Crost with a revoked driver's license or totaled car it was a great way to get home after walking into town. In the old days it was cheaper and faster than calling a taxi from a pay phone. In modern Uber and cell phone times it still provided the added bonus of arriving home with a pizza. Stop by Miko's Party Store first and you could also bring home beer – a combination his family called a Double Crost.

Jack tipped the delivery driver, stepped over the crime scene tape, and carried the pizza and a six-pack onto his front porch. He sat down on the swing to eat, drink and assess his situation.

His two police saviors had come to the hospital earlier in the day to see how he was doing and give him updates. They still didn't know if the State Police had found anything, or when the city inspector would check his house to see if he could live there. They told him about Jasper's alibi, and that they hadn't found Luc Novikov for questioning yet. Then the doctor who had examined him came in and said he had a mild concussion and could leave.

Jack was swinging back and forth.

He took a bite of pizza, washed it down with beer, and took inventory.

He was homeless, under police investigation and suffering from his second concussion in less than a month. Oh, and a killer who wanted him dead was on the loose.

It got worse.

Last night he left his laptop on the kitchen table; the only digital copy of the novel he had worked on for twenty years was lost in the fire.

And worse.

Maggie wouldn't talk unless they were discussing one of the many life-threatening tasks she gave him; it appeared the love it had taken him twenty years to find was dying. The first time he met her Maggie explained that in quantum mechanics you don't have a definite position until you collide with something else. He had definitely collided with something else, but still wasn't sure about his location or direction.

It was time for some deep thinking about where his life was going.

It was time for a ritual cleansing and rebirth.

It was time for a sauna.

SEVENTY

Deer Camp

"Where the hell are you?"

Jasper rarely yelled at Luc, but this time he really deserved it. Besides, they were talking on a phone and not in person, there was no chance of getting sucker punched.

"I'm at the deer camp cabin."

"Your uncle came by the house asking about the fire. The guy didn't die, he made it out of the fire and told the cops we did it. They're looking for you."

"Did he say anything about the college kid?"

"No."

"That's lucky for you, Jasper. Maybe he didn't trace the phone to our house. He must have figured out where we lived some other way. If he knew about the phone he would have told the cops"

"But why did he come here?"

"I dunno, I'm still trying to figure it out. He said Howdy Doody to us. He teaches at the college in Detroit that all our best customers go to. He was arrested there for possession. There's some kind of drug connection, I just need to find out what it is."

"What about the cops looking for you?"

"What did Uncle Vladdie say?"

"He told me to say our story is we were home watching TV all night. You need to say the same thing and we'll be each other's alibi."

"I like that, eh? He's got our back, we have an alibi, and nothing connects us to that fire other than a pill popping loser who picked a fight in the bar with you. Did they find the meth lab stuff yet?"

"Vladdie said the State Police were checking it out, but I haven't heard anything."

"It's there, they'll find it. Those state cops know what they're doing."

"What about the cops looking for you?"

"You worry too much, Jasper. I'll stop by Vladdie's house tomorrow morning. He can take my statement there."

"What are you going to tell him about going to deer camp? Why the hell did you take off before I woke up this morning?"

"I couldn't sleep, I was restless."

"Luc, you're taking more of those pills than you should. It's fucking you up, eh?"

"Bullshit. The pills are making me smarter, sharper. I see things you don't see, things nobody sees."

"Is that why you changed plans last night? Instead of framing the guy, we tried to kill him. This time it wouldn't have been an accident. What the hell, man?"

"Jasper, you need to relax. He didn't die, did he? We just scared him, that's all."

"We're lucky we didn't kill him, that's what you were trying to do. You used to be all about getting the details right, not taking any chances. Now you're doing all this crazy shit. It's the pills, man."

"I told you, there's nothing wrong with the pills. The pills are making us rich."

"You're not up there cooking, are you? We're supposed to do that together, it's a lot safer that way."

"We were running low on supplies after all the stuff we unloaded on those college kids. I'm making some more for our other customers. And some for me take along with me on my road trip."

"A road trip? Where are you going?"

"After I see Vladdie and get squared away with the cops, I'm heading south."

"South?"

"Detroit, eh?"

SEVENTY-ONE

Be Merry

Jack needed some scrap paper to start the fire in the sauna.

He knew exactly where to find it.

In the confusion after the fire and explosion he had left his briefcase in the cellar. Inside the briefcase was a paper copy of his novel; the only paper copy he had made. When his laptop was destroyed in the fire, it became the only copy of his novel left in the world.

Jack thought it would make fine kindling.

As a professor of literature he was well acquainted with symbolism. His novel was a symbol of his life for the past twenty years.

It wasn't very good.

If he wanted to change things around and make a clean break from the past, burning his dull, self-conscious, overthought novel would be a good place to start.

Jack found his briefcase in the same spot he had left it. The book was unharmed. He took his three remaining beers to the shed out back, got naked, and used it to light the fire.

The sauna ritual was soothing and relaxing, a much-needed break for his jangled nerves. He was hoping it also would somehow inspire and instill an extra dose of Finnish sisu in him. The Finns said sisu helped them defeat both the Germans and the Russians in World War II. He would need close to that level of sisu for the fight that lay ahead of him.

He wasn't sure what shape that fight would take, that was another reason to sauna.

It wasn't a strategy session, at least not in the conventional sense. He was still a fan of Sherlock Holmes, he wanted to be clever. But he was tired of thinking and disappointed with the results. His well-thought-out life had gone from disappointing to terrifying. It was time for a different approach: loosen up, lighten up, get crazy.

Sitting naked on a bench drinking beer in a hot room was a good start.

The writers he admired from the Sixties relied more on their own instincts than the tired conventional wisdom of the day, maybe that was the way to go. Let the heart rule for once instead of the head. Forget about dignity – he didn't have any left, and it was overrated anyway. Worrying about what others thought had not exactly worked out. Live in the moment, be spontaneous, go with the flow – that could be the path to a better life.

But was it the path to follow if someone was trying to kill you?

Jack was firm believer in the power of love and a strong advocate of non-violence, the great change catalysts of the Sixties. But he also was happy Murphy taught him the four fighting moves. He especially liked the answer Murphy had during one of their training sessions, when asked how he reconciled his Buddhist beliefs with a lifetime of violence.

"Buddha said, 'All beings tremble before violence. All love life. All fear death. See yourself in others. Then whom can you hurt? What harm can you do?'" Murphy said.

"The golden rule applied to violence," Jack replied.

"But sometimes I don't see myself in others," Murphy said. "If others are full of hate and want to do harm, you may have to do unto them what they would do to you."

By then Jack understood that Murphy often added his own thoughts to the teachings of Buddha. He had enough unique interpretations to start his own school, which Jack would happily join. Murphy's teaching here was clear: avoid violence, but don't rule it out.

What other alternatives did that leave him?

Protest was big in the Sixties.

Before he died and went to Helltown Jack had been planning a protest rally on the Wayne State campus. Not just against the obvious injustice done to him, but against lies, ignorance and hate in general. His heart attack interrupted those plans, and now they seemed far too grandiose. He needed to find a way to take on the lies and hate directed specifically at him before he took on all the hate in the world.

Jack dumped a ladle of water on the hot rocks and opened his last beer.

His approach to the Sixties had always been intellectual. But his toe-in the-water academic approach was a weak response to the tsunami of shit that was hitting the fan.

The last month had been especially crazy.

Maybe it was time to go with the flow and get crazy himself.

Luckily, he knew the best place on the planet to do that.

SEVENTY-TWO

Making A Statement

"Where the hell have you been?"

"Why does everybody keep asking me that?"

Luc had arrived at his uncle's house early in the morning, knowing that he wouldn't have left for work yet. He wanted to give him an official police statement about where he was two nights ago and leave, but his uncle wasn't having it. They sat on the back porch arguing in hushed tones as the sun slowly lit up Portage Canal.

"I'm asking you that because I want to know," Vladdie said. "You got cops looking for you, they want to know, too."

"I've been busy, taking care of business. You don't wanna know, eh?"

"Bullshit. You set fire to someone's house without checking with me first, try to kill him – I wanna know where you been and what the hell you were thinking."

"We were running low on inventory. I did some cooking."

"You're running low 'cause you're taking them all yourself."

"Who told you that, Jasper? He's lying."

"Yeah, he told me, but he didn't have to. You show up at my house at the crack of dawn looking like shit and talking crazy – you been up all night on them pills."

"I came here 'cause Jasper said you needed to get my alibi. Just take my statement and I'll get out of here."

"I told you, I can't just take your statement. I'm your uncle, I'm not on duty yet, you're a person of interest who's gone missing. I walk into the station and tell them I took a statement and let you go they're going to know something's funny."

"So what do I do?"

"You go home, get some sleep, get cleaned up and come into the station. I'll be there but you don't have to talk to me – you shouldn't talk to me. Tell them you went fishing and camping overnight, and the night before you were at home with Jasper."

"Why do I have to tell them anything? Didn't the State Police find the meth lab stuff we left? They should be arresting that asshole, not hassling me."

"The State Police haven't made a report yet. But it doesn't matter what their report says, you've been accused of arson. You need to give a statement. The only reason there isn't an All-Points Bulletin out on your ass right now is because I talked them out of it. They're holding off on it as a courtesy to me."

"Well, I ain't going in there, so you can forget about that, eh?"

"Yeah, you are."

"Fuck you."

The stinging slap surprised Luc, he surprised his uncle in return.

He slapped Vladdie back.

The two men sprang out of their chairs and collided with a grunt. They grabbed each other fiercely, holding on tight and at the same time grappling frantically for an advantage in leverage or pain. They spun around in a tight circle, careened into the outdoor grille, knocked over a small side table and slammed down on the wooden deck. Luc rolled on top and pushed up onto his knees to throw a punch, but his uncle kicked him off and scrambled to his feet.

Vladdie tried to kick his nephew in the head before he could stand up, but Luc grabbed his leg and pushed him backwards into the porch rail. With a curse Vladdie began punching down on the top of Luc's head. Still kneeling and hanging onto the leg, Luc remembered the college professor's devastating move against Jasper. He couldn't do it with his knee, but he let go of the leg with his right hand and threw a desperate uppercut.

His uncle screamed and fell to the deck holding his crotch.

Luc jumped to his feet and kicked Vladdie in the face. He kept kicking him until Vladdie stopped moving. Then he picked up a large glass ashtray that had fallen off the table and smashed it over his uncle's head. It broke in two, and Luc threw the half that was still in his hand over the rail into the canal.

He left without checking to see if he had killed his uncle.

SEVENTY-THREE

On The Road Again

"Where the hell are you?"

Murphy sounded concerned, which wasn't like him.

"I'm on I-75 south, just over the Mackinac Bridge, on my way to Detroit."

"Last night you said you weren't coming back. What changed your mind?"

Jack really didn't want to share the details of what had happened to him in the last 24 hours. He had plans to share and arrangements to make, and he wasn't in the mood for an angry "I told you so" lecture. But they couldn't move forward unless Murphy knew everything, so he raced through the story and waited for the response.

As usual, Murphy surprised him.

"Jack, you are a badass," he said. "You're like a love child who kicks butt."

"What?"

"I had you figured for a nerdy college professor, but you keep surprising me. I knew you'd be ready for a fight, you were great at what I taught you. But crashing through a wall, burying yourself alive – those are brilliant moves in a life and death situation. Where'd you learn to do stuff like that?"

A good question. Where did learn that?

"I guess it must have been all those Sherlock Holmes books I read growing up."

Murphy laughed for a long time before he spoke again.

"I'm proud of you, Jack. A lot of people would have freaked out and died in that situation. Now get your ass back here and let the police finish this thing."

"It's not that simple, Murphy."

"You said you told the Hancock police about those two losers. They attacked you twice, they're obviously the prime suspects for setting your house on fire."

"But I didn't tell you who they sent to question them."

"Oh shit. Uncle Vladimir."

"Yeah. Jasper, the big dumb one, told him they spent the night watching TV at home after their fight with me. That was it."

"They're not in jail?"

"No. It gets worse. Luc, the nasty little shit, is on the loose. They can't find him."

"How do you know all this?"

"The two cops who found me stopped by the hospital to see how I was doing."

"They can't all be bad up there, the uncle might be working on his own. Wait a minute – did you tell them those two losers killed the college kid?"

"No. I told you, at that moment the State Police were going to search the ashes of my house to see if I was running a meth lab. A respected member of the local police was on the scene and out to get me. A crucial piece of evidence had disappeared. It didn't seem like a good time to bring up a closed-case suicide and call it a murder."

"You did the right thing. That's a battle for another day. The fact that the bad guys don't know that we're on to them gives us a tactical advantage."

The long silence on the phone was enough to give Murphy a clue.

"Jack, they saw you hanging around their house, but that doesn't prove you know anything. Maybe you were just pissed because they beat you up. I know you said Howdy Doody to them. You didn't tell them anything else, did you?"

Another long silence.

"I might have said something to Uncle Vladimir."

"Oh shit, Jack. What did you say?"

An even longer silence.

"I said I knew his nephew and his friend killed Ajeet Nirmal."

It was Murphy's turn to not respond.

Jack drove past the exit for Indian River, which meant he had another four hours to go before he was home. Four hours until he flipped the crazy switch, unless he got an early start by stopping at Tony's in Birch Run for a BLT with a pound of bacon.

"You're not making this easy for us Jack," Murphy said at last. "I'll check with my State Police contact, see what's going on. Then we can figure out what to do next."

"I know what to do next Murphy," Jack said.

"Yeah? What's that?"

"You ever read *The Electric Acid Kool Aid Test*?"

"I'll be honest with you, professor, I don't do a lot of reading these days."

"Not a problem. Call Maggie, and tell her we are going to have a meeting. She'll answer your call, but not mine. Tell her I know how to bring Ajeet's murderers to justice."

"How you going to do that?"

"I'm going to go Merry Prankster on their ass."

SEVENTY–FOUR

Near Death

"How'd you know I was here?"

Vladdie was lying in a hospital bed, his head wrapped in bandages. His eyes were blackened and nearly shut, his lips were swollen, his right arm in a cast and sling.

It hurt to talk, but he needed information from Jasper.

"Two cops came by this morning looking for Luc, to tell him about you."

"Dumb shits. They knew Luc wasn't around."

"Yeah. They figured he wouldn't be there, but they showed up anyways and told me about you. I guess they thought I'd be talking to Luc, tell him you were here."

"Probably got the place staked out in case he shows up."

"Yeah. I'm pretty sure there's a couple of plain clothes guys in the lobby. I never seen 'em before, but they sure look like cops. They ain't foolin' nobody, eh?"

"Young guys?"

"Yeah."

"We just hired a couple of rookies, guys you and Luc wouldn't know. That's probably them."

With great effort Vladdie reached across his body and picked up a styrofoam cup from the raised bedside table next to his bed. He sipped ice water from a straw carefully before setting the cup back down.

"So did you?" he asked.

"Did I what?"

"Did you call Luc and tell him I was here?"

Jasper sat back in his chair and tried to think.

He didn't want to betray his friend, but he didn't want to lie, either. Vladdie was in no shape to hurt him at the moment, but Jasper knew from experience he was someone you didn't want to piss off. He struggled for a moment, then stalled for time by asking the obvious question he hadn't asked yet.

"Who did this to you?"

"I asked you a question, Jasper. Did you talk to Luc?"

"No."

"I can tell when you're lying, Jasper. You don't want to lie to me."

"I'm not lying. I didn't talk to him."

"But you tried to call him, didn't you?"

Jasper had hesitated to ask the obvious question because he was certain he already knew the answer. Fuck Luc, he was nuts, there was no sense covering for him anymore, especially not with Vladdie.

"I tried to call him but he didn't answer."

"But you've talked to him since you two idiots lit that fire, haven't you?"

"He called me last night. Said he was going to stop by your house in the morning and give you a statement for the police like we talked about, how me and him spent the night at home watching TV when the fire happened."

Vladdie rotated his head slowly so that he was looking Jasper in the eyes.

"I'm going to tell you something. You repeat it to anybody else you're a dead man, you understand?"

Jasper nodded.

"Luc came by my house this morning, alright. I told him he had to go the station to make his statement and he went crazy. Beat the shit out of me, made me look like this. I been carpooling to work with Matt Kotila, he stopped by to pick me up, otherwise I'd probably be dead. So you know I'm not fooling around here, eh?"

Jasper nodded again.

"I'm going to ask a simple question, and I want a straight answer: where is Luc?"

"He was at Deer Camp."

"I didn't ask where *was* he, I asked where *is* he."

"He said he was going to go south."

"South?"

"He's going to Detroit."

SEVENTY-FIVE

Card On The Table

"She said she was coming, right? That's what she told you?"

"Relax, Jack. Maggie will be here."

Jack had driven through the night to get home, slept a few restless hours, then got up and started cooking breakfast. Murphy arrived on time at nine o'clock, laughed at the offer of a mimosa, and instead supplemented his coffee with a large pour of the other Jack.

Maggie was late.

"You told her this meeting was to talk about how we are going to bring Ajeet's killers to justice, didn't you? That's the only way I can get her to talk to me these days."

"Yes, I told her. And she'll be here."

Jack was working on his third mimosa and had lost track of how many Irish coffees Murphy had when they heard the knock at his front door. When he answered it he was relieved to see Maggie and surprised to see her lab assistant.

"I hope you don't mind, I brought Robert along," she said. "He wants to help."

Jack led them back to the dining room where Murphy was waiting.

"Who's this?" Murphy asked.

"This is Robert Triffet, one of my graduate assistants," Maggie said.

"No offense, Maggie, but this isn't a lecture that anyone who is interested can audit," Murphy said. "We're talking about some serious, sensitive stuff here."

"Robert knows a lot about what these people are up to," Maggie replied. "He's the one who helped us track Ajeet's phone."

Murphy started to object again but Robert cut him off.

"They killed my friend. The police won't believe that until you find more evidence. I can help you do that."

Murphy looked at Jack and shrugged.

"Why don't we eat and then you can tell us what your plan is, Jack," he said.

Jack served breakfast and drinks all around. He wasn't a great cook, but he liked making breakfast and he wanted this meeting to begin as soon as possible. At least he did last night when he called Murphy from on the road.

Now he wasn't so sure.

As he dished out the eggs, bacon and pancakes Jack reviewed his sauna strategy in his mind. Without the beer, excessive heat and adrenaline rush after nearly being killed, the plans that had excited him last night didn't seem like much the morning after.

Even with the help of the mimosas, explaining them was going to be a problem.

He stalled for time as much as possible, offering seconds and thirds on the food and several refills on the drinks. Finally, there was nothing left to serve and no more dishes to be cleared. The room fell silent and they turned to Jack to hear his great idea.

"First of all, thanks for coming," he said. "This is going to be hard."

The long, awkward silence that followed confirmed his concern.

"All of my life, I have been an observer and an admirer," he continued at last. "I silently saluted those who took courageous stands, but I looked to established authorities and well-traveled paths to guide me. I was all about the tenure track."

Murphy and Maggie exchanged glances but said nothing.

"My life of quiet acquiescence has not worked out well," Jack concluded. "In the last month I have been disgraced, fired, killed, arrested and beaten up. Two nights ago I was nearly killed again, and the novel I worked on for twenty years was destroyed."

"That sucks," Murphy said.

"It wasn't that good," Jack said. "I'd like to start over."

"I'm sorry Jack, it's my fault. I shouldn't have gotten you involved," Maggie said.

Jack ignored her.

"Last night in the sauna I came up with a way to address these injustices, to take arms against a sea of troubles, so to speak. It's a change in plans, but more importantly a change in attitude. As you know, I'm big on the Sixties. So I guess the most appropriate analogy is that this has been my personal Vietnam. I've been using conventional methods and getting my ass kicked. It's time for unconventional warfare."

"Is that what the Electric Kool Aid book is about?" Murphy asked.

"Sort of. It's about a novelist, Ken Kesey, who traveled around the country in a bus in the Sixties with a bunch of his friends. They called themselves the Merry Pranksters. They took LSD and did crazy things to shock people into rejecting conventional thinking."

"You want us to take LSD?" Murphy asked.

"No, but I do want us to expand our minds. We keep trying to talk to the authorities and use proper channels, and we keep getting nowhere. It's time to reject conventional thinking. The name of the group – the Merry

Pranksters – inspired me. I lost my job because of a prank. I think it's time we paid the Wise Guys back with a prank of our own."

"How's that going to help bring justice to Ajeet?" Maggie asked.

"I thought about that. We're at a standstill with the bad boys up north, Luc and Jasper. We need to go back to square one, to the three students who got me fired. They're also the guys who sell Howdy Doody. It's their vulnerable point, and it connects them to Ajeet – it's what got him killed."

"We can't prove that, we don't have enough evidence," Murphy said.

"Exactly. Even if we did, the police and the courts are slow-moving bureaucracies, it could take years for any kind of justice to be served, or maybe none at all."

"So what are you proposing, Jack?" Maggie asked.

"Like I said, we need to prank them the way they pranked me. We'll get a video of them committing a crime: selling Howdy Doody to other students. But we won't give it to the police, we'll put it on a website and promote it with social media. We'll let indignant Internet trolls take them down."

The silence that followed was not a vote of confidence.

"That might help you clear your name," Maggie said finally. "But how does that help bring Ajeet's killers to justice?"

"Once we prove these guys are selling Howdy Doody, we can make the connection to the U.P.," Jack said. "At that point, with everything else we know and can tell them, I think the police would reopen Ajeet's case."

"How do we get a video of them selling drugs?" Murphy asked.

"You said they're having a big party next Sunday, an after party for the Movement festival," Jack said. "I'm guessing it will be somewhere in the Packard Plant ruins."

"That makes sense, they talk about the Packard Plant all the time at the Old Miami, and that's where I followed them to. But I lost them."

Robert started to say something, but Jack interrupted him.

"Maybe you can listen to them this week, find out where the party is," he said.

This time Maggie cut off Robert when he tried to speak again.

"Or maybe the guys in the U.P. will talk about it," she said.

"The guys in the U.P.? You're bugging them too? How'd you do that?" Jack asked.

Murphy and Maggie exchanged glances again, and Murphy replied.

"It's the same unit I use at the Old Miami. You can put it anywhere, no limits on distance, just send it a text with your phone to hear it. It helps to be able to see them so you don't waste time listening to nothing when they're not around. That's why I hang out at the Old Miami – well, it's one of the reasons."

"You haven't answered my question: how'd you get a bug in place in the U.P.?"

"I put it there, Jack," Maggie said. "You remember when Murphy said there was something I could do to help him up north? Turns out it was going to the Hoist House and planting a bug at the table where Luc and Jasper always sit."

"How'd you know where they sit?"

"After they tried to frame you Murphy followed them around. He looked in the Hoist House window and saw where they sat every time they were there."

"Those guys are killers, one of them knows what you look like. That's incredibly reckless and dangerous."

Maggie laughed.

"That's what I keep telling *you*, Jack. I went there during the day, Murphy said they wouldn't be around then. I wore a big floppy hat and sunglasses just in case."

"Murphy could have made the plant, you didn't have to do it."

"I'm a lot less conspicuous than Murphy, and I don't have ex-cop written all over me. The bartender tells them about the Sidney Greenstreet lookalike who sat at their table, and they might have checked it for bugs. I'm dying anyways, so what risk is there really?"

Jack looked at Maggie and tried to say something, but nothing came out.

"Sidney Greenstreet? The fat guy in *The Maltese Falcon*?" Murphy asked. "I've heard that before, you might have something there, Maggie. I'm not sure I can say the same thing for your plan, Jack."

"What's wrong with my plan?"

"The Packard Plant site covers 40 acres, there's all kinds of buildings and tunnels. I've listened to these guys talking for weeks and they haven't talked about where the party will be, my guess is they never will. We can't do anything if we don't know where it is."

"If you let me talk, I've been trying to tell you something," Robert said. "I know where it is."

He took a laminated card out of his pocket and put it on the dining room table.

It was a picture of Howdy Doody posed in front of the Detroit skyline.

SEVENTY-SIX

Chase The Devil

"There's no way I'm going to follow Luc to Detroit, he's nuts, eh?"

Vladdie could barely move in his hospital bed, so physical intimidation was out of the question. Deprived of his signature persuasive technique, he decided to try a radically different approach – he would ask Jasper to do the right thing.

"Luc is in trouble and he needs your help," Vladdie said. "You have to do this for him – you owe him."

"He's the one who dropped a guy off a bridge and burned a house down."

"And you're the one who hung onto the dead kid's phone like an idiot and brought the nutty professor back into the picture."

That one stung like a slap to the face, but Jasper continued to fight back.

"Even if I followed him down there, he's not going to listen to me. He's all messed up on Howdy Doody. We thought that shit was safe to take, but it's not."

"You're right, he's all messed up. He's going to do something stupid and get caught by the cops. If they connect him to what happened on the bridge and at that house what do you think happens to you? You're an accomplice, you're going to jail."

Jasper sat in the visitor's chair and said nothing, but his grim expression told Vladdie he was coming around. It was time for the knockout punch.

"If you won't do it for Luc, do it for me."

"For you?"

"When I found you guys cooking in the hunting cabin, I could have busted you like I have a thousand other punks making meth. But I didn't. I covered your ass, showed you how to do it right, helped you make a lot of money. You owe me."

"Luc says you owed him cause of his dad."

If Vladdie could have moved he would have punched Jasper. Instead he turned his head slowly to look directly at him, and delivered his final blow in a low whisper.

"I was a rookie cop just starting out, and selling a little cat on the side. Everybody was doing it back then. Somebody I sold to got caught and ratted me out, and they found the lab I set up in the old sauna behind our house. They were going to kick me off the force and press charges, so Luc's dad stepped up. He scared the rat into changing his story, saying he sold him the stuff, and then he told the cops the lab was his."

"What a dumbass. Why'd he do that?"

This time Vladdie couldn't help himself, he raised his arm to hit Jasper but the intense pain that shot through his body stopped him. After a moment he spoke again.

"He was my big brother. He didn't want me to lose my job. He thought he'd get a slap on the wrist, but it turns out that was right when they started coming down hard on cat. He ended up in Marquette. That's where you'll go if Luc screws up again."

"Luc says his dad died in prison."

"That's right. You know how he died?"

"No. Luc wouldn't say."

"Somebody tried to make him his boyfriend. He said no, and they killed him."

Jasper began to turn pale, so Vladdie moved in for the kill.

"You have a choice, Jasper. Go to prison and get a boyfriend, or go to Detroit and save us all. What's it going to be?"

"Fuck you. I'm going to Detroit."

SEVENTY-SEVEN

Rules For Radicals
(Jokes For Pranksters)

The party flyer told them a lot, Robert told them the rest.

The headline on the 6x9 inch laminated card read, **It's Howdy Doody Time**. Smaller type proclaimed it an **After Movement Party** and gave the exact **Time** and **Date**. **Location** was little more cryptic: it read, **Packard Plant Complex, Motor City Nut Park**.

"Where's the Motor City Nut Park?" Maggie asked.

"It's an area inside the Packard Plant site. To get there you drive under an enclosed walkway that goes from the second floor of one building to another one across the street," Robert explained. "If you're going to the party you park your car by that overpass and somebody takes you into a building and down into a tunnel. They lead you to this giant underground room where the party is."

"Why do they call it Nut Park?"

"Someone tried to reuse some of the buildings years ago, they put big letters on the side of the overpass that spelled out, 'Motor City Industrial

Park.' Over the years the letters in Industrial fell off or got stolen until all that was left is 'N-U-T.'"

"I saw that sign, it was right near where I lost them," Murphy said. "It's a big place, how do people know where to find that overpass?"

"Word of mouth," Robert replied. "As they put it, 'If you're cool enough to go, you're cool enough to know.'"

"How do *you* know all this?" Murphy asked. "You been to one of their parties?"

"No, but Ajeet had. He told me about them."

Murphy turned to Jack, who hadn't spoken since Robert put the card down.

"Problem solved, we know where the party is," he said. "What's your plan, Jack?"

Jack replied without taking his eyes off the card.

"That photo is exactly what I saw when I was up there."

"When you died?" Maggie asked.

"When I got arrested," Jack replied. "The view I had when I climbed up on the roof matched this photo perfectly. They took this photo of Howdy Doody where I was standing."

"They might have photoshopped him in," Murphy said. "You can do anything with photo software these days. Some of the divorce cases I've worked on had fake photos show up during the settlement talks, nasty pictures of things that never happened."

"This happened, Murphy, I know it. Don't ask me how, I just do. They stole Howdy Doody from the DIA, brought him up there and took his picture."

"Maybe they did. They're clever little shits, I'll give them that," Murphy said. "But if they're that smart it just means your plan has to be that good. So what's your plan?"

Jack looked up from the card and directly at Murphy.

"When we had breakfast at the Coney Island you told me the security guards at Henry Ford found the door to the roof unlocked the week before we were there."

"That's right. They checked it out, didn't find anybody, but it kinda spooked them. That's why security was so tight when you went up there."

"Do you know what day they found the door unlocked?"

"It was Thursday night, why?"

"That's the night I died."

That stopped the conversation around the table for what felt like forever.

"I know this is important to you," Maggie said finally. "What do you think happened, Jack?"

"I think they stole Howdy Doody and brought him up on the roof to take this picture. There's three of them, they probably left one down below to watch for security guards. He saw someone coming and signaled them, they panicked, dropped the dummy, and hid. That's when I showed up, right after I died. That's why I didn't see them."

"Why take crazy risks and go to all that trouble for a party flyer?" Murphy asked.

"They're adrenaline junkies," Robert said. "And they make a ton of money selling that drug."

"Can you prove that?" Murphy demanded.

"To you, or to the police?' Robert replied.

"To the three people sitting around this table with you."

"Ajeet told me they like to climb on rooftops and crawl through tunnels, run around the city like it's an obstacle course, pick fights to show off their martial arts skills, all kinds of crazy stuff like that," Robert said. "He also walked me through the numbers on what they make selling Howdy Doody. Taking a big risk to come up with a clever ad for it makes all the sense in the world."

"Okay, Robert, I believe you," Murphy said. "I saw them go off on some poor dudes at the Old Miami for no reason. They have some fair fighting skills, which they used unfairly, beat the shit out of them. For what it's worth, I believe you, too, Jack."

"If you believe me it's worth a lot," Jack said. "It means you believe I left my body lying on an operating table, went through a solid wall, flew through the air, and saw something that was happening on the roof of the building next door."

"If that's your truth, why shouldn't I believe you?" Murphy asked. "The important thing is you have a plan to move forward. If you don't mind, can you tell us what it is?"

Jack picked up the flyer, looked at it closely, and set it back down before he spoke.

"I told you my plan. We should get a video of them selling drugs at their party and put it on the Internet. That's all I got."

Once again, the conversation stopped.

"That's not really a plan, Jack," Murphy said at last. "It's just an idea – a half-ass idea to tell you the truth. Have you thought this thing through at all?"

"I told you, I'm tired of thinking. I'm raising my freak flag, going with the flow, becoming a Merry Prankster. Hippies were into love, altruism, honesty, joy and nonviolence. And a little mysticism, too. What's wrong with that?"

"It doesn't bring criminals to justice," Maggie said.

"Actually, there's another book from that era that I teach that's also inspiring me – *Rules for Radicals* by Saul Alinsky."

The blank stares around the table told Jack he should continue.

"Saul Alinsky was a community organizer who fought to give marginalized people a voice and some justice in this world. I'm a big fan of his Rule #4: Ridicule is man's most potent weapon. He once threatened to stage a fart-in at a Rochester Philharmonic concert to get the attention of the city's establishment."

"A fart-in?"

"The protesters were going to eat large quantities of baked beans and go the concert. The city backed down, gave them what they wanted. Another time he threatened a piss-in at Chicago O'Hare Airport. They were going to occupy all the toilets and urinals until they got the city to come to the bargaining table."

"So your plan includes attacking them with bodily functions?" Murphy asked.

"No. My plan is video them selling drugs and put it on the Internet. I want to make it funny, too – make them look ridiculous."

"You want to make them look ridiculous?" Maggie asked. "We're trying to catch a killer, Jack."

"I'm drawing the line against hate – are you with me or not?" Jack replied.

Murphy laughed.

"Buddha said, 'A trusted friend is the best relative, a liberated mind is the greatest bliss.' If you're all in on being some kind of fucking hippie, I'm all in with you."

They reached out and executed an old school thumb grab handshake that made it look like they were arm wrestling in mid-air.

"I'm glad you two boys are bonding so nicely," Maggie said. "But I'm a scientist, not a hippie. We're not hitchhiking to Woodstock here, we're crashing a party to narc on the hosts. We need a real plan, not just some literary references from the Sixties."

Jack was tempted to point out that she was the one who kept getting serving up the joints, but instead he went with the flow.

"I dig what you're saying, Maggie," he said. "Let's make a real plan."

"Any successful operation starts with good intelligence," Murphy said. "Robert, tell us everything you know about the party."

"What do you want to know?"

"Start at the beginning – how long have they been doing this?" Murphy asked.

"Three years. They started when they were freshmen. They found the underground space when they were running around, doing their parkour thing on the Packard site."

"They like going into tunnels, too." Murphy said.

"Yeah, that's how they found this place when nobody else had. The first couple of parties were smaller and more secretive, because what they were doing was illegal – they were trespassing. Now they are legit and a lot more out in the open."

"How did that happen?"

"You remember a few years back, a developer from Peru bought the Packard complex. He's got plans to turn the buildings into office space, artist's lofts, restaurants, stuff like that. They're supposed to start the restoration next year, but in the meantime the first thing he did was hire security guards to stop the scavengers and scrappers from stealing anything more from the place."

"Let me guess: the security guards busted the party." Murphy said.

"They stumbled onto a rave two years ago just as it was breaking up. But it turns out the guy who bought the place has plans to put in nightclubs, including a techno club. He wants to attract young people, make it a hipster hangout, so he made a deal. He lets them have two or three parties a year in the space, no charge. They're even talking about negotiating an arrangement to help manage one of his clubs when it opens."

"Does this guy know about the drugs?"

"No. They pretend the parties are still illegal and underground, even though they aren't, to make them seem cool. But the drugs aren't part of their agreement, so they keep that to themselves."

"They sell them there?"

"Yeah. Ajeet brought them down from the U.P. At first they were just something fun to do, they gave them away. But then people started asking for them. The guys figured they would make the parties more fun and help cover the expenses, so they sold them. Now they're the main reason they have the parties – they make a lot of money."

"Do the guys we're after – the three Wise Guys – handle the deals themselves?"

"No. They mingle with the crowd and take orders. They have a secret phrase they use to make sure you're cool and they don't have to ask you directly if you want to buy drugs. If someone gives them the right answer they send them down a hallway to a smaller room away from the party. There's usually two guys there who work for the Wise Guys, they make the sale and take the money."

"How do you know that?" Maggie asked.

"I told you, from Ajeet. He told me all about this stuff from the beginning. At first he was all excited, like a little kid going to Disneyland. Then he started getting weird, angry. It was all about the drugs and the money. By the end he was trying to figure out a way to rip them all off so he could have more of both. That's why they killed him."

"In the last year or so his behavior became increasingly erratic," Maggie said. "You said he was taking the drug himself, that would explain it."

"It's bad stuff, it messes you up. I tried to get him to quit taking it, but I couldn't. We'll be doing everybody a favor if we stop these guys."

"All we gotta do is get a hidden camera into that back room," Murphy said.

"It's not going to do any good if all we get is footage of some flunkies," Jack said.

"I got that part figured out," Murphy replied. "The tough part will be getting the camera in. Usually I put it in a briefcase, but we'd look funny with a briefcase at a party."

"No offense, but all of you would look funny no matter what you brought to the party; you're not exactly their regular crowd. Even if you did fit in – which you don't – they know you. They don't know me. I'm the one who has to carry it in."

"That's very brave of you, Robert," Maggie said.

"We still gotta figure out what to carry the camera in," Murphy said. "You can't just hold it in your hand. Maybe a purse – young guys carry purses these days, right?"

"Not in Detroit, they don't," Robert replied. "But I know someone who might come to the party with me. She could carry the purse for us."

"Are you talking about Donna?" Maggie asked.

"Yeah, how'd you know?"

"I've seen the way you look at her."

"Is it that obvious?"

"Yes. I hate to say it, but I don't think she looks at you the same way."

"You think I don't know that? I've been trying to work up the nerve to ask her out for a long time. At least I'll have a good excuse if she turns me down for this one."

"So, assuming the course of true love runs smoothly, and Robert gets a date, we're all set as far as getting the camera in," Murphy said.

"Oh, wait a minute," Robert said. "I forgot – Ajeet said they search people pretty thoroughly before they come in. They don't want them bringing in guns, or drugs or booze of their own. They pat you down, look in purses."

They sat quietly for a moment, their plan foiled by the simplest of precautions.

Then Murphy laughed.

"What if I could get the camera to you after you got to the party?" he asked.

"How can you do that?" Jack asked.

"I got a guy," Murphy replied.

SEVENTY-EIGHT

Notes From Underground

"Are you writing this down?"

Melcher was pointing his flashlight right at Baltimore, he could see he wasn't writing anything down, that's why he asked.

"That's a dumbass question. You're looking right at me. You can see I'm not."

"So…"

"So why'd you ask me?"

"I thought you were going to start taking notes, like we said. The party's this weekend, we got a lot of shit to do, a lot of things to remember."

"This isn't our first party. We know what we're doing. I'll write something down when you say something worth writing down."

Melcher and Casper looked at each other, but said nothing. The three pointed their flashlights in front of them and continued their walk-through of the immense underground room that served as their rave location. They had done the hard physical labor – cleaning out debris, stringing up lights, securing the newly discovered main entrance – before they threw their first party three years ago. But this party was different: the stakes were higher, the risks greater, the potential rewards immense.

They were taking everything to a higher level.

It was their last party before the developer finalized his plans for the initial mix of nightclubs and entertainment venues in the complex. They hoped to become permanent partners, organizing raves and private parties while they continued their studies – lawyers made good money, law students didn't.

This was their chance to show what they could do.

"You've checked the course?" Melcher asked.

"There was a bunch of broken glass on the roof right before the jump, but we cleaned it up," Casper said. "The course is ready."

"Did you get the extra spotters we talked about, Baltimore?" Melcher asked.

"I'll take care of it, don't worry."

"So you didn't get them?'

"I said I'll take care of it."

Melcher stopped walking and turned on Baltimore.

"This party is important, we can't afford to screw it up."

"I'll take care of it, like always," Baltimore said. "What's wrong with you, man?"

Melcher looked at Casper again before he replied.

"There's nothing wrong with me, but there's something wrong with you. How many Howdy Doodys have you taken in the last week?"

"What are you, my dad? I took some with me when we stashed the party supply down here. I've been using them to drum up business at the Traffic Jam, like I always do."

"You been giving them to customers, or taking them yourself?" Casper asked.

"I give them to customers, free samples, come to our rave. Maybe I took a few myself, so what? They keep you awake, help you study."

"Just don't be taking too many of them, okay?" Melcher said. "We have to put on a first-rate rave to impress this guy. And we have to sell a lot of Howdy Doody to make our money back."

"Duh," Baltimore replied.

"That's why the scavenger hunt is so important," Melcher continued. "We're taking the parkour outside of this dump for the first time. We need extra help to do that, people we can trust. That's one of things we need you to do."

"Alright, alright. Don't worry about it. I got it covered."

Baltimore pulled out his notebook and wrote something down. They all nodded, relieved to be in agreement, and continued their walk. Their flashlight beams cut through the darkness ahead of them, revealing concrete walls and empty space. At the far end of the room the lights fell on a raised area that resembled a loading dock. When it came fully into view, Melcher had another question.

"You got the bus and equipment bags so the scavenger hunt finalists will look like a hockey team when we get to the Joe, right?"

Without answering Baltimore took out his notebook and wrote something down, and they continued their walk. By the time they had finished the walkthrough, Baltimore had made a dozen entries in his notebook. They were all identical.

MELCHER IS AN ASSHOLE

SEVENTY-NINE

Plan Be

"So that settles it. We're going to call it Plan Be, spelled b e."

For someone who was determined to be a free spirit Jack was really getting into the planning process. It felt good to be doing something positive, initiating the action for once instead of waiting around for more bad things to happen to him. When everyone else thought they were done, he insisted on giving the plan a name and going over it one more time. By then they had reviewed it so many times they had lost count and lost interest.

"Murphy, you're going to get the video camera to Robert and Donna by meeting them and switching purses," Jack said.

"Yeah."

"Where are you going to meet them?"

"I told you, I don't know yet. It depends where the tunnel I take to get there comes out. I'll know more after I talk to my guy."

"Who is this guy anyways?" Jack asked.

"He prefers I don't give out his name, he's sensitive about working with the police – even retired cops like me. Don't worry, if there's a tunnel under the Packard Plant he'll know about it."

"There's definitely a tunnel," Robert said. "Ajeet told me that's how these guys stumbled onto this space. There also was a stairwell that led down to it in the old days, but that was covered up when a section of the roof caved in."

"And the Wise Guys found a tunnel that led to it, you're sure of that?" Jack asked.

"Yeah. It's in a remote part of the tunnel system, and it was almost covered up with mud. That's why no one had found this room for years. They cleaned up the stairway entrance and put a lock on the door to keep everyone out, like they owned it."

"But they don't own it. The police won't shut the party down, will they?"

"I told you, the real owner is okay with it."

The edge in Robert's voice caused Maggie to speak up.

"Jack, we've been over and over this plan. I've got work to do. Unless you have something new to add, this meeting is over."

"There's one other thing I've been thinking about," Jack said.

Murphy, Maggie and Robert all groaned.

"I don't have a role to play in catching these guys on video selling drugs, but I want to be involved somehow," Jack continued. "I think I have a way to do that. You said they have a parkour contest, where they run around the Packard complex."

"Yeah, they climb on roofs, go through tunnels, jump on things," Robert said. "The people with the best times are given a clue that tells them where to find a prize. It's always been somewhere in the complex, but this year they said it would be at another famous Detroit landmark. Ajeet sent me the message to see if I could figure out where."

"We know where it will be, but we don't know what it is," Jack said. "You said in the past it was always cash and something cool, like Sennheiser headphones. And there was always a special surprise gift no one talked about, not even the winners."

"That was part of the deal – when you signed up and paid your entry fee you had to promise not to tell anyone what the special surprise was."

"I'm guessing it was Howdy Doody pills, why else wouldn't they want people to talk about it?" Jack asked.

"What if it was?" Murphy asked.

"If the surprise gift is Howdy Doody and we could shoot a video of the winner finding it we'd have more incriminating evidence to put on our web site."

"That sounds like the beginnings of a bad idea, Jack." Murphy said.

"We know where they're hiding the prize, we know it will be dark out. If I was there with one of your night vision cameras, I could hide and catch them in the act."

"If that's where I think it is I'm totally against doing you doing it," Maggie said.

"I'll be above the immortals," Jack said. "On the roof of Joe Louis Arena."

EIGHTY

The Principals
Of Entropy

The guy who could get him through the tunnels and into the rave had a strange history and a complicated relationship with Murphy. But his response to Murphy's request was simple and straightforward.

"There's no way. We're not going to help you."

He was sitting in Murphy's office, a young man who looked like he could use a good night's sleep and a hot meal. Tall and thin, with thick glasses and slicked down black hair, he was nearly as disheveled as the office itself.

"I told you no on the phone," he continued. "Bringing me here is a waste of time."

Murphy ran his business from a room above O'Cac's, a rundown bar in Corktown, a Detroit neighborhood settled by Irish immigrants after the potato famine in the 1840s. They sat at a large desk covered in newspapers, manila folders, paper cups and a partially disassembled handgun. In the far corner there was a table and chairs, and a telescope that could be used to look out the front or side windows.

Music from the punk band Red Dwarf vibrated the floor beneath their feet.

"Hear me out before you say no, Cody," Murphy said. "The client I'm helping out is a good guy."

"The college professor you told me about? I saw him online screaming horrible things at his students. He checked all the boxes for things I could hate about someone."

"That's not who he is. Three of his students didn't like their grades, so they recorded him reading nasty quotes from a book and put it online. They made it look like he was screaming at them. If you help me you'll be helping an innocent man get justice."

"It doesn't matter if he is a good guy or a bad guy, the Principals of Entropy are not going to help you."

"Why won't you help me?"

Murphy regretted the question as soon as he asked it. He could see Cody straightening up in his chair, about to recite the POE sound bite.

Murphy hated the POE sound bite.

A few years earlier Cody Brown had guided Murphy through an abandoned steam tunnel under the city, which helped him save the life of a client who was a public relations executive. The grateful executive then worked with Cody and the organization he led, transforming them in the public mind from a weird and possibly dangerous fringe group into a civic-minded pillar of the community.

The makeover started with a logo that featured a silhouette of the Detroit skyline with the letters POE above and the word 'Evermore' below. It also included the sound bite, a short description of the group they repeated over and over again to the media and the public with a cult-like fervor.

"The Principals of Entropy believe that by supporting what Detroit *was*, we can make what it *will be* even greater," Cody said. "Let's not get rid of our old structures, let's preserve them and show them to the world."

Cody made the standard dramatic pause at this point before finishing.

"Let's turn our blight past into a bright future!"

Murphy had waited politely and patiently for him to finish.

"I've only heard that a hundred times, Cody," he said. "We get it, you guys want to promote... what it is you call it? Eco-tourism?"

"We're not environmentalists, we're opposed to anyone who wants to get rid of our so-called blight. We want to promote the city like it's ancient Rome, and get tourists to visit the ruins here. We call it 'Entro-Tourism.'"

"You told me what that was, but I have to be honest – I forgot it immediately."

"It's like eco-tourism, only instead of visiting what nature has created, you visit what mankind has destroyed. Entropy theory says that over time everything falls apart. Why not take advantage of that, invite people here to see it: entro-tourism."

"That's all very nice, but you still haven't told me why you won't help me."

Cody leaned forward and looked around, as if someone could possibly hear them over the thundering apocalypse being summoned from hell by the band below them.

"This is private, right? I don't want anyone but you to know."

"I'm a *private* detective. It's my job to keep secrets."

"The POEs are entropy's pals – we spell principals with a p-a-l – because we are *supporters* of decline and degeneration. We are opposed to projects that repurpose old buildings, and prefer that they be preserved in all their glorious ruin. But sometimes we have to compromise our principles – p-l-e – and make a deal with the devil. We've been in secret negotiations with the developer who bought the Packard Plant. In exchange for our not protesting or sabotaging his development efforts..."

"What you used to do before you became good citizens."

"...he is working with us to preserve some areas and buildings there *as is.* If he found out we helped sabotage an officially sanctioned event at Packard it would kill our deal. Then he'd make it *all* bright, shiny and new."

Murphy saw his opening and went for it.

"He'd never know you helped me. You just take me through the tunnels to where the party is, then leave."

"I don't know, Murphy. It would be hard to find your way back without me."

"I was an Army Ranger. I was in a lot of tunnels in Vietnam. I know how to find my way around."

"I don't know Murphy…"

"Listen Cody, you're worried that this developer might clean up that shithole completely. The dealer who's supplying drugs to this rave killed a student, and tried to kill the professor. If you can get me to that rave with a camera it won't just help clear my client's name, it will give us the evidence we need to put away a murderer, maybe stop him before he kills again. So what are your principles when it comes to murder?"

Cody shook his head and frowned.

"Why is it always life-and-death with you, Murphy?"

"I don't know. I just seem to attract these situations. Maybe it's the company I keep. So are you going to help me or not?"

"What would your buddy Buddha tell me to do?"

"Buddha said, 'I do not believe in a fate that falls on men however they act; but I do believe in a fate that falls on them unless they act.' What do you say?"

Cody shook his head again, but this time he smiled.

As he spoke the band stopped playing, so his answer was loud and clear.

"Let's turn our blight past into a bright future!"

EIGHTY-ONE

Murphy's Laws

"Tonight's the night. Are we ready to go?"

Jack heard the rhythmic thumps and muffled screams of rock music echoing faintly over the phone, but his question remained unanswered.

"Murphy, are you there?"

"Yeah."

"Are we ready to go?"

There was another long pause filled with the distant sound of rock music.

"Chaos is inherent in all compounded things," Murphy replied. "Strive on with diligence."

"Is that a Buddha quote?"

"Yeah."

"What the hell does it mean?"

"Let me put it a different way: No battle plan survives contact with the enemy."

"That's not Buddha."

"Helmuth von Moltke, German military strategist. He was chief of staff of the Prussian Army for 30 years in the 1800s. Mike Tyson updated the saying when he fought Evander Holyfield in 1997."

"Okay, I'll bite… what did he say?"

"Everybody has a plan until they get punched in the face."

"Thanks for the history lesson, but I'm still not following you. Are you saying we're not ready for tonight?"

"No. What I'm saying is the best-laid schemes o' mice an' men gang aft agley."

"I know that one, Scottish poet Robert Burns. The best-laid plans often fail. You mean us?"

"I'm not saying we're going to fail, Jack. I'm just saying that when the mission starts shit happens."

"Who said that?"

"I did."

"So you *do* think Plan Be is going to fail?"

"I didn't say that. I'm trying to tell you that things don't always go the way you plan them so you won't be surprised when that happens. You have to be ready to improvise, think on your feet. I have confidence in you, you're good at that, Jack."

"When the going gets weird the weird turn pro," Jack said.

"I like that, did you make that up?" Murphy asked.

"No, that's Hunter S. Thompson, *Fear and Loathing in Las Vegas*,"

The music in the background got louder and the screaming intensified. Then it stopped and Jack could hear cheering and applause.

"Are you in a bar, Murphy?"

"I'm in my office."

"Have you been drinking?"

"Have you been breathing?"

"Okay, dumb question. I know you'll be ready. Is your guy ready?"

"He's ready, don't worry about us – we'll be there. How about that Robert kid, will he be there?"

"He'll be there. He's scared but he's determined to get justice for his friend."

"And the girl? She still cool about going?"

"Yes. It turns out she's been waiting for him to ask her out for a long time."

"Hell of a first date. Did she practice using the camera like I showed you?"

"She did, she'll do fine. They're not in any real danger are they?"

"I don't think so. These guys are punks and bullies, but they're not killers. It should be fine. How about you and Maggie, you ready?"

"We're ready. But I wish you wouldn't have encouraged her to come with me."

"I told you, when you're sneaking around on private property, it helps if you are a couple, it's less suspicious than a guy by himself. You got your story ready?"

"I proposed to her at a Red Wings game years ago. We came back to see the building one more time before they knock it down."

"That's a good story, I hope you don't have to use it."

"I hope so, too. And I hope your friend leaves the back door open like he said."

"He will."

Everyone had opposed Jack's crazy idea to set up a hidden camera on the roof of Joe Louis Arena. When he insisted on doing it, Maggie insisted on coming along with him. At that point Murphy gave up and confessed he knew a guy who could help them.

"It seems weird that a Detroit cop would help us sneak into the Joe," Jack said.

"He's a good friend, and he knows it's for a good cause. Justice will be served."

"I hope he's more reliable than your friend at Henry Ford Hospital."

"He's stationed at the Joe for games and concerts. He knows the place like the back of his hand. Just do what he said and everything will be fine."

"I will. Any other last-minute advice?"

"Try not to get caught. You've already had one arrest for trespassing on a roof. You don't need another."

Jack started to say his previous arrest was Murphy's fault, but thought better of it.

"I've gone over every detail of what we need to do again and again with Maggie. I'm sure she's sick of hearing me repeat myself. I just wish she wasn't coming with me."

"And she wishes you weren't going in the first place, but she insisted on going with you, and she is…"

Murphy stopped himself, but Jack finished the sentence in his head.

Dying of cancer.

"The people who collect the prize will be college students, not hardened criminals. Just stay out of sight and make the video."

"I will."

"And don't do anything stupid."

Jack didn't respond to this request.

EIGHTY-TWO

Rave On

First dates made Robert nervous.

He really liked Donna, which made him more nervous.

They were about to secretly film a drug deal, which terrified him.

As they walked across the cracked asphalt toward the skeletal remains of a massive concrete building he struggled to calm himself. Slowing his breathing and his stride, he turned to the determined-looking young woman walking beside him.

"Are you sure you want to do this?" he asked.

"Yes, I'm sure. Ajeet was my friend, too."

Like advanced to love.

When they reached the building a young man waved them through a doorway with instructions to turn right at the first hallway. A few lights strung overhead lit the way as they walked down a bare concrete corridor. The walls were covered with spray-painted graffiti that was beautifully rendered, wildly imaginative and incredibly obscene.

"This looks like an art gallery for the criminally insane," Donna whispered.

He was now certain he was going to marry her.

At the end of the hallway on the right a heavily tattooed couple patted them down. As he was being searched Robert looked up and saw a gaping hole in the concrete floor above them. He could see all the way to second floor ceiling, and he realized he looking at the reason this above ground entrance hadn't been found until now.

The woman frisking Donna nodded at the small polka dot purse hanging from her shoulder. Donna offered it up and the woman rummaged through its contents, then waved them through another door that led to a staircase. At the bottom of the stairs a big guy sitting on a stool took their cover charge cash and pointed to a narrow hallway behind him.

They could feel deep bass notes thudding in the distance as they walked for what felt like forever. Then they rounded a corner and went through one last door.

Robert wasn't sure if they had arrived in heaven or hell.

Hundreds of writhing bodies were jerking spasmodically to painfully loud electronic music in an immense concrete cavern of a room. As his eyes adjusted to the flickering colored lights he could see what looked like a loading dock at the far end. A DJ wearing headphones stood there pumping his fist in the air behind a table stacked with turntables, mixers and laptops. The entire length of the right side of the room was a wall of smooth, graffiti-free concrete, on the left side there were several doorways and a scattering of tables and chairs.

Robert leaned into Donna to speak.

"We're a little early for the purse exchange. Do you want to dance?"

Donna nodded and they found an open spot and began moving to the music. Hesitant and slightly awkward at first, they quickly lost their inhibitions and were swept up in the hypnotic rhythm.

Definitely heaven.

Robert wasn't sure how long they danced before he awoke from his dream-like trance and remembered why they were there. He nodded toward the sidewall and they made their way to two folding chairs. As they sat down he checked his watch and had his first 'oh shit' moment of the night.

They were a half hour late.

As he turned to tell Donna they had to go a guy in an MC5 tee shirt stepped out of the crowd and yelled "What time is it?" over the music. Robert looked at his watch again and was about to yell out the time when he had his second 'oh shit' moment of the night.

It was the secret phrase.

Which meant he had to give the secret response.

"It's Howdy Dowdy time," Robert said.

MC5 nodded his head sideways in a 'follow me' gesture.

Oh shit.

They had lost track of time dancing, they should have had the camera by now.

For a moment Robert panicked and his mind went blank. Then he remembered what Murphy had told him about the location of the tunnel entrance. It was a slim chance, but it was their only chance. He stood up and spoke directly into the young man's ear.

"We have to go the bathroom first," he said.

Their new friend shrugged and nodded and walked off toward the front the room. Robert grabbed Donna's hand and followed, carefully counting the number of doorways they passed and stopping at the fourth one. In their last briefing session Jack told him that the Porta Johns were down this hallway and that, according to Murphy's guy, the tunnel entrance was in a room just down the hall from them.

Robert felt a wave of relief when MC5, walking ahead of them, stopped in front of the fourth doorway. They exchanged head nods and he led Donna down the hallway, feeling more relieved when MC5 didn't follow them. Not far ahead a row of Porta Johns lined the wall on the left, and as planned he and Donna occupied the last two in the row.

He wasn't sure what Donna was up to, but after all the excitement he wasn't going to fake this part. A few moments later, feeling truly relieved, he stepped outside and waited for Donna to join him. When she did they moved quickly down the hallway, looking for the door to what used to be the boiler room. They had given him a lot of directions to remember, but this one was easy – first doorway on the left.

It was a much smaller room filled with a series of raised concrete pads that once supported long-since removed furnaces, fans and machinery. A five-foot high brick wall ran parallel to the back wall for half its length.

This was the place.

Robert ran to the back of the room and rounded the corner of the brick wall. At the far end of the walled-in space he could see the four-by-four foot opening they had described to him, the place where he was supposed to meet Murphy.

This was definitely the place.

Murphy definitely wasn't there.

EIGHTY-THREE

Subterranean Homesick Blues

Tunnels made Murphy nervous.

Buddha and Jack made him calm.

Going after bad guys made him happy.

They started out walking in a relatively spacious tunnel with a concrete floor and red brick walls that rose into an arch overhead. It reminded Murphy of a similar tunnel his guide had taken him through a few years ago, which was somewhat comforting.

But it was still a tunnel.

"We're starting out in the old Administrative Building," Cody explained as they walked. "It's huge – 121,000 square feet – and it's the first building they'll renovate."

"This looks like the other tunnel you took me through."

"You caught a killer that time. Think you'll do it this time?"

"If you get me to where I'm supposed to be I will."

"You're right about the two tunnels – they're very similar. That tunnel was owned by the City of Detroit, this one is private, but they're both steam tunnels. In the old days they used to them to send steam heat to buildings. They also had water pipes and electric lines running through them. Most of that stuff has been taken away by scavengers."

"Thanks for the history lesson. How far do we have to walk?"

"It's a ways still. This tunnel runs along the north side of the complex, then crosses under a road to the south side, which is where we're going. The room they're holding the rave in is an old bomb shelter they built in World War II. No one had been in it for decades until your friends stumbled onto it."

"How come no one else found it? Isn't that what you guys do?"

"We knew it was there from old documents, but the main entrance on the first floor was buried under debris. The tunnel entrance wasn't completely covered, but it had a lot of mud and water in front of it. And it runs slightly uphill, so you can't see to the other side. But what really kept people out was the fact that it's not very big."

Cody swung his flashlight around and looked over at Murphy, as if something just occurred to him.

"Why are you looking at me?" Murphy asked. "How small is this tunnel?"

"Pretty small."

They walked on in silence.

Murphy could feel the calming effects of the Jack beginning to wear off. He was not eager to revisit his previous small tunnel experiences. He'd been around death for most of his life as an observer and initiator, and on several occasions as a near participant. It didn't scare him; nothing did really – except for small, enclosed spaces.

After walking for what seemed to Murphy like a very long time they made a turn down a somewhat smaller side branch of the tunnel.

"We're heading under the road now," Cody said.

By training and experience Murphy knew that one of the first rules of any clandestine mission was keeping talk to a minimum – nervous chatter could be fatal. But he needed to do something to keep his mind off the walls that were closing in on him.

"So tell me again, Cody, why do you guys hang out in places like this?"

"The Principals of Entropy believe that by supporting what Detroit *was*, we can make what it *will be* even greater. We say let's turn our…"

"Oh geez no, don't tell me your sound bite again. I want to know why you think a shithole like this is so great."

"People go to Athens to see the Acropolis. They go to Rome to see the coliseum. This is Detroit's coliseum. Michigan Central Depot train station is our Acropolis. We have beautiful old churches, theaters, mansions; all abandoned and in ruins."

"You really think people would come here to see that stuff?"

"They already do. But they have to sneak around, and they don't know what they're looking at. The POEs would change that: get rid of the vandals, set up tours, charge people to help pay for preservation."

"People would pay to see this?"

"Why not? You have to admit there's something fascinating about these places, something that draws you to them. You've felt it, haven't you, Murphy?"

"When I'm above ground, sure. Not down here."

"You all right? I remember last time you had some problems being in the tunnel."

"Yeah, I'm all right."

Murphy's mind was racing to find something other than tunnels to talk about.

"Kind of funny, they're spending money to restore this pile of junk and tearing down a perfectly functional Joe Louis Arena. What do the POEs think about that?"

"We're okay with it," Cody replied. "If you have yesterday's newspaper you throw it away without a problem. A newspaper from 100 years ago you keep."

"The Joe is yesterday's news."

"That's right. If they let it sit there for another 50 years we'd be interested in it. If they knock it down next month, we don't care."

Murphy was about to say the POEs were crazy but Cody pointed to the right with his flashlight and went around a corner. Murphy followed him into a tunnel that was slightly smaller than the one they had been walking down.

He was not pleased.

"These tunnels keep getting smaller," he said.

"This is nothing," Cody replied. "Just wait."

Murphy could wait.

They were walking single file, ducking slightly to avoid the ceiling. Streaks of mud and water began appearing on the floor, eventually covering it completely.

"The floor has cracked a bit in this part, it lets in ground water," Cody explained.

Murphy did not want an explanation.

A few more turns and they were there: at ground level, its floor sharing the layer of mud and water that filled the main tunnel, was an impossibly small square hole.

"Holy shit," Murphy said. "Why in the name of Siddhārtha Gautama would anyone crawl into that hole?"

"Who?"

"Buddha."

"It was worse before your college boys found it," Cody said. "They dug out a lot of mud and dirt that was covering it."

"My question still stands."

"They're parkour fanatics. They pride themselves on doing dangerous things no one else would even think about doing."

Murphy turned his flashlight up to Cody's face.

"How do you know all this stuff?" he asked.

"The POEs love old ruins, we hang out in them as much as possible. We also keep an eye on what's happening, make sure people respect their surroundings."

"You spy on people."

"We watch things. If people show up we watch them."

"I'm not accusing you, I'm admiring you. So what's next?"

"This is as far as I go. You go through this tunnel; it's about 20 feet long. On the other side is a big tunnel, like the one we started out in. Turn right and about 30 feet down on the left is another square bypass tunnel, twice as big and half as long as this one. Go through that and your friends should be on the other side."

Murphy swung his flashlight beam down from Cody's face to the tunnel entrance.

"You don't see a problem here?" he asked.

"I know you don't like small spaces, but this tunnel is short and you…"

"I'm not claustrophobic, I'm post-traumatic," Murphy interrupted. "But that's not the problem. In case you haven't noticed I am a somewhat portly older gentleman, what some would call a big fat guy. There's no way I can fit through there."

"You can fit, Murphy. If I have to I'll shove you from behind."

"As delightful as that sounds, I'm going to have to pass."

"You talked me into coming down here because you said you were after a killer. So now you're going to give up and let him get away?"

Murphy brought his flashlight beam back up to Cody's face for a moment, then back down to the small square hole in the wall. He held the light there for a long time – then he sat down in the mud.

"What the hell are you doing?" Cody asked.

"You remember the last time we did this, I freaked out and had a flashback, had to sit down and meditate to get my shit together. This time I'm going to do the meditation first, maybe that way I won't have a flashback. You can leave now, thanks for your help."

"I'm going to stay if you don't mind, Murphy. Make sure you make it through."

"That's fine, just don't say anything. This might take a while."

With that Murphy closed his eyes and began his journey.

He started by taking in deep breaths through his nose and exhaling through his mouth. Slowing his breathing down, he began a slow scan of his body from head to toe, noticing physical and emotional feelings, letting thoughts come and go. After that he spent a long time observing his breathing, noticing how his chest rose and fell.

Then he went home.

It was a place he had spent years creating in his mind, a perfect private beach where he could feel safe and serene no matter what else was going on in his life or his head. He could feel the sand and the hot sun, hear the waves and the wind. It was a place he hadn't been to in a long time, and when he returned he realized how much he missed it.

He stayed a long time.

When he finally opened his eyes Cody stepped forward anxiously.

"You did that for a long time," he said.

"I needed to. I'm ready to crawl in that damn hole now."

"What time did you say you would meet your friends?"

"Twenty one hundred, why?"

"Is that nine o'clock? Because my watch says it's nine thirty."

EIGHTY-FOUR

Beer League Night

Jack drove slowly down Steve Yzerman Drive looking for an illegal parking spot.

The Detroit River was on his left, Cobo Hall on his right.

Maggie was riding shotgun.

"I think there's a place between Cobo and the Joe where we can park," he said.

"Is it legal to park there?" Maggie asked.

"No, it isn't," Jack replied. "But it isn't legal to sneak into the Joe and climb on the roof, either, and we're going to do that, too."

When they reached the alley between the two buildings he turned right and stopped beside the curved outer wall of Cobo Hall, under a sign that read "No Stopping, Standing, Parking."

"You think it's smart to park here?" Maggie asked.

"Smart hasn't exactly worked out for me," Jack said. "I'm going all-in on stupid."

Maggie laughed, which made the world a better place.

Jack began another recitation of the list of things they needed to have and do to complete their mission – a list of details looking for a plan. He stopped when Maggie rolled her eyes; apparently a dozen repetitions was enough. They got out of his car, crossed the alley and started up the stairs to the row of red doors that served as the southeast entrance to the Joe. Jack was praying Murphy's friend had kept his word.

"The door on the far right should have its lock taped open," he said.

"Just like Watergate?" Maggie asked. "That turned out well."

Jack was happy to see their common interests included gallows humor.

The door opened as promised, Jack removed the red duct tape from the lock, and they ducked inside. The wide corridor was empty but fully lit, and he could hear shouts and the crack of hockey sticks through the red rubber curtains across the aisle. The curtains kept the cold air from escaping through the entrances that led to the seats, which was good. But the sounds coming through them meant there were players on the ice.

That wasn't good.

"I didn't think anybody would be here tonight," he said.

"Isn't the Red Wings season over?" Maggie asked.

"Yeah. It must be a beer league, it's too late for kids to be playing."

"A beer league?"

"Amateur teams sponsored by a bar. They can rent ice time here."

It was too late to worry, too late to go back. Jack turned to his right and started walking toward the elevators. On an off night their next move would have been easy: get on the elevator and go to the fifth floor. But tonight obviously wasn't an off night; there was an usher standing behind a lectern in the elevator lobby.

"Can I help you folks?" he asked.

Murphy had insisted Jack take Maggie with him, and that they dress in business casual clothes. He said a well-dressed couple would arouse less suspicion if someone saw them, but he didn't tell them what to do if that happened.

Jack had to figure that out himself.

Quickly.

"I'm glad you're here," he said. "Our son has a game tonight and my wife suddenly remembered she might have left her camera in our suite after the Hall and Oates concert last week. Do you mind if we go up and take a look? We'd love to get some pictures of him playing."

"I'm sorry, sir, the suite level is closed. These elevators are only for physically impaired fans who want to sit in the upper sections."

Jack knew no one was going to sit in the upper level to watch a beer league game, the handful of friends and family who showed up would sit close to the ice. This usher was here to make sure no one got on the elevator unless they worked at the Joe.

It was obvious he and Maggie weren't employees, so how could they get on?

Get on – get it on?

It might work.

"I'm going to be honest with you, we don't really give a shit about our son's game," Jack said. "He's 22 years old, still living at home and playing hockey with his drunken friends. We've been watching him play since he was a Mini-Mite, we have thousands of pictures – that's not why we're here."

"So why are you here?"

Jack looked around and leaned into the usher.

"Instead of watching a boring game we thought it would be fun to go fool around in our suite," he said quietly. "What do you say, can we have a little alone time?"

To further plea his case he handed the usher a $20 dollar bill. A moment later they were getting into the elevator and pushing the 5 button.

"What did you tell him?" Maggie asked.

"I told him we wanted to go to our suite and fool around."

"That's clever, but we could be up here for hours. He'll come looking for us."

"I didn't give him a suite number; and he's not going to look on the roof. And he won't tell anyone else because he shouldn't have let us up here in the first place."

The elevator doors opened and they stepped into a small white room. A gray hallway stretched into the distance; on one side there was a plywood wall and the other a chain link fence topped in barbed wire. Behind the fence were pallets of food, beer, condiments, napkins, cups – the supplies needed to feed 20,000 people.

Jack recited what Murphy had told him as they walked.

"This is the highest floor in the building, it's above the arena. They mostly use it for storage, but the kitchen and the broadcast facilities are also on this level. The ladder to the roof is down toward the other end of this hallway on the right."

"From the outside it looked like there were two levels to the roof," Maggie said.

"There's a long, tall structure that divides the roof in half. It's built over this hallway, that's why the ceiling is so high here."

"So there's a roof on one side, a higher roof that runs the length of the building, and another roof on the other side of that."

"Yeah."

"So which roof is the prize on?"

"I don't know."

"And where are you going to set up a hidden camera? If there any place to hide?"

"I checked Google satellite photos and there's what looks like heating or cooling units next to the top structure in one corner of the roof, with ductwork that goes into the building. Maybe we can hide there."

"It's good to know you have a well-thought-out plan," Maggie said.

They both laughed.

The ladder was bright yellow and built into the wall. Fifteen feet above them it stopped at a narrow ledge in front of a yellow metal door.

"You have the camera and tripod, right?" Jack asked.

Maggie rolled her eyes and patted her large purse; these were two of the items on the list that Jack had repeated ad nauseam before they started. Jack nodded and headed up the ladder, swung the door at the top open, and waved Maggie up. They walked out onto a tar roof, a silver wall looming behind them, the lights of the Detroit skyline sparkling in front of them. Even at night the collective light from all of the surrounding buildings made it fairly easy to see.

"It's beautiful," Maggie said.

They stood for a moment taking it in. To their right the towers of the Renaissance Center glowed in an eerie blue light, straight ahead in the distance the golden tower of the Fisher Building shined brightly. The roof itself was unremarkable – an empty expanse of black tar surrounded by a three-foot high retaining wall on three sides; on the fourth side the twenty-foot-high middle section.

There was nowhere to hide a prize.

"What now?" Maggie asked.

"I suppose we should find a way to get on top of the thing in the middle, search the roof up there, and then climb down and search the roof on the other side."

Finding a way up was easy. When they finished admiring the skyline they turned around and saw a ladder built into the wall a short distance from the door. It wasn't until they reached the ladder that things got complicated.

Jack was already climbing the ladder when Maggie called out from below.

"Jack, look at this."

He climbed back down and looked where she was pointing. Someone had left a message on the wall between the rungs of the ladder, in letters so small Jack didn't see them. It read: *Over the top and then head strait, finding your reward will be grate.*

"Why are straight and great spelled wrong?" Maggie asked.

"Because the Wise Guys are dumbasses."

"Jack, they're law students. They're not dumb, they just don't like Sixties literature. This has to mean something."

"Over the top is easy – it means we have to climb over this thing in the middle and look for the prize on the other side."

"Yes, but what do strait and grate mean?"

"I don't know. Let's climb over to the other side, maybe they'll make more sense over there."

They climbed up one side of the structure, crossed 50 feet to the other side, found a ladder and climbed down. At the bottom they turned and surveyed the scene.

"Another trapezoid," Maggie said.

"What?"

"The roof on this side matches the other side. They're both trapezoids."

"Okay."

"You don't remember your high school geometry, do you? A trapezoid is a quadrilateral with two parallel sides."

Jack was staring at the roof in front of him, looking deep in thought.

"A quadrilateral is a shape with four straight sides."

"I think I got it."

"No offense, Jack, but Americans know so little about math and science these days. I think everybody should…"

"I'm not talking about trapezoids," Jack said. "I know what grate means."

"You do? Tell me!"

"There's a wall on all four sides of this roof."

"So?"

"So where does the water go when it rains?"

"I suppose there's drains."

"There are – big ones. I didn't really notice them on the other side, but you can see them clearly over here. They're covered by grates – g-r-a-t-e."

"You think they put the prize in a drain pipe?"

"That's the only place it could be, but which one? There's lot of them."

"Straight out would be a ninety degree angle from the wall," Maggie said.

She hurried off and Jack followed. Halfway across the roof she stopped at a round sewer grate that was two feet wide. By the time Jack reached her she had pulled a small flashlight from her purse and was looking down into the drain.

Nothing.

The white plastic pipe made sharp turn sideways two feet down, creating a level space that would be ideal for hiding a small package. But there was nothing there.

"I thought for sure we'd find it here," Maggie said.

"You had the right idea, but you're forgetting something. Strait was spelled s-t-r-a-i-t. We're not supposed to go straight from the wall."

"Then where do we go?"

"They built the Joe at an angle to the river."

"Yeah?"

"The Detroit River."

"Yeah?"

"The word Detroit is French for the strait."

"So we need to go back to where we started and go directly toward the river."

Before she finished the sentence Maggie was running back to the big wall.

She beat Jack to the ladder, oriented herself to the river and started running again. Jack changed course before he reached the ladder and cut across to follow her. She was almost to the corner where two of the short walls met when she stopped running and knelt down. He caught up with her just in time to hear her assessment of the situation.

"Shit."

Good shit? Bad shit? Bullshit?

Jack leaned over her shoulder and looked down through the grate.

It was there.

A small box wrapped in white plastic.

The prize.

"Should we open it?" Maggie asked.

"No. It has to be untouched, in the exact same spot. If anything looks different it might give us away. There's just one thing I need to check."

Jack reached down and pulled on the grate. It came off easily. He put the grate back on and looked around.

"This is perfect," he said. "We can set up the camera over there."

They walked along the three-foot wall back to where it connected to the twenty-foot high middle wall. In that corner there were a several large metal boxes with pipes, wires and air ducts coming out of them. They could set up their camera in the shadows behind these heating and cooling units and no one would see them.

A few minutes later the night vision video camera was sitting on a mini tripod between two of the metal boxes. Jack ran out and stood by the grate that held the prize, Maggie used the remote control to turn the camera on and check the focus, and they were ready to go.

When Jack returned he sat down next to Maggie.

It was delightful and painful, a reminder of how desperately he loved her and how steadfastly she refused his love. The good news was he had time, and he had hope.

"It will be hours before anyone shows up," he said.

"Jack, I'm not a princess. I've conducted experiments all over the world, in all kinds of conditions. If I have to pee I'll just go behind that ductwork over there."

Jack laughed and fell even deeper in love.

"That's not what I meant," he said. "We have time to…"

He stopped in mid-sentence.

There was someone on the roof above them.

EIGHTY-FIVE

Fat Guy In
A Little Tunnel

Murphy was a half hour late for a precisely timed rendezvous. In the Army or on the police force, that could be the difference between life and death. He hoped that wasn't the case tonight.

"I got to get going Cody, thanks for your help."

"No problem. Good luck."

Murphy knelt down and pointed his flashlight into the small square hole. As Cody had explained the tunnel was slightly uphill, all he could see was the floor rising into the distance. It would have helped if he could have seen through to the other side.

He pushed forward and his head and shoulders cleared the entrance. His sides scraped against the tunnel walls, but he pushed forward with his legs and moved ahead.

He was in.

Holding the flashlight in one hand, he pulled with his elbows and pushed with his legs and started up the slope. Cody shouted something into the tunnel entrance, but the large body squeezed into the small tunnel blocked his words. Murphy couldn't make out whether it was encouragement or a warning.

"I'm fine," he replied.

Which he wasn't.

Murphy's perfect beach was being swamped by a rising tide of panic. He continued moving forward, mainly because going back seemed physically impossible. He told himself that getting through this tunnel would have been difficult even without his memories of Vietnam. But those memories were flooding back, making the tunnel even more crowded. He hadn't tripped out into a full-blown flashback yet, but that possibility was becoming very real.

It was time to meditate.

There wasn't time, this wasn't the place, but the alternative was unthinkable. He closed his eyes, took a deep slow breath, and returned to his beach.

It was difficult at first, almost impossible. Thoughts, fears, memories and urgent tasks all came rushing into his mind. One by one he greeted them, thanked them for coming, and let them go. At last he was alone on the beach. He lingered there for a while, seized the moment, and opened his eyes.

He wasn't calm, but he could carry on.

He pulled and pushed with renewed urgency as the flashlight beam skipped across the ground ahead of him. Suddenly, there it was – the bottom edge of the other opening. He pushed harder and faster and it came completely into view, the most beautiful thing he had ever seen. A moment later he pushed the flashlight forward, gripped the sides of the entrance with both hands, and pulled himself out.

To his great relief he saw that Cody was right: it was a much larger tunnel, the same size as the first tunnel they had entered. He grabbed the flashlight and rose unsteadily to his feet; trying to remember which direction he was supposed to go.

Then he heard someone calling his name.

EIGHTY-SIX

The Going Gets Weird

Jack could hear the footsteps of someone walking in the loose gravel of the roof above them. He raised a finger to his lips, got up slowly, and looked around the corner of one of the big metal boxes he and Maggie were sitting between. As he stared into the semi-darkness someone appeared at the top of ladder that led down to their level.

It was Luc.

Even at a distance Jack recognized the devil who had cursed his days, adding injury to insult, since his fall from grace. It took a moment for the shock of Luc's unexpected appearance to subside, and another moment for Jack to think of the possible reasons he was here. When he did an adrenaline-fueled wave of fear surged through him.

He sat back down next to Maggie.

"Who is it?" she whispered.

"Luc."

"The guy who killed Ajeet?"

"Yes."

"What is he doing here?"

"There are a lot of possible reasons, but two are most likely. One is he heard about the prize and came up to find it."

"And the other?"

Jack hesitated. He didn't want to alarm her, but she needed to know the truth.

"He followed me up here to kill me."

Maggie gently squeezed his hand, and Jack was ready for whatever came next. He stood up and led Maggie to a spot where they could peer around the corner. She stood behind him and they watched as Luc began climbing down the ladder.

"We'll know in a minute," Jack said. "If he's after me he'll come straight at us. There's no other place to hide up here."

"Let's hope he's after the prize."

"Let's hope," Jack agreed. "Then he won't come back here, as long as we're quiet."

Jack thought for a moment and turned to Maggie.

"You put your phone on silent, right?"

A phone ringing at the wrong time would give them away. It was one of the items on the list that Jack had kept repeating.

This time Maggie did not roll her eyes.

"Shit," she said. "Sorry."

She began fumbling in her pocket for her phone and Jack turned back to check on their visitor.

Luc reached the bottom of the ladder and turned around. He looked back and forth across the wide-open space around him, then turned to look at the heating and cooling units in the far corner. Hidden in the shadows, Jack held his breath. After a moment that felt like forever, Luc turned back and looked straight ahead.

Then he started walking.

"He's walking straight out at a ninety degree angle, like we did," Jack whispered. "He's looking for the prize."

Then he heard a thump behind him.

Luc stopped.

EIGHTY-SEVEN

It's Howdy Doody Time!

When Murphy stepped through the short square tunnel into the boiler room he and Robert said the same thing simultaneously.

"Sorry I'm late."

Murphy knew there wasn't time for explanation or speculation. Why were they both late? What good karma delayed them the same amount of time so that one of them didn't give up and leave? Those things could be discussed later.

Right now it was time to exchange purses.

He unzipped his windbreaker and carefully removed a small purse hanging from a chain around his neck. Donna stepped forward and handed him her purse. She took the purse from Murphy and hung it around her neck. The two purses were identical, with a busy polka dot pattern used to disguise a small opening for the camera.

"Turn it on before they take you to the room where the drugs are," Murphy said. "Be sure to point it…"

"We got to go, Murphy," Robert said. "The deal's already going down."

Donna reached into the purse and turned on the camera, and she and Robert headed back to the front door. Murphy followed, giving last-minute instructions.

"Just act natural and be cool. Pretend you're buying a candy bar. I got your back, I put a microphone in there, too, so I can hear what's going on. This room you're going to, it's not too far away, right?"

"Should be right around the corner," Robert said.

"Good, then I'll get a signal. You remember what I told you to do if none of our suspects is in the room?"

They had reached the open doorway; Robert turned around.

"I know what to do, Murphy."

Robert and Donna disappeared through the door. Murphy stood there for a moment, then turned around and walked back to the tunnel entrance. He sat down behind the brick wall that blocked the entrance from view and took out his cell phone. In a moment he would know if their good karma was still working.

He dialed a number, then punched in a code.

Instant karma: he heard music.

The bug he put in the purse was engineered to minimize background noise and amplify voices. Murphy was pretty sure he would be able to hear them talking – if somebody would say something. He was beginning to think they were using sign language to make the deal when he heard a voice.

"So you gonna enter the parkour prize contest?"

Murphy didn't recognize the voice.

"I had a friend who talked about it a little bit, but I don't really know what it is."

They definitely were in business – that was Robert.

"For $20 you get to run a parkour – like an obstacle course – on the grounds here at Packard. If you finish it you get a clue that tells you where the prize is. Everyone who figures out the clue is taken to where the prize is and has a chance to find it."

"What's the prize?"

"They're not saying, but it's always worth a lot of money. I'm not supposed to say this, but it may even include some of what you're about to buy."

"Sounds cool, but I'm not really an obstacle course kind of guy. I'll have to pass."

"No problem, you're still going to have a lot fun tonight. We're almost there."

The music in the background faded away and there was a long silence. Murphy was beginning to wonder if they had walked out of range when he heard Robert speak again.

"I was hoping our hosts would be here, I wanted to thank them."

"They're busy right now, I'll pass it along. You owe me $80."

This was it.

From what was just said it was obvious that the Wise Guys were not in the room. In their planning sessions Murphy explained what to do if that happened. His plan was easy to understand, but difficult to execute. It was based on a simple premise – in any business when customers have a major problem the next level of supervision is called in to handle it.

The question was, did Robert have the courage and skill to pull it off?

"I'm not to pay $80 for this shit. That's a ripoff. I'll give you $20."

"Hey, man, I don't decide the price, I just collect the money. It's $80."

"That's bullshit. Who decides the price? Get them in here."

"Dude, I'm being real with you now – you do not want me to call the boss."

"And I'm being real with you – I'm not leaving, and I'm not paying $80. Call your boss so we can negotiate a fair price."

There was a long pause, then Murphy heard the guy who had been talking to Robert barked a command.

"Go get Baltimore."

A longer pause followed. Murphy thought he heard Robert whisper "get ready" but he couldn't be sure. A few minutes later he heard a new voice.

"You're the guy who has a question?"

"I don't have a question, I just don't want to pay $80 for a few pills."

"I'm afraid $80 is as low as we can go."

"That's bullshit. Are you the only one in charge? I want to talk to some-one else."

"You're talking to me, and I'm telling you $80 is cheap. We keep our costs low and we pass the savings on to our customers. You know how we do that?"

"No."

"Low overhead."

"Look, I just want to try Howdy Doody. I guess I can…"

"For example, we don't hire bouncers to take care of whiny ass punks like you. We do it ourselves."

Murphy heard some grunts and curses, and then a woman screamed.

EIGHTY-EIGHT

Give Peace A Chance

"Who's there?"

Luc sounded impatient.

Jack looked back at Maggie, a pained expression on her face, her cell phone at her feet. He raised his finger to his lips and shook his head.

"I know you're back there. Step out and let me see you."

Jack reviewed his options.

He could stay here behind the ventilation units until Luc came to them, or he could step out and hope Maggie wouldn't be found. As Jack sat in the darkness trying to decide whether to go or stay Luc raised the stakes and urgency of his decision.

"You're not going to like it if you make me come back there," he said. "I've got a gun and I'm not afraid to use it."

So much for peace and love.

Jack had spent the days since his sweaty sauna epiphany celebrating his transformation from someone who admired Sixties philosophy to someone who lived it. He believed his string of near-deaths, arrests and violent encounters had changed him for good – and for better. After decades of standing on the sidelines encouraging others to embrace the power of love, he would embody it himself.

His personal love-in had been liberating and exhilarating. But his first post-sauna encounter with hate was giving him serious doubts about his new lifestyle choice.

Luc was hate on steroids, an angry drug-addled loser with a gun. What chance did love have against that level of ignorance and animosity? Would it help to flash a peace sign and a smile? Give him a hug? Tell him a whimsical story inspired by psychedelic drugs?

Actually, yes.

Jack had zero chance of winning a traditional hate-on-hate fight; the gun tilted the odds completely in Luc's favor. But he might have a chance – infinitesimally small, but a chance – if he could blow his mind.

It was time for Plan J.

"Gimme a joint," he whispered to Maggie.

"What? What are you talking about? This isn't the time for us to smoke a joint."

"We're not. I'm going to smoke it with him."

"Are you crazy?"

"Yes, but I have a plan. There's no time to talk, just give me a joint."

Maggie reached into her purse and handed Jack a fat cigarette and a lighter.

"I keep these in my purse in case I get nausea from the chemo," she said. "How did you know I had them?"

"I taught college for twenty years, I know what it smells like when someone's holding. Stay here, whatever happens, don't make any noise."

"That's sexist bullshit. I'm not some little damsel in distress for you to save. I'm the one who dropped her phone, I'm the one who's dying, I should save you."

Jack's brain was fogged with fear, but in order for his plan to work he needed Maggie to stay put. He needed to say something cool to calm her down.

"I've already died once, it wasn't that bad," he said.

Maggie gave him a puzzled look.

"I'm not afraid of dying anymore, I'm afraid of not living," he said.

"Are you trying to impress me?" Maggie asked. "This isn't a James Bond movie."

"Last call," Luc shouted.

"Stay here, stay quiet, call the cops… please," Jack said. Then he shouted, "I'm coming out, don't shoot."

Jack walked out from behind the machinery and stepped out the shadows.

"Holy shit, it's the nutty professor," Luc said. "Looks like I'm getting two prizes for coming here, eh?"

"Hey, Luc. Can we talk?"

"Sure, we can talk all you want. Then I'm going to kill you."

Despite his talk of not being afraid to die, Jack had to wait for a wave of adrenaline-fueled fear to subside before he could speak.

"Can I ask why?"

"You have to ask? You snoop around my business, stalk my house, sucker punch me in the throat, and you have to ask? Put it this way, I just don't like you, eh?"

If Jack was going to die, he might as well get a full confession on camera.

"Is that why you burned my house down with me in it?"

"Yeah, that's why."

This next part was tricky. Jack assumed that Luc already knew what he had found out about Ajeet's death. If not what he said next would definitely sign his death warrant.

"Anything else?"

"What do you mean?"

"I know that you murdered the college student, Ajeet Nirmal. Isn't that really why you want to kill me?"

"I didn't murder him, it was an accident. We were having an argument on the bridge, and he slipped and fell off."

Jack was pretty sure he heard a gasp in the darkness behind him, so he spoke fast.

"If you haven't murdered anyone, why start now?"

"I told you why. I don't like you."

Jack slowed his breathing down and tried to stay calm. His plan was to stall long enough for someone else to come along looking for the prize; or an even greater miracle, for the police to arrive. Might as well stick to it.

"I believe the tradition is for the condemned man to have a smoke before he gets shot. Mind if I light one up?"

"You're a real funny fucker, aren't you? Go ahead, light up. Just do it slow."

Jack reached into his front pocket, pulled out the joint and fired it up.

"Death is a groovy trip, man," he said. "I should know, I've done it before. I can't wait to do again when I'm high."

Luc was standing ten feet away; it didn't take long for the smoke to reach him.

"You smoking weed?" he asked.

Jack exhaled and replied, confident that Luc would take the bait.

"Yeah, you want some? It'll take the edge off of Howdy Doody."

"What do you know about Howdy Doody?"

"I saw him the last time I died," Jack said. "TV show puppet in the 1950s. Nice kid. Also a recreational drug in the 2000 teens. Nice drug. Not illegal in Detroit yet."

"How do you know that?"

"It's a long story. You want a hit or not?"

Luc stepped forward and carefully took the joint from Jack with the hand that wasn't holding the gun. He stepped back and took several hits before returning it.

The plan was working.

"That's good shit," he said. "But I'm still going to kill you."

Don't panic.

Sharing a joint was just the start.

Stick to the plan.

"Can I ask you another question?"

"Go ahead professor."

"You said something about prizes. Is that why are you're here?"

"Yeah. I'm looking for something Ajeet's friends put up here. Why are you here?"

"Same reason. You having any luck finding it?"

"What does it look like, dumbass? You see me holding anything other than this gun? I'll find it *after* I kill you."

"I can save you a lot of trouble if you don't kill me first. I know where it is."

Luc thought it over for a moment, then gestured toward the open roof with his gun.

"Gimme the joint and lead the way professor."

"So you're not going to kill me?"

"I'll think about it. Lead the way."

Jack handed him the joint and walked slowly toward the far corner of the roof.

"How'd you get past the security guard by the elevators?" he asked.

"I took the stairs"

"Smart. How'd you figure out the number clue?"

"I'm a Red Wings fan."

"Me, too. We may have gotten off on the wrong foot, Luc. I'm starting to like you."

"Shut the hell up. There's nothing ahead of us. If this is some sort of trick I won't kill you until the fourth shot. You don't wanna know where the first three will go."

Once again Jack had to wait for the wave of panic to subside before he could speak.

"The prize is out here, trust me. And think about maybe not killing me, too. It's a groovy trip, but I'd rather take it some other time."

Luc, who was walking a few feet behind and to the side of Jack, finished sucking down the smoke from the last tiny nub of the joint. He exhaled it as he spoke.

"Find the prize and we'll talk."

When they were nearly to the corner Jack stopped.

"It's here, underneath the drain grate," he said.

"Bring it out. Slowly."

Jack knelt down, pulled off the grate, and set it aside. He leaned forward and grabbed the box with both hands, then lifted it out carefully.

"Set it down," Luc said. "Open it."

Jack sat back and set the package down on the in front of him. He tore the plastic wrap from the top of the box, lifted the lid, and laughed.

"What is it?"

Jack didn't reply, instead he reached into the box and pulled out a large ceramic head spotted with freckles and topped with red hair.

"What the hell is that?" Luc asked.

"You don't recognize our old friend Howdy Doody?"

"I know who it is, but what is it?"

"It looks like a vintage cookie jar," Jack said. "They probably bought it on eBay."

"I came all the way to Detroit and snuck onto the roof of Joe Louis Arena for a fucking cookie jar? I'm definitely going to kill somebody now."

"Hold on, maybe there's something inside it."

Jack set the jar down, grabbed the red hair and pulled the top off.

He started laughing again.

Forgetting the fact that he was holding a hostage at gunpoint, Luc sat down next to Jack and joined in the laughter. For a moment Jack considered trying to grab the gun, but decided instead to stick with his plan. He was going all-in on peace and love, and he had a feeling what he had just uncovered would help his chances.

Inside Howdy Doody's head was a festive mixture of candy, cash, freckled pills and tightly rolled joints. Luc picked out a Howdy Doody pill and swallowed it, then pulled out a joint and handed it to Jack.

"Spark this up," he said.

Jack did as he was told and soon they were passing a joint back and forth between them. As they did the idea of being killed seemed less and less real in Jack's mind. He hoped the same thing was happening in Luc's mind.

Maybe he could help it along.

"Do you get to the Kaleva Cafe much?" Jack asked.

"All the time for breakfast. Great pasties there too, eh?"

"Yeah. I spent my summers in Hancock when I was growing up. Went back and forth between two lost worlds of faded glory, Detroit and the Copper County in the U.P."

"What the hell are talking about, lost worlds?"

"Once upon a time Detroit and the Copper Country were both thriving global economic powerhouses that..."

Luc looked confused and bored. Jack urged his muddled mind to drop the social commentary and stick to the story.

"I loved Kaleva Cafe pasties. Do you know what Kaleva means?

"No."

"Kaleva was an ancient Finnish king, like King Arthur. He had twelve sons, who were giants. When the people of Finland converted to Christianity they chased them away because they were pagans."

"For real?"

"For real. These days in Finland if you see like a really big weird looking rock they say it was left by one of Kaleva's sons."

"Cool. I like stories like that."

Jack searched his brain frantically for another cool story.

Oh yeah. Been teaching it for years.

"Mysticism is underrated. One of my favorite stories is *The Teachings of Don Juan*. It's about a native American Indian sorcerer who uses weed, mushrooms and peyote to teach his students how to become a man of knowledge."

"Hell yeah," Luc said. "I would have got straight A's in that class, eh?"

"This guy says all paths lead nowhere, but he recommends a path with heart because it makes for a joyful journey."

"Sounds like a cool dude."

"He is a cool dude. He helps his apprentice turn into a crow."

"No shit, that's awesome. Where is this teacher?"

"He's from Mexico, but he met his apprentice at a bus stop in Nogales, Arizona."

"Too bad shit like that doesn't happen in the real world."

"Arizona is the real world."

"I mean like here in Detroit. Psychedelic teachers, crazy creatures. Shit like that."

"You ever hear about Nain Rouge?"

"No. What's Nain Rouge?"

"He's a little red devil who hangs around Detroit, supposed to be the sign of bad things happening in the city. He's been here for more 300 years, back to when the city was run by the French. Nain Rouge is French for red dwarf."

"Wow. You're blowing my mind, man. You think he's still here?"

"I don't know. They have a parade every year on the Sunday after the Vernal Equinox, supposed to keep him away. It's sort of like Detroit's Mardi Gras, but I'm not sure if it works or not. I'm pretty sure there's still a devil running loose in Detroit."

"That's so cool, eh?"

Jack nodded but said nothing. By now he could barely remember what his plan was – this shit was that good – but something told him to keep pursuing it.

"You can have the cookie jar and everything in it, I don't want anything," he said.

"I was going to take it anyways, but that's nice of you to offer, professor."

"So, you still going to kill me?"

"Depends. You believe me it was an accident on the bridge?"

"I do. You haven't murdered anybody yet. Don't start now."

"What about me trying to burn your house down?"

"What about it?"

"You going to tell the cops I did it?"

"You walk away tonight and don't shoot me, we'll call it even. I won't say anything to the cops."

Luc was sitting cross-legged next to Howdy Doody's head, the gun gripped casually in his right hand, which was propping him up. He seemed to be thinking things over. Jack sat across from him anxiously waiting to see if his offer would be accepted, and kicking himself for not asking for one of the little candy bars in Howdy's head as part of the deal.

"What the hell," Luc said finally. "Thanks to you I got what I came up here for. I guess I won't kill you. You want one of these candy bars?"

"Not killing me would be awesome. So would a candy bar. Thank you."

Luc pulled a Three Musketeers bar out of the cookie jar and tossed it to Jack, then took one for himself. As they ate them in silence, Jack heard a noise that he thought sounded familiar. At first he couldn't remember what it was, then it came to him.

It was someone walking across the gravel on the roof above them.

Jack looked up and saw the back of someone climbing down the ladder.

His plan had worked.

He had used flower power – love, joy, non-violence – to keep from being killed. Potent pot and stoner stories had helped, slowing down time until someone else showed up. Now, with a witness here, Jack was sure Luc would stick to his word and not kill him.

Until the newcomer reached the bottom of the ladder and turned around.

"This really is my lucky night," Luc said. "It's my friend Jasper."

EIGHTY-NINE

Tough Crowd

Murphy was certain it was Donna who screamed.

As he took off running he could hear the sound of fighting on his phone: muffled curses, grunts and the thud of punches landing. He ran out the door and turned right, running past a row of Porta Johns toward the main room. Through the open doorway ahead of him he could see the room was dark, its only sound a low, rhythmic thumping.

Murphy ran through the door just as the immense space exploded in a burst of shimmering high notes and bright colored lights. He stopped to get his bearings as the lights began keeping time with the rhythm of the throbbing bass line, turning on and off to reveal and conceal a rectangular concrete room packed with wildly gyrating dancers. He looked to his left in time to see two of the Wise Guys – Melcher and Casper – disappear into another hallway.

Murphy headed after them, pushing and dodging his way through young people expressing themselves with dance moves that ranged from the familiar to the bizarre and beyond. He reached the hallway in time to see the guys he was following turn into a doorway. He ran down the hall after them, pausing for a moment to catch his breath before he stepped into the room.

Running is not my strong suit, he thought.

Just inside the doorway a folding table and chairs sat in front of a stack of boxes. Beyond that a small group of people stood in a circle around someone lying on the floor.

"Murphy!"

Standing at the back of the group, Donna saw him and called his name. Everyone turned around to face him. Melcher, Casper and Baltimore were in the middle of the circle, closest to Murphy. As they turned he could see it was Robert on the floor; he looked conscious but dazed and bloody.

"Donna, come over here," Murphy said.

As she hurried over to him the look on the Wise Guy's faces morphed rapidly from surprise to recognition to anger.

"Hey, it's Jack Daniels, the bar fly from the Old Miami," Melcher said. "What's your fat ass doing at our party old man?"

"I came here to get my friends and leave," Murphy said.

"You mean this piece of shit would-be thief dripping blood all over our clean floor? Sorry, he has to stay with us for a while longer. He has to finish taking our customer satisfaction survey. It's what we give to dissatisfied customers to make sure they never come back again. You can pick him up at the main entrance in an hour or so."

"That's not acceptable, Melcher. He and this young lady are coming with me."

"You know my name? I'm beginning to think you've been spying on us. I'm not sure why you'd do that, but I don't like it. We may have to give you our customer satisfaction survey, too. We can use it to figure out what you are up to, old man."

"That wouldn't be smart. I don't want to hurt you boys, but if I have to I will."

In addition to the three Wise Guys, there were two other young men in the room. All five of them burst into laughter when they heard Murphy's warning. When they finally stopped laughing Melcher gave his final warning.

"I don't want to beat up an old man, but if that's what it takes to get you to explain what the hell you are doing here, I guess I will."

"Donna, make sure you get this on video," Murphy said. "I'm going to inflict substantial injury, and I want to make sure I can prove it was in self-defense."

Donna looked confused but did what Murphy ask her to do, raising her purse and holding it sideways.

"Oh, shit," Baltimore said. "She's got a camera in her purse."

"Not a problem," Melcher said. "As soon as I finish with this old man I'm sure she will be happy to give it to us."

Melcher stepped forward and struck a fighting pose – knees flexed, left leg forward, fists raised one above the other. Murphy knew the Wise Guys had martial arts training and had seen him beat up three big guys. But he believed they greatly overrated their abilities, that they wouldn't hold up to a well-trained individual who had life and death experience.

His theory was about to be tested.

"Buddha said the cause of all pain and suffering is ignorance," he said. "You don't know who I am or what I can do. Your ignorance is about to cause you great pain."

"I know this bitch called you Murphy," Melcher replied. "And I know a fat guy named Murphy is about to join his friend on the floor."

Melcher lunged at him, throwing a right jab from down low straight toward his head. Murphy casually blocked the punch with his left forearm and stepped down hard on Melcher's left knee with his right foot. The crunching sound that made was followed by a scream, which ended when Murphy followed through with his right elbow, striking Melcher in the chin.

As Melcher collapsed to the ground Casper leaped forward and swung a roundhouse kick at Murphy's head. Murphy grabbed his foot and twisted it 180 degrees, a move accompanied by horrific crunching and a high-pitch wail. He held the leg for a moment, then pushed Casper backwards over his fallen friend.

The other two young men were backing toward the wall behind them with their hands raised, pleading with Murphy to be cool, so he turned to face Baltimore.

He was too late.

Murphy has assumed Baltimore would join the fight, instead he took advantage of the few seconds it had taken to dispatch his friends to make a run at Donna. As Murphy turned he saw Baltimore grab Donna's purse, shove her and run toward the door. To her credit Donna recovered her balance and took off after him.

"Don't lose him, I'm coming after you," Murphy yelled after her.

Running is not my strong suit, he told himself once more. And these guys were the best at running over difficult terrain he'd seen since his Army days. The chase was going to be tougher than the fight, and if this punk got away everything they'd done was for nothing.

Murphy started running.

By the time he made it back to the main room he was gasping for air. He did a quick survey of the room, looking to his left toward the loading dock stage and sweeping around to his far right – where Donna stood a short distance away in front of the Porta John hallway. She was waving at him frantically; when he saw her and waved she stopped waving and ran into the hall. Murphy followed, doing more shoving and less dodging than he had done coming the other way.

Donna was on Baltimore's trail, and he needed to catch up to them both.

When he made it to the entrance and looked down into the hallway, he could see Donna waving at the far end of the line of Porta Johns. He took a deep breath and began jogging toward her, watching as she disappeared into an open doorway.

By now it obvious to Murphy that Baltimore had headed to the boiler room and planned to escape through the tiny tunnel. It also was obvious that if he didn't get there before Baltimore made it into that tunnel he would have no chance of catching him.

Murphy plodded past the Porta Johns, for a moment puzzled by the absence of long lines but then remembering this was a rave, not a kegger. When he passed the last portable restroom he turned left through the open doorway into the boiler room. He got there just in time to hear Donna shout a non-negotiable demand.

"Hey asshole, give me back my purse."

She was standing at the far end of the five-foot wall that ran parallel to the back of the room. At the other end, near the square passageway that led to the tunnel, Baltimore's head stuck out above the wall. He turned to look at Donna and give a two-word response.

"Fuck you!"

Baltimore ducked down and Donna took off running after him. Murphy fast-walked toward the far end of the wall, huffing and puffing like a cartoon train, certain that Baltimore would make it to the tiny tunnel before he could catch him. But as he rounded far side of the wall he was greeted by the first of many surprises.

At the other end of the wall, in front of the four-by-four foot opening, Baltimore was on the ground, wrestling with Donna and someone else. As Murphy jogged toward them Baltimore slapped Donna, knocking her backwards. He then landed several punches on the head of the other person holding onto him.

It was Cody.

Baltimore pulled himself free of Cody's grip and turned to duck through the short tunnel, but Murphy managed to grunt out a short warning before he did.

"Hey!"

The last Wise Guy standing looked up to see a lightning-fast haymaker with substantial weight and momentum behind it speeding towards his nose. With a sharp crack the lights were out and his getaway was over.

Several deep breaths later Murphy was able to gasp out a question.

"You guys okay?"

By that time Cody and Donna had both managed to sit up, nod and say yes.

A few minutes later and many breaths later, Murphy had another question.

"Cody, what the hell are you doing here?"

"I followed you through the little tunnel just to make sure you were okay. When I got to the boiler room entrance I eavesdropped and heard you talking to Robert and Donna, then you took off. I thought you might need help getting back through the tunnel so I stuck around."

"This guy has studied martial arts, he's a black belt in karate. What the hell were you doing trying to fight him?"

"I was waiting for you to come back on the other side of this tunnel when he showed up. I recognized the purse he was carrying and figured you wouldn't want him running off with it. When this girl yelled at him he turned around and I saw my chance – I ran through and tackled him from behind."

"Thanks, man. I appreciate your having my back," Murphy said.

He turned to Donna, the side of whose face was already beginning to bruise.

"And thank you, young lady. I blame myself for putting you in harm's way. I got cocky, figured it didn't matter if they knew you had a camera. I thought I could beat them all up before anything happened."

"You could have, you were amazing," Donna replied. "You did nothing wrong."

"That was a brave thing you did chasing after this punk," Murphy continued. "If he gets away with the camera, we don't have proof of anything, and maybe somebody gets away with murder. Not to mention I might end up facing assault and battery charges."

"If you mess with my date and steal my purse, I'm coming after you," Donna said. "Speaking of which, we have to go find Robert."

Murphy reached down to Cody and Donna and helped pull them to their feet. He was in the middle of introducing them to each other when a voice called out.

"This party sucks, Donna. Let's go somewhere and get a drink."

Robert stood in the doorway to the boiler room, dark circles forming under eyes, blood crusting under his nose, a smile spreading across his face.

NINETY

Friendly Fire

Jack was not happy to see Jasper.

He had spent the last half hour getting Luc to mellow out and not kill him. Or maybe it took a half-day or a half-minute, he couldn't be sure because time turned relative when you smoked pot. In any case he knew it was a miracle that would be hard to repeat, especially when Jasper recovered from his initial surprise and spoke.

"What the hell is he doing here?"

"It's cool, man," Luc replied.

"What do you mean, it's cool? He's been following us around like some kind of narc or something. And now he's up here with you."

"And you're here, too. How cool is that? How'd you know I was here?"

"'Cause you're nuts, that's why. All you been talking about is finding the prize. I hung out here all afternoon waiting for you to show up. I was going to try to stop you, but you got inside before I could catch up to you. It took me awhile to figure out how to get up here. And now I get here and you're best friends with this piece of shit."

"He came up here up looking the prize like me, eh? We're cool now."

"He kicked me in the nuts and punched your throat. You wanted to kill him."

"The nutty professor showed me where the prize was, so I told him I wouldn't kill him. Check it out..."

Luc lifted up the Howdy Doody cookie jar.

"It's got Howdy Doodys, cash, great weed and candy. Professor here says I can have it all, right professor?"

"Sure, no problem," Jack said.

"And he's not going to tell anybody what he knows, either – right?"

"That's right," Jack said.

Jasper stepped closer to where they were sitting.

"What a minute, what does he know?" he asked.

"He knew about that college kid and the bridge," Luc replied. "But now he knows it was an accident, that I was just trying to scare the kid."

Jasper froze.

He stood motionless, ten feet away, for a segment of time Jack couldn't measure – a moment, a minute, forever? Then he began pacing back and forth in a small, tight circle. The two-word phrase he kept whispering to himself was terrifying.

"Oh shit, oh shit, oh shit, oh shit, oh shit."

"What's the matter, man?" Luc asked.

"What's the matter? You've fried your brains on the drug we invented, that's what's the matter. It's made you crazy. You beat the shit out of your uncle, and now you're best friends with the guy who's trying to take us down."

"Vladdie's not dead is he? I didn't really want to kill him, I just wanted him to stop giving me crap and hitting me."

"Vladdie's not dead. He sent me here to stop you before you did any more stupid things and got us all in trouble. But it looks like I'm too late for that. It looks like I'm going to have clean up this mess you've made."

"What are you talking about?"

Jack knew exactly what Jasper was talking about. He assumed Jasper was carrying a gun, and started looking around for things to throw or places to go.

There weren't a lot of options.

He could throw the cookie jar at Jasper, maybe the drain grate. Very little chance of success there. Or he could jump over one of the nearby walls – good chance of making it, zero chance of surviving it. He fought desperately to clear his head and focus.

Jasper pulled out a gun.

Jack chose the grate.

It was sitting next to his right hand. He could grab it and throw it, maybe hit Jasper in the head, or at least buy some time to get the gun. Of course, if that happened, there was a good possibility Luc would shoot him in the back. Thanks to Howdy Doody, he was as crazy and unpredictable as Jasper said he was, no telling what he could do. Maybe he could talk Luc into turning against Jasper. If he could buy some time…

Jasper's next words put an end to Jack's calculations.

"This is for kicking me in the nuts."

With no time left for thinking, Jack grabbed the grate and threw it at Jasper as he rose to his feet. It was heavier than he anticipated and took longer to fly through the air than he wanted, but it had the desired effect.

Almost.

Jasper ducked, but still managed to get off a shot. Instead of hitting the middle of Jack's chest where it was originally aimed, the bullet tore into his left leg, spinning him around. He stepped forward and collapsed face first onto the ground. Behind him he heard footsteps and then Luc's voice.

"Dude, what are you doing?"

Another shot was fired. Overcoming a shockwave of intense pain, Jack managed to roll over onto his back. He could see Luc lying flat on his back, blood spurting from his chest. He looked over and saw Jasper walking his way, then standing over him.

Jack was looking straight up into a gun barrel.

"You fucked up, professor," Jasper said. "You got in over your head with some drug dealers in Detroit. They followed you here to kill you, and then they had to kill an innocent bystander who was playing a party game."

Jack started to explain that wasn't what happened, then realized Jasper was spinning a scenario he hoped the cops would follow. Maybe if he understood there was too much going on for the police to jump to that conclusion.

"You know, Jasper, the police…"

"Shut up. I don't want to hear any more of your bullshit. You're the one who caused all this trouble. You're the one who made me kill my best friend. Now you're going to die."

"Wait! Stop! Don't shoot him!"

Jack heard Maggie calling out, then heard footsteps running across the roof.

Then he heard another shot.

NINETY-ONE

No Deal

The video footage from the rave was vivid and promised to be violent.

Whether or not it was useful was another question.

"You guys did a great job, I'm proud of you," Murphy said.

"But…" Donna added.

"But what?" Murphy asked.

"You don't seem very excited. Is there something wrong?"

"First of all, I'm not an excitable guy, I'm a professional. But, yes, there is something wrong."

"What's wrong?" Robert asked.

"We wanted to get a video of a drug deal. This isn't a drug deal, it's a street fight."

"But we talk about buying the drugs, and he makes me an offer."

"You didn't give him any money, he didn't give you any drugs. No deal."

No deal, but they had made it out alive, which was a big deal.

After their confrontation with the Wise Guys, Murphy made it clear that he would rather fight his way out of the rave than go back through the tunnel. Cody wished them luck and left the way he came. Murphy, Robert and Donna walked out through the main entrance; no one bothered or even noticed them.

As agreed to as part of Plan Be, the three of them drove to Murphy's office to download their video onto a computer and wait for Jack and Maggie to join them and do the same. They had watched the video up to the part where Robert and Donna were waiting around for Baltimore to show up when Murphy made his grim no deal assessment.

Robert clicked on Pause and stopped the video before he replied.

"You're thinking like a cop, Murphy. We don't need evidence that will stand up in a court of law. We want to win in the court of public opinion."

"And this is going to help us do that?"

"It might. Social media is about attracting attention. This will definitely do that."

"Then what?" Murphy asked.

"I'm not sure. Maybe the Internet trolls will take them down after that. The main thing is to embarrass them and complicate their lives."

"I don't think these guys embarrass that easily," Murphy said.

"You haven't seen what happens when the other wise guys shows up," Donna replied. "It's after Baltimore sucker punches Robert and kicks him when he's down."

"Like I said, a street fight. A dirty fight, but just a fight."

"But when the other two show up, they start yelling at him," Donna continued. "They say he's been taking too many Howdy Doodys, that he's going nuts."

"That's interesting," Murphy said.

"It gets better. They tell him to save them for the customers, quit taking them himself. Robert is on the floor bleeding and they are talking about how the drug they are selling makes some people hateful and violent."

"They weren't yelling at him when I showed up."

"They stopped as soon as they saw you," Donna said. "You were an outside threat, that was a discussion they had among themselves."

"Let's take a look at it," Murphy said. "I don't know anything about social media, but if what they said about the drug is on the video then it's back in my territory – that's something we could go to the cops with."

"It's Jack's plan, we can ask him what he wants to do," Donna said.

"Speaking of Jack, where is he?" Robert asked. "Shouldn't he and Maggie have been here by now?"

"Oh crap, we forgot something," Murphy said. "They're up on the roof waiting for one of the parkour contestants to claim the prize."

"And the three guys who run the contest are probably headed to a hospital right now," Robert said. "There isn't going to be a contest."

"Should I call and tell them?" Donna asked.

"I wouldn't do that," Murphy said. "They're up there on that roof illegally, and Jack's already in trouble with the law. A ringing phone or a ding from a text might give them away. If they were smart they silenced their phones, but we can't count on that."

"So what do we do?"

"Nothing. If they made it onto the roof then their biggest problem will be getting back down without being caught," Murphy said. "No one else is going to go up there tonight. They'll figure it out eventually; in the meantime they're perfectly safe."

Donna was starting to reply when Murphy's phone rang.

NINETY-TWO

The Principal Of Uncertainty

Lying on his back, high on pot, bleeding and in pain, it was difficult for Jack to keep track of what was happening.

He was pretty sure Jasper hadn't shot him; if he had been shot at this close range he would be dead. Jasper was looking up, his gun was pointing forward. Maggie had screamed and a shot was fired.

Jasper had shot Maggie.

Ignoring the searing pain in his leg, Jack rocked forward and grabbed Jasper's legs. Jasper slammed down on top of him and they fell sideways to the ground, and Jack began punching and kicking his would-be killer with the leg that could still move. He kept punching until he heard Maggie screaming again, this time much closer.

"Jack, stop, he's dead."

Jack stopped punching and pushed his attacker off of him. When he did he could see a hole in his back that was spurting blood. The shot he heard had killed Jasper.

"You're not shot," Jack said.

"No, I'm not, but you are," Maggie replied. "Let me see your leg, I'm going to put a tourniquet on it to stop the bleeding."

With great difficulty and pain Jack pushed away from the dead body and swung his left leg around. Maggie knelt down, pulled off her belt, and tied it around Jack's calf above his wound. He winced when she tightened it, but his bleeding stopped immediately. The pain helped him focus as he tried once again to clear his head and figure out what had happened. As he reviewed the sequence of gunshots he arrived quickly at the overlooked but obvious fact: Luc shot Jasper *after* he was shot himself.

Jack rolled over, pushed up onto his hands and good foot, and started moving toward Luc in a low crouch.

"Jack, what are you doing?" Maggie demanded

"Luc is still alive."

"Are you crazy? He's a killer, he's got a gun."

"He just saved our lives."

Luc was on his back, eyes closed, the identical twin of Jasper's dark wound in the middle of his chest. Jack laid down next to him and carefully removed the gun from his hand before gently shaking his shoulder.

"Luc, are you still with us?" he said quietly. "Can you hear me?"

Luc opened his eyes and turned his head toward Jack.

"Can you believe that fucker shot me?" Luc whispered. "Some best friend, eh?"

"You saved our lives, thank you."

"No problem. I hadda take out the guy who killed me before I kicked, eh?"

"Hang in there, Luc. You're going to be okay. We'll get you out of here."

"Bullshit. Jasper's a good shot, he don't miss. I'm dying for sure. You said you died before. Was that bullshit too?"

"No."

"Tell me what it's like."

"Like I said, it's nice. You kind of float around, you feel real peaceful, and you see family and friends who died before you."

"If I see Jasper I'm going to kick his ass."

Luc laughed, then closed his eyes and coughed up blood. Time was running out for Luc, and for Jack: if he didn't ask now he would never know.

"Luc, I have a question: why didn't you kill me?"

"What makes you think I wasn't going to?"

"But you told Jasper…"

"Jasper was a dumb shit. When stuff happened and we had to change plans on the fly he never could follow along. I guess he couldn't tell I was putting you on."

"So you were going to kill me all along?"

Luc stared at Jack for a long time, then he smiled.

"No, I'm bullshitting you professor. You and I were going to be best friends."

Luc started laughing again.

Then he coughed up more blood.

Then he died.

NINETY-THREE

Funny Story

Jack did what people did on TV when someone died, feeling Luc's wrist for a pulse that wasn't there. When he turned to find Maggie she was standing over him.

"Did you call the police?" Jack asked.

"Funny story," Maggie said, sitting down.

"I can't imagine anything being funny about any of this, but go on."

"When you first walked out here I called 911. I was scared and flustered so I blurted out we were on the roof of Joe Louis Arena with Howdy Doody."

"What happened?"

"They hung up on me. So I calmed myself down and called back and told them my boyfriend was being held at gunpoint by a drug dealer who had already killed someone. That got their attention. They said they were sending officers here and wanted me to stay on the line, which I did until the shooting started and I ran out."

"You said I was your boyfriend?"

"Don't get too excited, I was just trying to get someone to come here. I thought it might help if I made it more personal."

Jack was going to hide his disappointment by complimenting her quick thinking when Maggie continued.

"But, yeah, maybe. That stupid action movie line you said made me think. I'm still afraid of dying, but I'm even more afraid of not living."

"So I'm your boyfriend? That's awesome!"

Maggie responded by punching him in the arm.

"Life is precious, you don't take crazy chances and squander it. What were you thinking, smoking pot with a killer?"

Jack took a deep breath and exhaled slowly. His leg hurt like hell, but he couldn't pass up this chance to explain himself.

"When you have a theory in physics, you do an experiment to see if it's true. I taught Sixties literature for 20 years, and in that time I came to believe in the power of love."

"Like the hippies?"

"Something like that. I told my students that love could conquer hate, but I was just reciting a dry academic theory, I wasn't living it. Then I had a vision in the sauna."

"It was probably a heat stroke."

"I decided to really bring love into my life, to be open and spontaneous, to laugh a lot, and have a sense of wonder. When I saw Luc I decided to put my new lifestyle to the test. I went Merry Prankster on his ass. I basically was trying to stall for time. It's not like I had a lot of other options."

"So that was your experiment? Hold a love-in with a murderer?"

"It worked, didn't it?"

"He said he was going to kill you all along, but Jasper interrupted him."

"Then he said he was kidding. Who knows? I'm still here. And if we're going to start lecturing people for taking foolish risks, how about you? You ran out shouting at somebody who had just shot two people."

Maggie held his gaze for a moment, then looked down as she spoke.

"You had done so much and risked so much for me. Also, I realized something."

"What was that?"

She looked back up at him.

"How much I loved you."

Jack propped himself up on his elbow and reached out for her. She leaned forward and they embraced and kissed. Their moment of bliss ended when Jack yelled in pain.

"Oww."

"Sorry. Probably not the best time to make out. You need to get to an emergency room. Where are the police? I called them a while ago, it shouldn't take that long."

Maggie took out her phone to call the police again when they heard it.

Sirens.

And then a voice calling down from the upper roof through a megaphone.

"This is Joe Louis security. You are violation of the law, you are not supposed to be on this roof. The police called us, they are on their way. We are coming down to escort you inside."

Maggie yelled back.

"We have a wounded gunshot victim down here, and two fatalities. The wounded person needs immediate medical attention."

In the dim light they could see the small group of people who had gathered on the upper roof duck behind the wall. After a long pause the megaphone voice spoke again.

"The police will be here shortly."

Maggie looked at Jack.

"You alright? Can you wait?"

"Yeah, I'm okay. While we're waiting why don't you go retrieve the camera. I have a feeling we're going to need that video to help explain all this."

"Good idea. I'll be right back. Don't move."

Jack was pretty certain he couldn't move even if he wanted to, which he didn't. As he watched her walk away he pulled out his phone and turned it on. Taking no chances of it making any noise at all, he had gone beyond silent mode and turned it off completely before they started.

When it was fully powered up he punched in a number and spoke.

"Hey Murphy, it's Jack. We're going to be a little late."

Part Three

Einstein Was Right

"Einstein said that if quantum mechanics were correct then the world would be crazy. Einstein was right—the world is crazy."

—Daniel M. Greenberger

NINETY-FOUR

Shaggy And Velma

"This discussion reminds me of the talks I had with my wife after she died."

"That's nice, but please stop proposing to me. I'll let you know when I'm ready."

"It's the health thing, isn't it?"

"Does she still visit you in your dreams? Because I won't do it if she still is."

"You shouldn't talk like that, even as a joke. But the answer is no."

"What do you think happened?"

"I guess she said all she needed to say. It was time to move on, for both of us."

"No, I mean how do you explain her presence in your dreams?"

"Her being there is easy to explain – lots of people dream about loved ones who have passed. What's hard to explain is how she told me what was going to happen before it did. Having a premonition come true is like going through the looking glass. You can never look at things the same way again. Dying is even stranger."

"How did death change you?"

"For starters, I'm just happy to be here. Simple things bring me joy, or awe."

"Like a hippie."

"Hard to say exactly what caused the change, everything blends together. I'm much more tolerant of people, I feel the connections we have with everyone. I even have a new trick I use to get closer to people. It's kind of morbid but it works."

"What's that?"

"I pretend I'm at their funeral, but when I walk up to the casket they're alive."

"That is morbid. And weird."

"Yes, but it works, even with people you don't like. When you go to someone's funeral you think of all their wonderful qualities and you minimize the bad things. Why wait until they die to feel that way?"

"Do you do that with me?"

"I don't have to with you."

"That's sweet. You're a good man."

"For thousands of years all the religions in the world have been telling us the same thing – be nice to people. It's so simple and obvious that we tend to ignore it, but it works. When I do something nice for someone, it comes back to me ten-fold. Murphy says it's karma. I can't explain it, but I know it works."

"Quantum physics presents us with all kinds of things that we can't explain. You and I made particles connect across time and space. That defies all logic and conventional wisdom. Einstein called it crazy. Physicists assume – we hope – that someday we will be able to understand what's happening. That's why we keep coming up with theories and using experiments to test them."

"I don't think there are any experiments I can do that explain what happened to me. The only way for me to understand it is to go back."

"To die again?"

"Yes. I'm not in any hurry, but I'm not afraid."

"*I am. I'm afraid I'll get there before you, and I want to stay because of you.*"

"*Don't worry, you're going to be here a long time. The tests will be negative.*"

"*They won't have the full results for another week. How do you know that?*"

"*Call it a premonition.*"

NINETY-FIVE

The Comeback Kid

It had been nine months since Jack had been in Baxter's office.

Nothing had changed.

Everything had changed.

"Just sign the papers where they're marked, Jack, and the money's yours."

"It's not my money. I told you, I'm giving most of it to charities here in Detroit, and the rest is going to Murphy. It's a lot more than he asked for, but he was worth it. It's also good karma."

"So Murphy's got you talking about karma?"

"He said he didn't charge you anything for helping me because he owed you a great debt of karma he wanted to repay."

"He didn't tell you why he thinks he owes me, did he?"

"No."

"And neither will I."

"But he did agree to take the extra money. I insisted."

"Nobody is getting anything until you sign these."

Baxter spun the papers around on his desk; Jack leaned forward in his chair and began signing.

"The first time I asked you to bring a wrongful dismissal lawsuit against the university you refused," Jack said. "And then, when I didn't want to do it, you insisted."

"You didn't have a case the first time, they would have taken us to court and trounced us. With what happened later, and our video proof, they were happy to settle. Their big mistake was freezing your tenure. We could have gotten a lot more if you wanted."

"This is plenty. The main reason I agreed to the lawsuit was to clear my name and make sure this doesn't happen to anyone else. I have no hard feelings toward the university, their apology was sincere and sufficient."

"Spoken like a true English professor. Apparently the Wise Guys' apology to you was sincere and sufficient as well. They would have been expelled if you hadn't been such a strong advocate on their behalf."

"They're smart kids, they just need to channel it in the right direction."

"Smart enough to break into a heavily guarded art museum and steal an artifact."

"It wasn't as difficult as you'd think. Turns out one of their fathers is on the Board of Directors of the DIA, they had access to all kinds of inside information. They went through some old steam tunnels and came up in a courtyard."

"How'd they get into the building?"

"They bribed a janitor to keep a couple of doors unlocked, including the back door to the showcase where Howdy Doody was on display. It was just a puppet, they didn't have any high-tech sensors or anything like that around him."

"Still, they stole something from an art museum."

"After that they brought him up on the hospital roof to take his picture, then they took him back and left him in a storage area. They called it their 'Heaven and Hell Hack.'"

"After all that and everything else they did you still defended them to the university. And you never put the video online like you said were going to."

"It wasn't necessary. They finally learned what I was trying to teach them all along."

"What lesson is that?"

Jack finished signing, spun the papers back around, and leaned back.

"Conquer anger with non-anger. Conquer badness with goodness. Conquer meanness with generosity. Conquer dishonesty with truth."

"Oh my lord, Jack – Murphy's got you quoting Buddha now, too?"

"Sometimes. It's all about love, Baxter. Love conquers hate."

"Like the peace rally you had with the guy who was going to shoot you?"

"It didn't end up peaceful, but yes, that's a good example."

"I hope you never have a better example. That guy could have killed you."

"It turns out Howdy Doody has some serious side effects. If you take it long enough it makes you angry and violent. It drove Luc out of his mind, I think the pot we smoked helped calm him down. One of the Wise Guys, Baltimore, was messed up on it, too. He had to go through rehab before they let him come back to school."

"Hard to believe a goofy looking guy with carrot top hair could make people so nasty."

"There are a lot of ugly things going on these days. The world is crazy."

"Is that why you left town?"

"It was time for a fresh start. The U.P. seemed like a good place to begin my second life. Michigan Tech isn't a liberal arts school, but they love my course. I've lightened up, like you always told me to do, and the students have responded to my new approach."

"You really have turned into a hippie."

"It gets worse. Did I tell you I'm building a geodesic dome on the spot where they burned my family's house down?"

"You mean the Buckminster Fuller thing? Like the big ball at Epcot?"

"Yeah. It should be done by spring, then Maggie and I are moving into it."

"How's Maggie doing? Does she like teaching at Tech?"

"She loves it."

"And her research?"

"Her paper was controversial, but people have already duplicated the results. She's going to do it again in the spring with a lot more comebacks."

"Comebacks?"

"People like me, who've had a near-death experience. We started calling them comebacks and it stuck. She's actually in town with me, meeting with Robert and Donna."

"The students who helped you get your rave video?"

"Yeah. They're going to run the experiment in the salt mine here in Detroit, and Maggie will run it in the copper mine in Hancock."

Baxter hesitated a moment, looking across the desk at his old friend.

"And how's Maggie's health?" he asked finally.

"She's in remission. We're hopeful."

"That's great news, Jack. I'm happy for both of you."

"I've assured her that death isn't that bad, it's a transition. But we like where we're at and we want to stay as long as we can."

"Amen."

Jack reached into the backpack sitting at his feet.

"I've got something for you," he said. "I've written a novel."

He placed a book on the desk and spun it around so that Baxter could see the title.

Far Out Man